RAINBOW KISSES

DEVILS HOCKEY

Rowdy Hearts

Rainbow Kisses

Rebel Secrets

Rocky's Story

RAINBOW KISSES

DEVILS HOCKEY

STEPHANIE JULIAN

MOONLIT NIGHT PUBLISHING

For my hockey family.
May we spend many nights freezing together in uncomfortable seats watching our favorite guys crush the opposition.

ONE

Brian

STARING out the door of my rented duplex, I watched my older sister flash a strained smile at the rideshare driver before she opened the back door of the car and got out.

I already had an ache in the pit of my stomach, which had started the second I saw her number pop up on my phone about half an hour ago. For a split second, I'd considered letting it go to voicemail, but I knew I couldn't.

This was why I'd moved to Allentown from Anderstown. To be closer to Lindsey and my niece, Maddy. To be here for them. To get to know my niece better, do all the things I couldn't do living three hours away. Dance recitals and soccer games and chorus concerts and whatever else Maddy might decide to do.

But mainly, it was to make sure Linny knew she had someone she could count on to be there for her. To back her up. That's what brothers did. At least, that's what they were supposed to do. But not me. I hadn't been around much the past ten years because I'd been playing hockey.

So I'd picked up the call, and after our usual careful greetings, she'd asked if she could stop by. I'd said sure. Of course. And that familiar ache immediately started to eat away at my gut.

Now, when I saw how skinny she was, I had to take a breath before I could dig deep to find a smile. Which turned genuine the second she saw me and smiled back.

"Oh my god, I almost didn't recognize you with all that hair," she said as she reached the porch and held open her arms for a hug. "Though you still can't grow a beard, can you? It's been a while, Bri-bri."

The nickname immediately took me back to my childhood, as did the smell of cigarette smoke clinging to her like perfume. I stepped forward and wrapped my arms around her too-thin frame and squeezed, not too hard though. Didn't want to hurt her, and I had at least a hundred pounds and a foot of height on her.

Her arms circled my waist, and we stood there for several seconds, just holding each other. But I knew this wasn't just a quick social call.

"Hey, Linny." I didn't ask her how she was doing as I pulled away and waved her into the living room. I could see that for myself. "It's good to see you. Come on in. You want something to drink? I got water and lemonade."

She smiled up at me, her grin lopsided as she nodded. "Sure. Whatever you're having. Thanks." Her gaze whipped around the room, assessing everything. A habit I didn't think she'd ever break. "Nice place. Kinda bare though. Don't feel like celebrating the season, huh?"

Christmas was only a couple weeks away, but I didn't decorate. Why should I? I lived alone. Hell, I didn't even own Christmas decorations.

"It's just a short-term rental, 'til I decide where I want to settle. It came furnished."

I headed for the back of the house, to the kitchen, listening for her footsteps to make sure she followed me. That was my old habit, making sure she hadn't stopped somewhere to pocket something.

I immediately felt like an asshole for even thinking that.

"Not working today? I thought you had a job."

Her voice held a note of something I couldn't place. Panic? Nerves?

"I do. I'm working at the lumberyard. Pays pretty well. All those years of hockey were good for something, I guess. I can deadlift a hundred pounds of concrete mix, so...yeah. I'm pulling a Saturday shift, so I'm off today."

She sat on a chair at the table while I pulled out a couple cans of lemonade.

"Do you miss playing?"

Crossing to the table, I took a few seconds to answer that while I sat down opposite her.

"Yeah." *Understatement of the year.* "But I needed a break." *Not exactly true.*

Linny nodded, gaze flashing away. "You gonna go back? Or you gonna use that degree you got in...what was it? Math?"

My gut clenched. "Don't know that a team would sign me right now. And I never got my teaching degree so..."

Her eyes narrowed, and she nailed me with a look that made me feel ten again and in trouble for breaking a window with a puck. "You never did tell me what happened."

I took a swallow of lemonade before answering. "Disagreement with another player on the team. Decided I should probably take a little time away."

For a second, I thought she'd ask what had happened. But that wasn't us. We didn't like to rehash shit. We just moved on. So she nodded, her head dropping forward, eyes downcast as she put her clasped hands on the table. Not in prayer, because we didn't do prayer either.

I took a deep breath and braced for impact. When she looked up again, I saw the look I'd been expecting since she'd called. Desperation.

Setting my hands on the table directly opposite hers, I met her gaze head-on. "What's up, Lin?"

To her credit, she didn't beat around the bush. "I need help."

Yeah, I'd expected that. "How much?"

She flinched like I'd hit her, something I'd never fucking do, not ever. And I felt like a total asshole for jumping to that conclusion. But we'd done this before. Way too many times. A couple bucks here and there. Sometimes a couple hundred. Always for Maddy.

Shaking her head, she blew out a breath and visibly straightened her shoulders.

"I don't need money. At least, not..." She paused, sinking her teeth into her bottom lip and sucking more air. "I need you to take Maddy."

My brain skidded off track, and I swore I heard the screech of a needle over a vinyl record. "You need what now?"

Her eyes had gotten watery, but the tears weren't flowing, at least not yet. "I need you to take Maddy for me." She took another breath, and I knew there was more. "I found a program, a good program. But it's inpatient. Six weeks." She blinked, willing those tears to just disappear. "I need to kick this monkey off my back for good. I have to do it for me. For Maddy. This is my chance. But I need your help."

Linny was an alcoholic. Had been for years. Ran in the family from our dad. I'd somehow dodged that bullet, but Linny... Linny had fought this demon for fucking years.

Jesus. This was totally not what I'd been expecting, and my mind raced.

She wanted me to take my niece. Maddy was twelve. What the *hell* did I know about caring for a twelve-year-old girl? My mouth opened, but words wouldn't form, my brain just clicking like it was stuck.

She pressed on before I could think of anything to say. "I can't leave her with Mom and Dad. You know that."

Yeah, I did. Our mom would love to have Maddy, but our dad was a fucking powder keg who could blow at any second. It's why neither of us went home, like, ever. Still... How the hell did *I* become the best option to care for a twelve-year-old girl?

Maybe because you're her only other family.

My sister took an audible breath. "I know it's a huge ask, but I need to know she's gonna be taken care of while I'm gone. And you're the only one I trust with my daughter."

My heart flopped like a landed fish at the sincerity in her voice.

When we were kids, it'd just been her and me, a united front against our drunk dad and our codependent mom. But the teen years had hit Linny hard, and I'd been so wrapped up in playing hockey and school I hadn't understood what was going on with her until it was too late. She'd never once blamed me for leaving for college and leaving her behind. Even though she was almost two years older than me, I'd always taken care of her. But I still felt guilty as hell sometimes for making that decision to go away to college and to stay away to play hockey.

She continued to stare at me with that look, and I knew what my answer had to be. Knew what I had to do.

"I'm out of options, Bri." Linny's voice held a despair I'd never heard from her. "I need to do this for Maddy. I need to do this for me. And I need your help."

I reached across the table and took her too-thin hand. "Of course. Anything for you and Maddy. Anything."

THE DOOR CLOSED behind Linny fifteen minutes later, after we'd gone over the legal details. She'd come prepared. She'd had legal documents for me to sign and Maddy's school records, everything I'd need to take legal guardianship of my neice. The program she was working with had helped her with everything.

Now, I sat on the ugly-ass, uncomfortable-as-hell couch and stared at the beige wall. No pictures. No window. Just a bland blank canvas. The neighbor's television blared the news through the thin wall. The volume battled the traffic noise from the busy street. Usually, I could block it all out, but right now, it combined to make me twitch.

This was no place for a twelve-year-old. It wasn't what

you would call a great neighborhood. Hell, no one would call this a good neighborhood, but it was what I was willing to pay so I wouldn't have to put a dent in my hard-earned nest egg.

I was going to have to move. Like, immediately. But where?

Linny's apartment was in an even worse neighborhood. She'd told me that, after the first few weeks of school this semester, she'd pulled Maddy out and enrolled her in online classes. When she'd found out Maddy was being bullied, she'd ripped the school principal a new one then demanded another option. For all her faults, Linny had always made sure Maddy was taken care of.

Linny loved her daughter. I'd never questioned that. And while I'd worried that Linny's drinking would become an issue, I'd let myself think she'd been holding it together. Obviously, she hadn't.

How had I missed it?

Because you hadn't been fucking looking.

Shit. I couldn't go down that rabbit hole now. I had shit I needed to figure out. I needed somewhere for Maddy and me to live. Somewhere safe. Somewhere with a little breathing room for both of us, where I'd have backup if I needed it.

I could only think of one place.

I picked up my phone and dialed.

"Hey, man. I need help."

TWO

Rain

"WHAT DO YOU MEAN, is it supposed to look like a penis? Of course, it's not supposed to look like a penis."

"You sure, Rainy? Because it looks like a penis to me. Might've been a while since I've seen one, but I'm pretty sure I still know what they look like."

Taking a deep breath, I shook my head then let it rest on my hands, fisted on top of each other on my desk. Monday morning after a game weekend was always quiet. Practice was optional, and a week before Christmas, no one wanted to spend more time here than they had to. Which made it the perfect time to get some work done.

Except everything seemed to be going wrong today.

"Fred." I tried to hide my sigh but wasn't completely sure I succeeded. "Do you see the Devils' logo anywhere on that proof?"

The other end of the line went silent. Fredricka Gaines

had taken over her parents' sporting goods company last January. And while it hadn't been a disaster, this wasn't the first hiccup. And it wouldn't be the last because I wouldn't even think of using another company unless Fred's company went under. The Devils were loyal like that.

Some would say to a fault, but... Well, anyway.

"Um, no. No, I don't."

"Then I don't think that's our proof."

Silence from the other end of the line. Then, "Shit. I'm sorry. You're right. Of course, you're right. Let me look in my email again.

"No problem. Hey, I'm going to send it to you again right now, then we can go over it together."

"Yeah, that's probably a good idea."

Fred went quiet, and a picture of her popped into my head. Strawberry blonde ringlets to her waist, pixie features, and all of five feet, the woman was a whirlwind of energy, constantly in motion, her brain always working. Brilliant, funny, and the most disorganized person I knew. But she always managed to get whatever she needed to do done. Even if it was down to the wire.

Then Fred sighed, long and loud. "How do you do it, Rain? How do you keep it all together? Somedays I feel like I'm drowning."

Fred sounded so absolutely forlorn, I wondered for a second if she was going to quit right there and then. And I couldn't live with myself if that happened.

"You're doing fine," I said, my voice calm and collected. "Give yourself a break. I've been doing my job for almost five years. You've been in yours a year."

"But you always seem so in control of everything."

I wanted to laugh, but I didn't want to seem flippant as I clicked the button to resend the email with the logo. Which I'd sent last week. "Not all the time. Sometimes, I'm just faking it."

"No way. I don't believe that."

It was more true than she'd ever know, or that I'd ever admit, but that was part of the job. Making it look easy and then working my ass off to make it happen.

Sure, I manifested that shit like a boss. But, yeah, my ducks were in a row and no squirrels allowed. When those suckers popped up their heads, I made sure to bop them like I was playing Whack-A-Mole.

"Seriously, sometimes you just gotta believe it's all going to be okay and then jump into the deep end and hope you don't drown."

"Well, I feel like I'm drowning in the shallow end right now."

"Then snap out of it, because I need you to make sure you got the right proof. Check your email. That's all you need to do right now. I don't trust anyone else to do our specialty sweaters."

Another huge sigh.

"Yep, it's there."

"Now open it and make sure there are no penises on the proof."

There was the laugh I wanted to hear.

"You're right. No penises. But... Wait, are these shirts pink? And do those bats have heart bodies?"

"Yes, they are and yes, they do. Do you like them?"

I'd designed them myself, and I thought they were some of my best work so far. But they weren't our normal style.

They were a little softer, a little less in your face than our normal logo. Since Dad had given me carte blanche to design the specialty sweaters when I'd come to work for the team, I'd stuck to the tried-and-true variations of the grinning devil's face that was our regular logo.

This year, I'd wanted to do something different.

"Rain, these are too good to be on hockey sweaters. You totally missed your calling. You should've been an illustrator."

My lips curved in a happy grin. "Thanks, Fred. I'm glad you like them."

"I love them. Seriously, these are quality. I'll try not to screw them up."

"Stop it. You're not going to screw them up. I have faith in you. Hey, I hate to cut this short, but I've got a meeting with Rowdy and Dad, and I need to make another call before then. Text me, and we'll make a date for lunch after Christmas."

"I would love that, Rain. And thanks."

"No problem. I'm here. Whatever you need. Just ask."

I hung up, making a note to follow up on the proofs in a couple of days. And to make sure Fred didn't need anything. If she did, she knew she could count on me.

Dad needed me? Be right there. Mom needed me? I'm on my way. My brothers? Hell, even they knew if they called, I'd drop what I was doing and be at their side. Friends needed a shoulder to cry on or a bridesmaid to stand up for them? I stock tissues and ice cream in bulk and I'm always up for buying a new dress.

But lately, some of those friends had begun to suggest there was a correlation between my lack of a significant other and my good friend status. Like, maybe I used friendship to avoid relationships.

Well, what was wrong with that? Considering how my last relationship had ended, who could blame me? I wasn't eager to jump back into the dating pool. I didn't need a man to make my life complete. So there.

Sticking out my tongue at no one in particular, I grabbed my planner to see what was next on the to-do list, even though I knew damn well what it was. I'd been avoiding this for a week, but now I absolutely had to get this done.

Picking up my phone, I pulled up my contacts and found the one I needed.

After the third ring, I thought I was home free, but then it connected, and a gruff voice said, "Lawrence. What can I do for you? I've only got a couple minutes before I have to leave."

Gritting my teeth, I took a breath before speaking, because my smart-ass tongue had gotten me in trouble many times before, and I just didn't have time to deal with this asshole the way I wanted to right now.

"Wyeth." I made sure my tone was friendly, with just the right amount of fuck-you. "I'm calling about the sweaters for the March home-and-home games. I plan to send over the designs later this week—"

"I'm sure they'll be fine. I'm good with whatever you come up with."

My mouth dropped open, but I couldn't think of a damn thing to say. Usually Wyeth, who owned the Bentonville Badgers, had to stick his two cents into everything. Didn't matter if it was as simple as changing one word in a slogan or wanting a complete design overhauled a day before it was due to the printer.

Then he continued. "Just send them to me when they're done. We'll talk then. Have to go."

And he hung up. Leaving me rubbing my temples at the tiny hammer that had started to beat there.

In my mind, a mental picture of Harry Wyeth formed, and it wasn't flattering. If I didn't know the man well, I'd think he was handsome. Sandy blond hair, blue eyes, and a stocky build. A carbon copy of his dad. But his smile tended toward mean, and his eyes were arctic blue, cold and calculating.

Harry had always reminded me of a sleazy salesman who wanted to sell me something I didn't need and wasn't going to leave until I bought it. We'd had a lot of dealings together over the past three years, since we'd occupied basically the same position for our dads' companies. We'd been able to work together without too much friction, but when he'd taken over all hockey operations after his dad's death a year ago, his true nature had come out.

His dad had been old-school but never condescending. Harold Wyeth had struggled with having women in hockey, except as cheerleaders, of course. But at least he'd been respectful. Harry, however, had inherited all his dad's bad qualities and none of the good. Which made every interaction with him something I dreaded.

Not that I couldn't handle him. I could. I just really, really, really didn't want anything to do with him. But if the damn man didn't stop hanging up on me every time I called, like I was one of his damn lackeys, he was going to learn the hard way that I was not all sunshine and light, like my name might imply. After dealing with me on a bad day, some people (namely my brothers) had suggested I change my name to another natural phenomenon: Lightning. All jagged edges and a flash of angry growl.

Sometimes it was good to know they feared me, but I never doubted their love. Not my brothers' or my parents'. But anyone else, besides my closest friends... Yeah, I had a real hard time believing a word out of their mouths. It made for rocky relationships. But could you blame me? I mean, my last relationship had been a total bust, but that was mostly my fault for dating a hockey player. Again. Obviously, I hadn't learned from the first disaster.

Another man's face popped into my mind. A man with auburn hair that he kept short because otherwise it got curly, hazel eyes, and a nose that'd been broken not just once, but a couple of times, including once by my brother, Rebel.

Damn the man for continuing to pop up in my thoughts when I least expected it and for no reason whatsoever. Except for the fact that he had coldcocked my shitty ex, who I should have known was an asshole. But no, of course I hadn't listened to my brother Rebel, who thought he knew how I should live my life better than I did.

Except he hadn't been wrong about Mo Zelinsky, had he? As much as I hated to admit it, Rebel had been right about Mo. Total dick. Supreme asshole who looked like god's gift to women.

Brian... Not a dick. But also... Gone. After he'd cold-cocked Mo, who'd been the captain of Brian's old team, Brian had disappeared. I'd asked Rowdy, just once, where Brian had gone. Rowdy had said, "Home," like I was supposed to know where that was. And since I didn't want Rowdy to wonder why I was asking about Brian so much, I broke down and asked Rebel, who'd shrugged and grunted, which was guy speak for, "Don't know, don't care."

Sometimes I slapped Rebel upside the head just because I could, and because I'm sure he deserved it for something.

So I'd searched for Brian online and found out he hadn't played at all the rest of last season. And he wasn't on a roster this season. Anywhere in the world. Trust me, I'd checked. And his social media hadn't been updated for at least a year.

Okay then.

You really need to stop obsessing.

"I am not obsessing," I muttered under my breath as I pulled up the Devils' social media accounts and added a few more posts to the queue. The season had started more than two months ago, and while Dad wasn't worried about it, ticket sales were down slightly. I know, I know, high school football was just winding down and the holiday was almost here—

"Rainbow! Come up here for a minute."

My dad's voice boomed down the hallway, scaring the shit out of me because I hadn't realized he was here. We weren't supposed to meet for another hour.

I muttered, "Oh for fuck's sake," while putting a hand over my chest as my heart pounded against my ribs.

"Dad! This is why we installed a phone system!"

And yes, of course, I yelled back at him without using the phone. Because that was how we rolled around here. I hadn't known anyone else was in the building, which was kinda creepy, because anyone could've walked in and murdered me. Hey, it could happen. There had to be some people out there who didn't like me. Probably none who wanted to take an ax to my—

You know what? I should probably lay off the crime podcasts for a while.

"That wouldn't be as much fun!" my dad yelled back. "Just come up here."

With a heavy sigh, I pushed away from my desk, my dreams of a quiet, uninterrupted morning dashed. Oh well, there was always tomorrow. I said that a lot around here.

Halfway up the hall, I yelled, "What's the problem?"

I got to his door before he had time to answer. And what I saw in his office made my mouth drop open and my brain skip like a needle on a scratched record.

"Brian? What the hell? Where have you been? What happened to you? And why the hell didn't you—"

I stopped before I could finish that question because it would raise way too many other questions from the other occupants of the room. Mainly, my brother Rowdy. Who was staring at me like I'd just revealed I was a secret superhero.

My dad's brows were arched and curious too.

Snapping my mouth shut, I focused on my dad, because I didn't want to have to deal with Rowdy. That was a conversation I wanted to avoid.

"What's going on?"

Dad paused for a second before he said, "Just wanted to let you know we're bringing Brian on for the rest of the season."

The bottom fell out of my stomach. At least, that's what it felt like. And my lungs constricted until I felt like I was going to suffocate. I had so very many questions, most of them for

Brian, but I couldn't ask them, not with Dad and Rowdy in the room.

I slid a quick glance at the man who had punched his then-captain because the guy was being a dick to me. And then he'd left the league and disappeared before we could discuss it. Before I could yell at him for stepping into my business. And thank him for coldcocking the aforementioned dick. What the hell I'd seen in that man, I couldn't tell you now. Maybe I'd been blinded by his looks. Maybe I'd dated him because I knew it would piss off my brother Rebel, who still treated me like I was twelve and should follow his every order. Which I never had, anyway.

So I asked another question farther down the list. "I thought we had a full roster?"

I looked at my dad with raised brows because I *knew* we had a full roster, but that sounded more diplomatic than, "How the hell can we hire this guy? We don't have the space for him."

Had something happened to another member of the team? Why hadn't anyone told me? I wasn't just in charge of marketing, I was also serving as the entire HR department because our full-time HR director, Tabitha, was out on maternity leave and wouldn't be back for a few months.

Dad just shrugged. "We'll make it work. I'm sure you'll figure out something."

My mouth dropped open again, and my brain replayed his words on a loop. *You'll figure it out.*

"Dad—"

"Rain," Rowdy's quiet voice cut in, and my gaze shot to him. "Put me on the DL."

Brian's head whipped around to Rowdy. "Wait, no. That's not what we agreed to."

I'd been no slouch in college. I'd graduated cum laude. And while most people thought I was a spoiled brat who should keep my mouth closed a little more than I did, I knew when to actually do it.

Brian and Rowdy went back years, to college. Brian had joined the Devils a year before Rowdy, and they'd played together for a year before Brian moved to Anderstown for his third year. I'd never learned why Brian had left the Devils, but I knew it had something to do with Rebel. Who had never breathed a word of it to anyone. At least, not to me.

"What exactly *did* you agree to?"

I asked because I was too curious not to. And yeah, it was because I'd had a secret crush on Brian from the first moment he joined the team.

I'd been a senior in high school, working at the arena in the concession stand, because my parents believed it built character to work from the ground up. Of course, they were absolutely right, but I'd bitched because I was seventeen.

Truth was I'd loved being at the arena. Still did. It was my second home, just above my actual home and Crack One Open, the local coffeehouse/radio station/weekly newspaper, where I helped out my friend Erin occasionally.

I'd been at the arena the day Brian had walked in to sign his contract. He was a year older than Rowdy, whom he'd met at Penn State, where they'd both played for the college team.

It'd been August, my senior year about to start, and I'd been in Dad's office, helping him with his computer, which he always seemed to screw up somehow. Brian and Rowdy had walked in, Rowdy's mouth going a mile a minute about something and Brian just nodding his head, his lips curved in a half grin.

The bottom had dropped out of my stomach, kinda like it'd done just now, and I'd realized what lust at first sight meant. I was seventeen, and while I wasn't exactly boy-crazy, I liked guys. Mainly older guys who played hockey and would never give me a second look because they were scared off by my older brothers or my dad, or all three. I'd managed to date a few adventurous local boys, but I knew I was going to college in a year, so I hadn't been looking for a steady boyfriend.

But I took one look at Brian and thought, "Gimme." The fact that he'd never done anything other than smile at me and make sure there was always five feet between us still pissed me off.

He'd been older. And quiet, which wasn't normal for the players who made this league their home. He and Rowdy had been complete opposites, which was probably why they'd been such good friends, along with Rebel. At first. When Brian had left for Anderstown after several years with the Devils, Rowdy had been visibly depressed, something that rarely happened.

But Rebel had been glad to see him go. And I'd never found out why.

Now, Brian and Rowdy exchanged a look, communicating without words. After a few seconds, Rowdy's brows rose, and Brian sighed.

I knew that sigh. I gave it a lot. Rowdy had won this round of whatever the hell was going on.

When Brian turned to look at me, I honestly thought my

knees would give out. That secret crush I'd been nursing for years rushed back with a vengeance, making my blood heat and various parts of my body tingle. He'd always been kind to me, the younger sister of his best friend. And I knew how cliché it sounded, that I'd held on to this crush for a damn long time. But when he looked at me with those beautiful eyes that hid secrets, all I wanted to do was fix whatever he needed fixing.

And I could. I could fix whatever problem he had. He just needed to let me. Everyone let me.

After another couple of seconds, he finally cracked. His gaze dropped to the table. "My sister's enrolled in a...program for the next few months, and I have custody of my niece until she's finished. I couldn't think of anywhere safer for Maddy than here. I want Maddy to be around people I trust. A place where I know she'll be safe after school when I've got a game or practice. I need to—"

"Sure. I can make this work. No problem."

The words were out of my mouth before I realized I was going to say them, but that was okay because I meant every one of them. My brain had already started to work over solutions. Because that's what I did. I fixed things. And if I couldn't fix it... Well, I just didn't have all the facts, and when I did, I would fix it.

From the look on Brian's face, he didn't like needing help. I got it. Men hated to ask for help. Especially professional athletes who thought they could handle everything. But I knew, because I'd been an off-ice member of this team for six years, that most of these guys wouldn't be able to fill out the paperwork needed to join the Devils without me.

Now, I wasn't saying these men were stupid. I'm just

saying some of them didn't have the smarts god gave a squirrel. Nice guys, but geez, some of them would never be able to comprehend the inner workings of a contract, and in our league, most of the guys did not have an agent looking out for them. They had me.

I did *not* count Brian among those guys. The man had a brain, and a sharp one. He'd been a math major, if I remembered correctly. He'd talked about teaching at some point. High school, I think. But he'd loved hockey more.

Until he'd punched out his former captain and left the league last year. And it'd been my fault. Because I'd been stupid enough to date the asshole.

"I don't want any special treatment."

Of course he didn't. That wasn't the kind of guy he was.

I smiled and shrugged, trying to look like everything was fine. "Brian, you're not the first guy we've brought on midseason." I didn't add that he wasn't even the first guy Dad had hired simply because he needed a job or a fresh start. There was always wiggle room in our league. Rules were rules, sure, but sometimes the guidelines were more like...just not there.

Lifting a hand, he shoved it through his hair, his gaze shifting away from me before staring at the ceiling for a quick second.

Then he looked at Rowdy, who grinned at him, then at our dad, who nodded, looking stoic, like Dad always looked, except when he looked at my mom. Finally, Brian looked at me and sighed. And I wanted to bat my lashes at him and swoon. Which wasn't happening.

"Ok. Just show me where to sign."

THREE

Brian

"THANKS AGAIN, Colonel. I know this was—"

"Unexpected, yes." The Colonel shook my hand, patted me on the back, and basically pointed me toward the door. "But it's nice to have you back, Brian. Rainy'll help you figure out all the details."

Rowdy walked me to the door of the Colonel's office, his arm around my shoulder.

"I've got a few things to finish up with Pop, but why don't we plan to meet for lunch? Rain should be done with you by then, right?"

Rowdy glanced at his sister, the woman I'd been avoiding looking at since I'd signed the papers making me a Devil again. I already had way too much baggage with her and now I'd basically had to beg for a job, and she had to clean up the mess.

Okay, maybe not beg, though I still felt like I was getting

preferential treatment. But this wasn't just about me. It was about Maddy too. And what was best for her.

And St. David was best for Maddy.

"Shouldn't take that long to do the paperwork. Just come down to my office when you're ready. It's the last one at the end of the hall." She made a face at Rowdy that I couldn't figure out then shot me a smile that made my gut flip. "It's got my name on the door and everything."

That smile sent my blood flowing south. Which was totally not happening. Nope. I bit my tongue and willed my dick to behave. But I couldn't quite rip my gaze away from her quick enough. The look Rowdy leveled at me let me know exactly what he was thinking. So I ignored that and held out my hand, which he took with a slight smirk. If we were on the ice, he'd totally get an elbow in the gut for that.

"Thanks again for everything, Rowdy."

"Whiskers, if you say thank you one more time, I'm going to make you do the Rookie Rumble."

My brain stumbled over that one, and my expression must have shown it. Rowdy's smile became downright diabolical.

"What the hell is that?"

"Something we started last year. But I think I'll let you find that out on your own."

"I'm far from a rookie."

"Yeah, but you're a Devil again. You know we don't do rules here."

I shook my head, feeling my lips curve for the first time in a while. "Just guidelines, huh?"

"And those are more like suggestions." His expression turned serious then, which didn't look as wrong as it would've a few years ago. "Look, I know you've got a lot on your plate right now, but we've got your back now. Concentrate on Maddy and hockey. That's all."

Good advice. And yet, I couldn't stop thinking about the one woman I really shouldn't be thinking about. Not only because she was this man's younger sister, but because I needed to be present for my niece. She needed all my attention when I wasn't on the ice.

And when you are on the ice?

Well, that's why we were here. Because I knew this town and these people. They wouldn't let her struggle or disappear. They'd look out for her when I couldn't.

"Thanks, Rowdy. I appreciate everything you've done for me. For us."

"Don't thank me too much." His grin widened. "You still gotta play hockey for the Devils."

I wasn't lying when I said, "That might be the best thing I've heard all week."

Rowdy huffed. "Let me know if you still think that after the first few days. We're on a winning streak so practices have been a little more, uh, intense."

My eyebrows rose in surprise. "Winning streak, huh? That's new."

Rowdy's expression brightened even more. "Yeah, it is, and I like it, so we're trying something different this year. Actually trying to improve our game."

Well, fuck. To say I was out of shape was an understatement. But I didn't figure I'd be playing all that much anyway, so I wouldn't drag the team down.

"You'll get up to speed in no time." Rowdy clapped me on

the back. "Find me after you're done with Rain. We can catch up."

"Hey, can I get a rain check on that? I left Maddy in the hotel room—"

"You know you could've brought her along." Rowdy shook his head. "Look, why don't we plan to get together for dinner this week. Tressy and Krista would love to meet Maddy, and you and I can catch up. How about Thursday night at the Tea Room? I'll check with Tressy and let you know what time."

"Let me make sure Maddy's okay with that before I agree." Since her mom was in rehab for alcohol, maybe the kid wouldn't want to go to a bar, although the Tea Room was more than a bar. "Shouldn't be a problem, but—"

"No problem. Just text me and let me know."

I nodded. "Thanks, again, man. For everything."

"Trust me, you won't be thanking me after your first practice." Rowdy's expression made my eyebrows rise. "Which, did I mention, is at ten tomorrow morning? But please stop thanking me. I told you you're actually helping me out here."

Shaking my head, I managed a true smile. "Can you point me toward Rain's office?"

Rowdy's smile turned sly. And knowing. And yeah, that was not happening.

"Last door on the left. She'll have the paperwork you need to sign."

I turned to look where he was pointing.

"And Brian?"

"Yeah?"

"Give yourself a break."

Nodding, I turned and headed down the hall, my mind

already consumed with the need to see her again. No, not need. That was ridiculous. I didn't *need* Rain. I wanted her. Two very different things. And considering I couldn't do anything about that want, I just needed to be professional.

Yeah, like professional and St. David Devils go together.

I stopped just before I reached the door then knocked on the jamb. The door was already open, but I didn't just want to walk into her office.

"Come on in."

I took a breath. "Hey, Rain." I was going for casual, but I probably ended up sounding like a dick. She looked up from whatever she was doing on her laptop, her eyes caught mine, and I thought, *yep, this is gonna be torture.*

Her smile twisted my gut into knots and the welcome in her warm dark blue eyes sent my blood pressure skyrocketing. It was only through sheer determination that I did not get a hard-on. Give me a pat on the back.

"I've got the papers you need to sign." She waved at her desk, and I hoped like hell I didn't have to sign all the papers covering it. It looked like the damn printer had just kept spewing papers for hours. "Sit down, and we can make this as painless as possible."

I huffed out a laugh because just being in the same room with her was proving to be painful, considering the ache in my crotch. Taking the seat on the other side of her desk, I looked at the stack of papers she'd placed on the edge of the desk closest to me.

"If you want to read through them, I can go through each one—"

"Not necessary." Rowdy had already given me his word that I wouldn't be traded, and I knew how much I'd be making. Nothing else mattered. "Just give me a pen and show me the dotted line."

I sensed her hesitation before she grabbed the pen beside her mouse and handed it over.

"Brian?" She paused. "Is there anything I can do to help?"

I should've known she'd ask. That was the kind of person she was. Of course, she wouldn't come right out and ask what was going on, even though I knew she had to be curious as hell. And I knew Rowdy hadn't said anything to her about signing me because she'd been genuinely surprised to see me.

Looking up from the legalese that was making my eyes cross, I caught Rain as she bit her lip. And that pit in my stomach threatened to swallow all my internal organs. *Fuck.* My heart began to race, and my gaze got stuck on her mouth. And that definitely wasn't good because she was sitting there staring at me, knowing that I was looking at her lips.

Shit. I didn't want to make her uncomfortable. Because she wasn't into me. She'd never been into me. And I definitely didn't want to make this weird.

Taking another breath, I said, "Honestly, I don't know. I don't know if I know what I need yet."

She didn't answer right away, even though I knew she must have a thousand questions. But she didn't push or prod. Just nodded and gave me a genuinely kind smile.

"If you do, I'm here for you. For...whatever."

If she only knew...

"Got any friends with twelve-year-old daughters?"

Her mouth dropped open, and her eyes widened in complete and utter shock. Then I realized what I'd said.

"Fuck. No. Sorry, that came out totally wrong. Shit." I

sighed, scrubbing a hand through my hair. "They're for my niece. To make friends with. She's twelve. She's part of the reason I came back. Well, most of the reason."

Rain blinked, and I could practically see her brain spinning. "Okay," she said, drawing the word out to at least three syllables.

"Yeah, sorry." I sighed and shook my head, as if that would help get my brain on track, frustration an ache in my gut. "I don't mean to be cryptic. It's just... I don't really talk about this shit with a lot of people. Rowdy and your dad know what's going on but..." I blew out a hard breath. "My sister's in an inpatient program for the next month and a half, maybe two months. I've got custody of Maddy until then. I love my niece, but I'm out of my league with a kid her age."

Rain held my gaze while she sorted through the information I'd just given her.

Then she said, "She's a tween."

Since that wasn't at all what I'd been expecting to hear, I said, "A what?"

Rain's lips quirked into a little smile. "That's what kids her age are called. She's almost a teen. It's a rough age."

"God, that's an understatement. Don't get me wrong, I love her to death, but I'm fucking terrified of screwing this up. Screwing her up. That's why I came back here. Because I know there are people here who won't let me fail. People who will look after Maddy when I can't be around. People I trust."

One of those people was sitting right in front of me, eyes wide and maybe a little wet. "Brian. I'm so—"

I held up my hand to stop whatever she was going to say. "I didn't tell you that for sympathy. We don't need sympathy. But I do owe you an apology."

Now her brows drew down hard. "What? Why?"

Now or never. "For laying out Zelinsky. I'm not sorry for punching him. The bastard deserved it. But I am sorry for making it awkward for you."

Rain stared at me wide-eyed for a second before shaking her head. "You didn't. Make it awkward, I mean. Honestly. I never heard from the bastard again after that night, so I should thank you."

I blew out a frustrated sigh. "You don't have to—"

Standing, she walked around her desk and sat in the chair next to mine. Then she put her hand on my arm. And my libido sat up and practically begged for her to pet me.

"Yes, I do. Because I *am* thankful. But I really hope you didn't leave the league because you thought I would do something to get you in trouble. The only reason I didn't say anything about that night was because you left the team the next day and no one seemed to know why. Mo never said a word, at least not that I got wind of. If he had, I would've made sure everyone knew he'd ended up on the floor after you punched him. I just didn't know what to do when you disappeared."

"I'm really sorry—"

"Brian. Stop. Seriously. Stop saying you're sorry for sticking up for me, or I'll think you didn't mean to have my back and just slipped and ended up flattening Mo accidentally."

The smile on her lips and in her eyes rocked my world. Seriously, I thought for sure the floor was shaking. I could only stare back at her and debate the wisdom of kissing her.

It wouldn't take much for me to lean over the arm of the chair and smash my lips against hers and kiss the hell out of her, like I wanted to do. I also knew that would be the worst thing in the world. I'd prove to be just like Zelinsky, taking something she hadn't given permission to take.

And this was the worst friggin' time for me to be lusting after a woman, even if that woman was Rain Lawrence. Especially since that woman was Rain Lawrence.

"Now," she continued when I couldn't think of a damn thing to say, "you need to sign the contract so we can get you and Maddy on our health care plan. Then we can figure out the school situation. Where are you staying? I'm sure we can find you— Wait, let me get a pen so I can start making a list."

Then she smiled and my gut clenched.

"Don't worry," she said. "We'll figure this out."

FOUR

Rain

"DOES this outfit look like I'm going on a date? Because this isn't a date."

I held a plaid, button-down shirt over my chest and turned to face down my toughest critic. And one of my very best friends.

Caity Lopez gave me a look that expressed exactly what she was thinking. Which, of course, she then had to put into words because she couldn't help herself.

"No one would think you were on a date wearing that shirt and those jeans. Not even in St. David. Have a little respect for the fact that you're going to be spending time with a guy who isn't your brother."

I sneered. "Ugh. You suck."

Caity flipped me the bird. "But I'm right. I'm always right. Besides, Brian Fiskers is a fucking sweetheart and the kind of guy you wanna climb like a pole. I mean, those arms alone make me want to lick them."

I stared at Caity, who lounged on my bed just like she had when we were teenagers trying to decide what to wear to the school dance. Not that Caity ever had to ask my advice. She could make a plain white t-shirt and a hand-me-down pair of jeans look designer.

With waist-length, wavy red hair, cinnamon-colored eyes, and a body with curves for days, Caity had grown up with four older brothers who'd beaten down any guy who'd so much as looked in her direction in high school, but they'd also taught her how to fight for what she wanted.

And what Caity wanted, Caity got.

"Wait. Do you have a thing for Brian?"

Holy shit. Did she? Had I totally missed the fact that Caity had feelings for Brian? And why did I feel like I just took a punch to the stomach?

Caity rolled her eyes, huffing out a sigh. "Please. You know me better than that. Not my type. Too quiet. Besides, I know you've been lusting after him for years."

"I have not." The words automatically popped out of my mouth. "He's a friend."

Caity made a rude noise that sounded like a cross between a snort and a hack. "Yes, you have. And you want him to be more than just a friend."

"No, I haven't. And no, I don't." My nose wrinkled. "Well, not lusting." As Caity laughed, I tossed the shirt I was holding at her. "So I like the guy. Doesn't mean I'm lusting after him."

I didn't know why I was lying. I did lust after the man.

Though I'm not sure it'd been years. Okay, definitely not more than a couple of years.

"Just admit it," Caity said. "You want the guy. And there's nothing wrong with that. You're allowed to like guys. Even guys who play for your daddy's team."

My heart shriveled a little inside. "Yeah, like that ever worked out well for me."

Caity grimaced. "Damn. Sorry. I forgot. But you were too good for that douchebag anyway."

With a sigh, I turned back to my closet. "That *douchebag* is now playing for the NHL, and he and his wife just started a charity for sick kids. Or something like that."

Not like I was following Rodney Chisholm's career or anything. I followed him on social media like I followed all the former Devils who'd actually made it to the NHL. There weren't many of them, but Roddy had had something special. And he'd broken my twenty-one-year-old heart when he'd left.

"Okay, so maybe he outgrew his douchebag tendencies. You're not still pining after Chisholm, are you?" Caity's voice held disbelief. And a little bit of worry.

"No, of course not." And I wasn't. I pulled out a sweater and held it up as I turned around. "I've been over him for years. But obviously I didn't learn my lesson the first time. I'm not going to make it a third."

My second strike had been dating Mo, another hockey player, who'd turned out to be an *actual* asshole, instead of just a young cocky player who'd had a few missteps but had turned his career around. Like Roddy.

At least I'd managed to keep the affair with Mo secret from *almost* everyone.

"Still don't know what you saw in that dick." With a sigh, Caity pushed off the bed, came over to stand beside me at the closet, and started rifling through my clothes.

"Oh hon, we need to schedule a shopping trip and soon. The team has a competition in Philly in January. You should come with us. We definitely need to update your casual wardrobe with something that isn't jeans, white shirts, or plaid."

I stifled a grin. "What do you have against plaid? And you know I can't. The winter festival is in January, and I have too much to do."

"I don't have one damn thing against plaid. If it's flannel. And on a guy. Oh wait. What's this?"

Reaching toward the back of the closet, Caity grabbed a shirt I'd pretty much forgotten I'd had. Cream silk, a little lower cut than anything I wore for work, and a splurge I'd made the last time I'd gone shopping with Caity. I hadn't worn it more than a couple of times since then. Mostly because I didn't really have an occasion to wear it. It wasn't something I could wear during the offseason, which meant the summer. And during the season, I wore clothes that kept me warm in the arena, which meant jeans or chinos and t-shirts and sweaters. And flannel.

Okay, maybe I was in a little bit of a rut.

"Wear this." Caity shoved it at me. "You should want to look good for *yourself*. Doesn't matter where you're going or who you're going with. When you look good, you feel good."

"When did you become a life coach? Fine." I took the shirt out of her hand and flounced away toward the bathroom with an exaggerated huff that made Caity laugh.

"And if you want to look good for Brian," Caity shouted after me, "there's no shame in that, either."

CAITY LEFT WITH A HUG, a smack on my ass, and the admonition to have fun. Or had it been a threat? You could never tell with Caity.

I walked out my front door fifteen minutes later to meet Brian at the Tea Room. The pub was only a few minutes from my home by car, and I was, of course, going to be early. I was always early. For everything. Daddy always said if you were on time, you were late, and my brain had metabolized that at a young age.

I took my time weaving through the small development where my house stood. St. David sat in a little valley created by the surrounding hills, covered with old-growth forests. A few farms remained in the valley, the fields brown now. In the summer, corn and soybeans thrived, feed for the dairy farms in the area.

The town came into sight after I crested one last rise. I could just see the outline of the arena on the south side before I started to descend a little. And in the distance, I could barely make out my parents' home on the other side of town, a huge old mansion that they'd bought more than thirty years ago and renovated at the same time they'd built the arena that housed the hockey team. It sat right at the edge of town, a beautiful old wooden lodge where I'd spent all my life until moving into my own place a few years ago.

I passed a few larger houses along the side of the road before the businesses began. The heart of St. David's business district was all of about four blocks long, but the buildings could star in their own Hallmark movie, they were so damn cute.

The town had been built more than two hundred years ago, just a little cluster of buildings to support the farmers in the area, but in the fifties, some corporation had built a factory outside of town and St. David had expanded into what it was now.

Most of the businesses along Main Street were closed now, except for the pizza parlor, diner, and the Tea Room, which was where I was meeting Brian. My stomach gave a little flutter before I reminded myself that his niece would be there too. No fluttering allowed.

I found a space in the lot behind the building, zipping my puffy jacket before I got out of the car. The temperature hovered around forty degrees and was supposed to drop to about thirty later tonight. Shivering in the cold, I hustled for the door, head down against the wind whipping through the valley—and walked straight into someone's back.

"Oh my god, I'm so sorry."

Low, male laughter reached my ears as a large hand cupped my elbow when I tilted to the right.

"It's okay, Rainy. No problem."

Brian stared down at me, his mouth holding a hint of a grin.

I nearly sighed in complete and utter appreciation of his handsomeness. Even the little bump on his nose where it'd been broken, probably more than once, made me want to trace it with my finger in sheer appreciation. Luckily, I noticed the smaller shadow by his side before I did anything ridiculously stupid.

Drawing in a quick breath, I took a step back as I smiled at the girl.

"Hi, you must be Maddy. I'm Rainbow. It's nice to meet you."

The young girl looked up at me, her eyebrows arching as she looked between me and her uncle. It took a second, but finally she said, "Hi."

I couldn't tell if she was shy or distant or just disinterested, but I planned to cut her some slack considering the circumstances. She'd had to uproot her entire life in the past couple of days. I couldn't even imagine.

And holy crap, she looked enough like Brian that people might think she was his. From the auburn hair to the hazel eyes to the shape of her face.

"Well, why don't we get inside before we freeze." I smiled a little too brightly, trying too hard to be friendly and probably looking like an idiot. "I'm ready to eat."

Brian had the door open before I'd finished speaking, waving Maddy and me in ahead of him.

"I called ahead and asked Mitzi to save us a table in the back, where it's quiet." I waved at the Tea Room's owner, Mitzi Naugle, who'd spotted us from across the room and began to weave through the tables on her way to us.

"Brian! It's really good to see you again. How've you been?"

For the first time, Brian smiled, a real smile that reached all the way to his eyes and lit them up, making my mouth dry.

"Good to see you too, Mitz. It's been a while."

Mitzi wrapped her thin arms around his broad shoulders, having to reach up onto her tiptoes to do it. My eyes widened in shock, because Mitzi didn't give out hugs to just anyone.

She was a tough old lady, though I would never say that to her face because... Well, she might spank me like I was six. Or make me wash dishes in the kitchen, like she'd made most of the teenagers who'd lived in this town when they'd screwed up.

You really didn't want to get on Mitzi's bad side. She was sixty-something, as far as anyone could tell, and showed no sign of slowing down any time soon. And no one would dare suggest it.

Stepping back, she gave me a nod then turned her attention to Maddy, who looked like she was trying to hide behind her uncle.

"And who's this?"

The other thing about Mitzi was that she could charm birds out of the sky when she wanted. She had a way with kids that was uncanny. They trusted her implicitly.

Except Maddy seemed to be the exception to the rule. She shrunk even closer to her uncle, one thin hand reaching around his arm. To Brian's credit, he didn't force her to be sociable, and Mitzi didn't push herself on the girl.

"My niece, Maddy." He put his arm around the girl's shoulders. "We're moving to town for... well, a while."

Mitzi's smile never wavered. "Well, welcome to St. David, Maddy." Then she transferred her attention back to Brian. "Glad to have you back. The team could use a little age and wisdom this year."

"Well, I don't know about wisdom, but the age thing might come back to bite me."

Mitzi's laughter filled the room, where only about half of the tables were full. It was a Monday and Christmas was a week and a half away. The drinking crowd would show up around eight or so. Until then, it'd be quiet.

"Son, when you're my age, we'll talk. Until then, suck it up." Mitzi jerked her head to the left, glancing at me. "The table you asked for is set up. You know where it is."

"Thank you, Mitzi."

"No problem. I'll send Chrissy back to take your order in five."

Mitzi moved back to the bar, and I started walking, nodding and smiling at the couple in the corner, who were season ticket holders, and waving to the family celebrating a birthday on the other side of the room. I'd seen the family at games occasionally, though not often.

"Just give me a sec," I said to Brian, "I'll be right back."

I made a quick detour, digging into my purse for the ticket vouchers I always kept there.

"Hey, happy birthday, Colin. I just wanted to stop and give you a little present." I smiled at the little boy wearing the party hat then glanced at his parents and held up the vouchers. "Tickets for a Devils' game. Good for whenever you can use them."

The tickets also came with free snacks and drinks, but I didn't mention that. People sometimes took it as an insult.

While the parents thanked me, Colin asked if I wanted cake, which, at any other time, I would've gladly accepted. "I didn't eat yet, but thank you, Colin. Have a good night."

With a little wave, I headed toward the back room. Brian and Maddy were already seated at the table I'd asked for. I saw Maddy say something to Brian, saw him nod in response, but as soon as I got close, she went silent, her gaze flashing up at me for a second before looking back down at the table.

I slid into my chair, trying not to show the nerves that started to bang around my stomach.

"Did you guys get a chance to look at the menu?" Which was stupid, because Brian had been here before. Countless times. "Well, not you, of course." I waved a hand at Brian, probably looking like an idiot, and addressed my next comment to Maddy. "The burgers are great, and the chicken pot pie is the best in the state. Although it's not really a pie. It's the Pennsylvania Dutch pot pie so it has noodles and not pie crust."

And now I was rambling. This was off to a great start. Maybe I should just get down to business. At least I had a list I could follow.

I reached behind me for my purse before I realized I'd put my coat over top of it and had to rearrange things before I could dig notebook out of it.

"So, I made a list because—"

"Of course, you did." Brian full-out smiled at me for the first time and the bottom dropped out of my stomach. "You've got a list for everything, don't you?"

I attempted not to wrinkle my nose at him, though if he were one of my brothers, I would have kicked him under the table.

"Lists help me stay organized." I hope that didn't sound as prissy as it had in my head. "And not forget anything. And I made a duplicate for you, so you don't have to take notes."

Now he actually chuckled, and I wanted to sigh at the sound. I was pathetic.

"I appreciate it. I know there's a lot I need to do to get Maddy settled here."

From the corner of my eye, I saw Maddy shift in her seat,

bending her head so her long hair covered her face even more.

"I'm sure moving in the middle of the school year is tough. Where were you going to school before, Maddy?"

I didn't want to not include her in our conversation, but I also didn't want to poke at her and make her even more uncomfortable than she already seemed. She surprised me by answering, though she didn't look at me.

"In Allentown but I did remote for a couple months." She shrugged. "I told Uncle Bri I could homeschool again. Not a big deal."

I glanced at Brian to see him shake his head, just once. Got it. Not something Brian wanted to do.

"Well, I think you'll like our school. I'm sure it's a lot different than a big city like Allentown. My graduating class had about a hundred and fifty kids. There are a few more kids now, but it's really not that big. I'm sure you'll fit right in."

Ugh, why couldn't I stop saying stupid shit? I know I would've hated if anyone told me I'd "fit right in." I'd only just met this girl. I had no idea what she was like and what her interests were.

"Sorry, that was a stupid thing to say."

Now I had the attention of those sharp hazel eyes, so like her uncle's. And I thought maybe I might've gone up a little in her estimation. Maybe.

"Did you like going to a big school?" I asked.

Maddy thought about it for a few seconds, before shrugging. "Not really. Most of the kids were stupid and didn't really want to learn anything."

Which implied that she had. Good to know.

"Yeah, I had some of those kinds of kids in my school but, because it's small, they didn't dominate. Know what I mean?"

She thought about it for a second then shrugged and looked down again. Obviously, I was going to have to do a little more work with Maddy before she opened up to me.

"If you want, I can go with you tomorrow to help you get signed up." I glanced at Brian. "I mean with both of you. It's really not that involved, but sometimes it helps to have someone else there to help with the forms if the office staff is busy."

"I'd appreciate that," Brian said. "I don't want to screw up some form and have them send you to the elementary school."

Maddy looked up long enough to roll her eyes at her uncle, though I thought I spied a little bit of a smile now.

"I think they'll be able to figure out where I belong by my age."

"I don't know, kid. I could accidentally put the wrong birth year or something. I'm not sure I like the thought of you going to the high school."

Her head tilted to the side. "I'll be in the high school?"

"Actually," I said, "you'll be in the junior high, but they're the same school, so..."

Now I had her attention. "Really? That's kinda cool."

Since I didn't want to disabuse her of that thought, I just nodded. "It also means you get to pick what classes you want to be in, and sometimes you can choose upper-grade classes if there's room."

Now I saw real interest in Maddy's eyes, and I bit back a triumphant grin, even as I wanted to pump my fist in the air. I'd discovered my first clue about Maddy. Then she shrugged and looked away again, as if she didn't want to be excited.

"Probably all the interesting classes are full already. Doesn't matter. I won't be here that long anyway."

Now I was at a loss, and I looked over at Brian, who didn't look like he knew what to say either. From what he'd told me, it could be six weeks to two months..

"Well, I know the principal," I said. "I can ask to talk to her tomorrow and—"

"No." Maddy broke in, her eyes wide and a little frantic. "You don't need to talk to the principal for me."

I opened my mouth to say it was no problem, that I knew the principal, and she was a really nice person, but something in Maddy's expression made me pause and regroup.

"I don't want special treatment."

Her mouth flattened with determination, and she reminded me more of her uncle with every minute.

"Sure. No problem, but you'll probably meet her when we get you registered tomorrow. Like I said, it's a small school. She likes to get to know all the kids."

And I'd lost her again. It was like she'd flicked a switch and shut down.

I hated to lose. And though this definitely wasn't a game, I hated knowing Maddy was so closed off. When I looked at Brian, his expression as he stared at his niece showed pained frustration. I just wanted to reach over and squeeze his hand, tell him it would be okay. But I couldn't do that in front of Maddy because... Well, just because.

Time to switch tactics.

"So, Brian. I had a few thoughts about your living situation."

I didn't get to say anything else because our server appeared out of nowhere, head bent over her notepad. Which just meant I hadn't been paying attention.

"Hey, Rain, how are ya tonight?"

"I'm good, Chrissy. How are you?"

The blonde, who'd graduated a few years behind me in school, shrugged, looking harried. Couldn't blame her. This was her second job, after the bakery, where she made some of the most delicious pastries in the state, and before her third job, which was working at the arena on game nights.

"Busy. Can't complain. No one listens anyway. What can I get you guys to drink?"

After we ordered sodas—and she did a double take at Brian—she nodded and hustled away.

I glanced back at Brian and found him staring at me. Our gazes locked for several seconds before I blinked, feeling my cheeks start to get hot.

Stupid response. Didn't mean anything.

I snorted silently. At least I could admit to myself that I still had a few (ha!) lingering feelings for the guy.

But then Maddy shifted in her seat, like she couldn't get comfortable, and my mind immediately went back to the problem of how to get this girl to relax. To make her feel like she belonged. Because she clearly didn't feel comfortable, and it was kinda breaking my heart.

"So," Brian said, "you have a suggestion for our living arrangement? That'd be great, 'cause the hotel's not ideal."

"Right, right." I snapped back into focus, my brain practically whirring like a plane propeller. My mom had made the analogy when I was a kid, and it'd stuck. "So, player housing is full, and we can't bunk you with another player for obvious reasons. Mom and Dad are renovating the guest house, so that's out, and I'm not sure you'd want to stay that close to Dad during the season, anyway. He'd always want to talk hockey and you'd be right there, like a sacrificial lamb."

Brian's brows arched, just slightly enough that I noticed how much darker they were from his hair. Huh. Anyway, I just shook my head and kept going.

"And let me know if you think this totally won't work for you, but Mrs. Travers converted her garage into an apartment that no one's renting right now. A couple of the Yingst kids had been living there while on *rumspringa*, but they went home a couple of months ago, so the place is empty. And I know Mrs. Travers is kind of, um, grumpy some of the time, but the garage is detached, so it's not like you'd be living in the same building."

I stopped to take a breath because I realized I needed to. Damn it, I'd been running at the mouth again.

"What's *rumspringa*?"

I turned to Maddy, smiling because she'd perfectly repeated the Pennsylvania Dutch word. "It's the time when an Amish teenager can be away from their family and live in the modern world and use modern things like cars and cell phones and computers without getting in trouble."

Maddy's brows rose in a perfect imitation of her uncle's. "Seriously? That's like a real thing?"

"Yep. The Yingst kids decided to go to school here for a couple of years. The youngest was a really good hockey player. The school team was sorry to lose him. And honestly, it's good for Mrs. Travers to have someone living so close. She hates to admit it, but she's getting old, and she could use some help sometimes. Not that you're there to take care of her. She wouldn't let you anyway. But sometimes she needs help getting packages and stuff inside her house and when her neighbors offer, she tells them she can do it herself, and no one wants to tell her she can't. If you're living there, you can just do it, and she might not yell at you for it. Then again, she probably will, but you'll learn to ignore her."

That faint smile was back on Brian's lips, the one that made me feel giddy. Such a stupid word, but damn, it was descriptive as hell.

Chrissy saved me from making a complete fool by gazing longingly into Brian's eyes when she returned with our drinks and took our order for dinner. Since I knew the menu by heart, I ordered my usual, fish and chips. Maddy went for chicken fingers and French fries and a side of applesauce, which made me smile, because it was exactly what Krista, my brother Rowdy's almost-daughter, always ordered. She was seven. It made me think that Maddy wasn't as old as she fronted.

Brian went for the tried-and-true burger with a side of alfredo noodles and broccoli.

Maddy looked at him like she was seeing a new side of him, and he shrugged. "I start practice tomorrow with the team. I'll burn it off in two hours."

He wasn't wrong, but it was obvious Maddy found this unusual behavior. Which made me wonder how much time she'd actually spent with Brian before he'd taken custody.

When Chrissy left again, I waited all of two seconds before asking him what he thought of my idea.

Shrugging, he sat back in his chair. "Honestly, we don't have a lot of options so I'm open to whatever you suggest."

Since I was used to my brothers and dad, who never

failed to question anything I suggested, my shock must have shown on my face, because Brian's grin grew, making my eyes widen even more.

"That's it? You don't have any questions?"

"No. I trust you, Rain. If you say this is the best option, then that's what we go with."

I didn't honestly know what to say to that.

Brian put one hand on the table and started to drum his fingers. "So what else's on that agenda of yours?"

Mentally going through the list I'd made, I picked an easy one. "I need your sizes for your uniform, but you can just text me those, and I'll have them ready for you tomorrow. We have a home game Friday night, which is nice, so you don't have to travel right away."

He flashed a quick look at Maddy. "Gonna need to figure out something about those travel weekends."

"Actually, I have a plan for that too, if it's okay with you. Maddy can stay with Mom. My mom," I added, when Maddy looked up at me with a question in her eyes. "My mom doesn't go to the away games anymore."

Maddy's mouth flattened. "I don't need a babysitter. I've been staying by myself for years."

"Mads." Brian's quiet voice made Maddy's head jerk around to him. "I need to know you're okay when I'm gone. I'll be away for two or three days at a time. I'm not leaving you by yourself that long."

I could tell Maddy wanted to argue. And I had the sense that Maddy had been taking care of herself for so long she thought she was more capable than she should be at twelve.

Brian and Maddy stared at each other for several long seconds while I bit my tongue against the urge to say something. I wanted to tell her how wonderful my mom was, how she loved to have company and would make her feel like family. Luckily, I didn't open my mouth and insert my foot, because I had a feeling Maddy wouldn't appreciate the contrast with her own mom. Or the reminder that her mom wasn't around.

Yeah, I was making assumptions, but I'm pretty sure I wasn't wrong.

I didn't want to stare at Maddy, so I kept my focus on Brian—and saw the absolute resolve in his expression. He wasn't going to budge on this. And he shouldn't. No matter what the conditions Maddy had been living in before, Brian wanted her to know he was taking care of her now. That was the kind of guy he was. The really good kind. My stupid heart fluttered.

"I can take care of myself."

The stubbornness in that young voice reminded me of myself at Maddy's age. I'd had two bossy older brothers constantly ordering me around. My mom had told me it was okay to do what I wanted to do, as long as I was safe and didn't hurt anyone. She'd wanted me to be able to stick up for myself, but with two older brothers and my retired-military dad, I felt like I had to constantly fight for my place as an independent person. Not as a little girl who needed protecting.

"I get that." Brian nodded, his voice still calm. "But I need you to do this for me. Because I won't be able to concentrate if all I keep thinking about is you all alone."

Maddy's mouth pressed into a taut line, and the silence stretched out between them for several long seconds before Maddy's eyes rolled so hard I swore I heard them rattling.

"Fine. We can see how it goes."

And now, I couldn't keep my mouth shut any longer. "You don't have to stay with my mom all the time. You can stay with me if you want. I mean, my place isn't as big as my parents', and I don't have a hot tub, but I've got Wi-Fi and a TV, and I can cook. Kind of."

That "kind of" was important because I didn't cook a lot. And I didn't cook as well as my mom, but I could make a mean mac and cheese.

Maddy gave me a look that implied she would be rolling her eyes at me if her uncle weren't there. But Brian's sly smile made my heart trip over itself. It was doing a lot of that tonight. Luckily, I thought I was doing a good job of hiding it, but I swore my bones wanted to melt into liquid with the warm and gooey feelings I had for him.

"Thanks," he said. "We'll figure something out by next weekend."

"Of course. After that, the league has a few days off for the Christmas break, and then the games that next weekend are away but they're not overnighters." I turned to Maddy so she knew I wasn't cutting her out of the conversation. "And if you're interested, the town holds a winter festival at the beginning of February. The team does a lot of volunteering to help with setup and activities. We could always use an extra hand."

Maddy shrugged, not meeting my gaze, arms crossed over her chest. "Not really my thing."

"Sure. No problem." I smiled, totally ignoring her scowl. Then I switched my attention back to Brian. "I don't know if you remember, but the players are asked to volunteer a few hours at the festival. At the nighttime skates, especially."

Brian nodded. "I forgot about that. I'm sure I'll have time to volunteer. Your dad still play Jack Frost?"

I grinned, shaking my head. "Actually, we have a new Jack Frost this year. Dad said he was getting too old, even though he secretly really loved it. But the cold was getting to be too much for him. So Dad roped Rowdy into taking over."

Brian shook his head, grinning. "Rowdy's really stepping into your dad's shoes, isn't he?"

"Yeah, he is."

Brian's gaze narrowed. "And you're okay with that?"

"Of course." The words were out before I even thought about what to say, my smile already in place. "That's been the plan for years. Why wouldn't I be okay with it?"

Brian sat back in his chair, crossing his arms over his broad chest. I had to force myself not to stare because, damn it, the man had a chest I wanted to pet.

"Because this is your team just as much as it is your brothers'."

No one had ever said that to me. I mean, I knew Dad and Rowdy appreciated everything I did to make the team run, but to have someone else say it...

"Thanks. It's nice to hear." Momentarily struck mute, I tried to get my brain to move past the fact that Brian had realized something I didn't think a lot of people did. This wasn't just my job. I loved the Devils just as much as my brothers and my dad did. It was my second home.

Seconds later, out of the corner of my eye, I saw Maddy look between the two of us, gaze narrowed. This kid saw way too much.

Shaking my head, I smiled again, this time making sure to

include Maddy. From the look on her face, though, she wasn't buying it.

"Anyway, I'm glad you're cool about helping out. I appreciate it. I know some of the guys think it's stupid, but I think the carnival gives the community something to look forward to in the dead of winter instead of just hibernating. And hockey. Of course."

"Of course." Brian's comment was dry but amused.

"Seems like hockey is the only thing this town has going for it," Maddy said. "Guess you're outta luck if you don't like watching grown men beat each other up."

If I hadn't seen the grin Maddy aimed at her uncle, I would've thought that was a dig. And maybe it was, but Brian reached over and ruffled her hair, and her grin widened reluctantly.

"Guess after a few weeks of living with me, you'll be happy to see me take a few knocks to the head."

The mask Maddy wore most of the time slipped and the love for her uncle shone through so brightly at that second, I swore I got a toothache from the sweetness.

"Nah. I love you, Uncle Bri." Then she paused, and her grin got that wicked edge to it. "But that could change in a heartbeat, so watch your back."

FIVE

Brian

MADDY WAS quiet for the first minute after we got in the car, looking out the side window so I couldn't see her expression. I had no idea what she was thinking about.

But then she turned to stare at me, and I knew exactly what she'd been mulling over.

"So, you got something going on with her, huh?"

I blinked, Maddy's question stumbling through my brain for a few seconds while I considered my answer. At least I could answer this truthfully. "You mean me and Rain? No."

Maddy made a sound between a huff and a snort, that I recognized as a perfect imitation of her mom. My lips started to twitch into a smile, but I managed to cover it.

"She's definitely into you."

Really? "No. She's not. We've just known each other for a long time."

Maddy's arms crossed over her chest. "And you're totally into her."

Shit. "No, I'm not."

Okay, that was a total lie. And there was that huff-snort again, which made me want to squirm in my seat like I was Maddy's age.

"Does she always talk that much?" Maddy continued. "I mean, oh my god, like, she never shut up."

"We had a lot to talk about."

"Does she always get so involved in everyone's business? Seriously, like, doesn't she have her own life?"

"She helps her family run the team. Pretty sure that counts as having a life."

"That just means she got her job *because* of her family. Must be nice not to have to worry about money and stuff."

I didn't say anything right away, because I heard the hurt and frustration in Maddy's voice. Life with Linny had never been easy, even though she had to know how much her mom loved her. Linny had always struggled with money. I'd helped as much as my sister would let me, but she only let me give her money when Maddy needed something. Clothes. Medicine. School supplies.

"Yeah, her family has money, but that doesn't mean she doesn't work just as hard as everyone else."

I glanced over to see Maddy looking at me with narrowed eyes. Those eyes were way too sharp for a twelve-year-old.

"You like her."

She sounded so much like Linny, I shook my head, which Maddy took to be my answer.

"Yes, you do."

"She's a nice person, so yeah, I like her."

"No, you want her to be your girlfriend."

Since I'd promised Maddy I wouldn't lie to her, and I had already totally lied to her just a few seconds earlier, I didn't respond to her statement. "What I *want* is to get us settled here, and Rain's going to help us do that."

"Why would she do that? She doesn't really know us."

"I told you I played here before. I got to know Rain then. But I was friends with her brothers, Rowdy and Rebel, first."

"Why do they have weird names?"

I barked out a laugh. "Wasn't there a kid in your class named Blue Sky?"

"Yeah, but her parents are stoners, and they had her when they were, like, eighteen."

Fair enough. "Rain's parents definitely are not stoners, and their other son is named Rocky."

"Seriously? That's just stupid."

"Well, when you meet the Colonel and Raffi, you can tell them that."

I obviously couldn't hear her roll her eyes, but I know she did. "Like I would ever. I'm not stupid. You need this job."

I had to laugh again as I pulled into the parking lot of the hotel. "Mads, stupid is not a word I would ever associate with you. You're way smarter than me."

Her snort echoed through the car. "Yeah, well, you're the only person who thinks that."

"Your mom thinks you're brilliant. And I'm pretty sure Rain doesn't think you're stupid."

Another sideways grin. "And I'm pretty sure you like her more than a friend. You're not really that great of a liar, Uncle Bri. Like, you really shouldn't even bother."

THE NEXT MORNING, I walked out of the school feeling like I'd just failed a job interview.

Rain walked by my side, strangely subdued and silent the entire time it took to get to my truck. We both got in and got seated, and I just sat there for a second, wondering what the hell had just happened.

"Wow, so that was...interesting," Rain said, staring out the front window. "I had no idea that would be so intense. I don't even think I need my coffee this morning."

"Good thing I'm going to practice later," I responded. "I feel like I need to do penance or something."

We turned and looked at each other, shaking our heads, and finally Rain started to smile, which made me smile.

"I'm so sorry," she said. "That was more like an interrogation than an interview. I mean, I guess they need to be sure about who's taking care of their kids, but damn, I thought he was going to ask for a vial of your blood to be sure you are who you said you are."

"I know, right? But hey, he seemed genuinely interested in Maddy, so that's a plus."

"I didn't realize we—you'd be talking to the assistant principal. I've only met him a few times at games, but damn, he's scary. I wouldn't want to get on his bad side."

Still shaking my head, I pulled my gaze away from the beautiful woman in my passenger seat and got the engine started. Maddy and I had met Rain in the front of the school about an hour ago. She'd walked over from the arena to meet us, because she'd said she wanted to get her steps in.

But now I was in an enclosed space with a woman I had

dreamed about last night, with Maddy's claim that I couldn't lie worth a damn running through my head. All of that jumbled together with the look on Maddy's face when I'd left her alone in a strange school in a strange town where she knew exactly no one, and I felt my chest constricting until I thought it would crack.

"She'll be fine."

Rain's voice wrapped around me like my favorite flannel shirt, warm and comforting. And fucking arousing. My hands reflexively gripped the steering wheel before I caught myself and relaxed them.

"I know. She's tough." I sighed. "Maybe a little too much."

"Give her time to settle in. Let the town grow on her. Of course, Mrs. Travers might give her a level of tough to aspire to."

Mrs. Travers owned the garage apartment Rain thought we should rent. And because there weren't a lot of other options in town, that's where we were headed next. The team took care of housing, so I didn't have to worry about being able to pay the rent, just if the place was a good fit for us.

And right now, pretty much anything would be better than living in a hotel. Maddy needed a place that felt like a home. Where she could have her own room. Where we could make dinner instead of eat takeout.

Rain gave me directions to Mrs. Travers's house, which was in the residential area a couple of blocks off Main Street, and when we pulled into the driveway, I knew just from looking at the garage that this would work. The main house was a small stone Cape, which looked like it could use a little sprucing up. But the garage, which sat at the end of the drive-way, looked newer and in great shape.

It looked more like a small house than a garage, with what looked like a full second floor. You could tell where the garage door had been replaced with a regular door and a full window, but otherwise, it checked every square for what I thought living in a small town should be.

"Is something wrong?"

Rain's hesitancy made me slide her a glance as I shook my head. "No. It looks...perfect."

Shit, maybe I shouldn't have said that out loud. This could still fall through. I hadn't met Mrs. Travers yet, and from what Rain had said, she was a tough nut. And I hadn't seen the inside. It could be a complete mess. But I had a feeling it wasn't. Rain wouldn't steer me wrong.

Rain's bright smile made me feel like I'd just skated sprints, but I smiled back and got out of the truck. Didn't want the moment to get awkward, and knowing me, it would get awkward fast.

Before I could make it to the front door, the door on the side of the house opened and a woman walked out, the cane in her hand looking spindly compared to the woman herself.

"Well, you must be the hockey player," she practically yelled. "Got that look. Rainbow, you here?"

I heard the car door slam before Rain said, "Yes, Mrs. Travers. I'm here."

Mrs. Travers had to be nearly six feet tall and probably weighed more than a few of the guys on the team. And I didn't mean she was overweight. No, she was solid. I'd been expecting someone frail and elderly. This woman looked like she could bench two hundred pounds.

"You know I can't see so well or hear so well, so come closer."

I obeyed without hesitation because I'd been raised to respect my elders. Even so, Rain beat me to her.

"Mrs. Travers, this is Brian Fiskers. I told you he'd like to rent the—"

"Yes, yes. He wants to rent the garage for the season." Mrs. Travers turned toward me and squinted. "I was told you had a teenager."

"She's twelve, but yes, ma'am, my niece is living with me. She's in school now."

"Hmm, so, not a teenager. She noisy?"

"No, ma'am. Not really."

"She's not old enough to stay alone, and I'm no babysitter."

Beside me, I saw Rain look up toward the sky.

"I'll be here most days after school." I planned to be, anyway. "We've already got a plan for her to stay with Miss Raffi when I'm gone for games."

"Where's her mom?"

My tongue got stuck on that one because I hadn't planned to tell many people what was going on with my sister. I'd known there'd be questions, but Mrs. Travers's blunt question took me back a step. Still, I didn't want to lie.

"Treatment center. For alcohol."

I didn't know what I expected her to say or do, but I braced for whatever. Despite my size and my personae on the ice as an enforcer, I really didn't like confrontation. That didn't mean I was a pushover. I just didn't want to have to deal with other people's attitudes.

Mrs. Travers stared at me for a few more seconds, like she was ticking off pros and cons.

Finally, she said, "Son's got issues with that. Been in and out of rehab a few times. Seems to be on the right path now." She shot Rain a look, who didn't look surprised. "No telling tales out of school, little girl."

Rain nodded. "Yes, ma'am." Then she shrugged. "I like Jimmy. He's sweet."

Mrs. Travers huffed. "Yeah, he is that." She turned back to me. "Well, it's ready to move in today, if you want. I'll open the windows and give it some air. Been closed up for a few weeks. I'll throw the bedding and towels in for a wash too."

I released a breath I hadn't realized I was holding. Guess I'd passed the test. "Thank you. We'll be over after I pick up Maddy from school. And you don't have to worry about the towels and stuff. We can do that tonight."

"I ain't got nothing to do today anyway."

My lips parted to protest again, but out of the corner of my eye, I saw Rain widen her eyes and shake her head just once. I shut my mouth.

Mrs. Travers had already turned to shuffle back to her home, now leaning heavily on her cane. Part of me wanted to offer my arm for her to hold as she walked, but she'd probably bite my head off if I did.

"I expect to hear from the team about rent today," she said before disappearing back into the house.

"Yes," Rain said. "I'll get payment set," the door slammed behind Mrs. Travers, "up."

Okay, I guessed we had a place to stay.

I looked at Rain, who looked at me like I might take off screaming. She should know me better than that. I don't run.

Although my past performance with her and Mo might suggest otherwise.

"Well, that went better than I thought it would." She gave me a thumbs-up and a bright smile that made me want to smile back. "I think she likes you."

That got a chuckle out of me, and I nodded my head toward my truck. I didn't say anything until we were back in the cab and pulling away. I didn't want my new landlady to accidentally hear something she didn't like and kick us out.

"Oh my god," Rain said, "I just realized you never went inside. We can go back—"

"If you say it's good, I'm sure it'll be fine for us. I trust your judgment. Besides, we don't have a lot of options, and this one is pretty perfect location-wise. It'll be fine. Back to the arena now?"

She nodded, still watching me like she expected me to do something. "You're going to be early for practice."

"Haven't been on the ice for a few months. I figure I can use the extra time."

A slight pause, but I could practically hear her brain clicking over her thoughts.

"Did you miss it? Playing, I mean."

She didn't need to explain her question. I knew what she meant.

Like I'd lost a limb. "Yeah, but I think I needed a break to realize how much I missed it."

"So you haven't skated since you left last season?"

"No, but I'm pretty sure I remember how."

Her quiet huff of laughter made my gut twist. "You always were good on skates."

"Yep, since I was a kid. Growing up in a small town with

an ancient ice rink as the only entertainment, and parents who think the busier you are, the less time you have to get into trouble, kinda seals your fate."

"Does your sister skate too?"

"She can, but she had other distractions by the time she hit high school. I loved hockey. She loved to party. We didn't have a lot in common as kids."

"So she's always had a…an issue with alcohol?"

"Yeah. She was twenty when she had Maddy. My parents didn't kick her out or anything. Linny just didn't want to follow their rules and moved out with Maddy's dad. They were okay for a year, maybe. And then it all fell apart. The guy skipped out on them, and Linny worked a lot of shit jobs, collected assistance and lived on food stamps for years. It was always a struggle for her, but she was stubborn. Maddy never went without food or clothes. She loves Maddy. I've never doubted that. But Lin always had just enough money for alcohol. What I've learned about alcoholism is that people can fully function while being alcoholics. But it always catches up to them."

"I'm glad she's getting help."

"Yeah, me too. I just hope it sticks this time."

"So this isn't the first time she's been in rehab?"

I thought back to the three other stints in different facilities, and the promises that this time it was going to be better.

"No, but this is the first time she's done inpatient."

"That's gotta be tough on Maddy."

"Yeah, it has been."

Since we weren't that far from the arena, we were already pulling into the parking lot. There were only a few cars in the lot, but I recognized her tan Subaru Outback, decked out with Devils hockey stickers and magnets. Her car served as a mobile billboard for the team. She probably had the backseat packed with promotional material, ready to hand out in a flash.

She'd always been the team's most devoted fan.

As I parked next to her car and shut off the engine, I stared at the service entrance, a familiar feeling settling over me.

"Brian?"

"Hmm?"

"I'm glad you're back. I just...wanted you to know."

I turned and caught her lopsided smile, which made me feel even more warm and fuzzy. And hot and bothered.

"I'm glad to be back."

It felt like home.

SIX

Rain

"HEY, Rainy Day. Can you stop by after work? There's something I want to run by you."

I had picked up the call without looking at the screen, but the second I heard the woman's voice on the other end, I started to smile.

"Oh no," I teased Erin Wright. "You didn't blow up your kitchen again, did you?"

"Jeez, one tiny fire, and no one lets you forget it."

"Well, you did put it on the front page of the paper."

"It was a slow news week, what can I say?"

I laughed at one of the people I loved most in this town. Erin had moved here about four years ago, and we'd hit it off immediately. Our type A personalities fit together like burgers and fries.

She'd come to help her grandfather, Will, shut down the small weekly newspaper and radio station he'd inherited from his grandfather. She'd ended up staying to help Will run it, very much over her parents' objections. They didn't talk much anymore.

More recently, she'd bought the tiny café next to the radio station/newsroom and had taken over the bakery herself. There'd been a learning curve. And there had been that one small oven fire that hadn't entirely been her fault. But, damn, the woman's baked goods were delicious. Between Crack One Open—I still thought the name needed work—and reporting for the newspaper and station, the woman never stopped.

Too bad she hadn't been able to make her business profitable. Yet. Between the diner just down the street and the Dunkin' Donuts a few miles away near the interstate interchange, there was tough competition.

"I don't think I have anything tonight." I grabbed my planner off the corner of my desk and flipped it to this week. I hadn't checked my schedule yet today, and sometimes I forgot I'd added something to my calendar. Not often, but it had been known to happen. "Looks like I'm free. What's up?"

"I've got an idea."

When other people heard Erin say that, they sometimes ran in the opposite direction. I'd literally seen one of the local handymen cross the street to miss her. And Erin was so damn sweet, she didn't even notice they were trying to avoid her. She just ran after them, strawberry-blonde hair streaming out behind her and green eyes blazing while she smiled and called out to them.

"Please tell me this doesn't have to be done until after the carnival because my plate is full until then. And Christmas is only a week away."

"You love all this shit with the holidays and don't deny it, because I'm not the one who put up their office Christmas tree on November first."

My gaze slid to said tree, twinkling in its perch of honor on its stand in the corner next to the window overlooking the arena. All the offices in the building looked out over the playing area, which meant if I walked over there now, I could watch Brian skate.

I'd been really good so far and hadn't moved from my chair. But my legs were literally twitching with the need to get up and stand by the window like Liv Tyler in *Armageddon*, hyperventilating as she looked out over the control room. Probably not the best analogy, because her father had just given up his life to save the world and I was just going to watch a hot guy skate, but anyway.

"Don't diss my tree."

"Then come over after work and let me run this idea past you."

I gave an exaggerated sigh, my smile spreading. "You know I will."

"Oh good. I really think you're going to love this one. Okay, don't want to keep you tied up at work. See you tonight."

I didn't have time to respond. She was just gone.

And now my concentration was completely blown, though I couldn't blame it all on Erin. Usually, I could ignore the faint noise from the ice. I was so used to it by now that it didn't even register. Most days. Today was not one of those days.

I could barely hear the sound of skates gliding over the

ice, or the tap of stick slapping puck, but now I got up and walked over to the window.

Brian stood at center ice, a bucketful of pucks scattered next to him. He wasn't wearing a helmet and every time he took a shot, he stopped to shake his unusually long, for him anyway, hair out of his face.

He'd always had a hard shot, and that hadn't changed in the time he'd been off the ice. He hadn't lost any muscle, either, if the way he looked in his gear was any indication. He looked massive, a solid wall of muscle—

"Rain, you here?"

I turned away from the window with a gasp, the sound of my dad shouting down the hall scaring the crap out of me. As always.

This time, I didn't even bother to yell back, I just gritted my teeth and stomped down the hall.

"If I didn't miraculously appear every time you yelled, what would you do?" I asked as I walked through the door of his office, not surprised to see Rowdy there. I smacked my brother on the back of the head, just because I could, as I sat in the chair next to his in front of my dad's desk. Rowdy returned the love by ruffling my hair.

I thought about sticking my finger in his ear, but Dad gave us the look, and we both resisted the urge to continue tormenting each other. It was our love language.

"You got some time to talk now?" Dad looked at me. "Something I want to hash out with the two of you."

My spidey senses tingled, because my dad didn't typically sound like this. Like he had a problem and no answer. Dad always had an answer for everything.

"I've already talked to your mom, but I wanted to talk to you two together."

Rowdy and I glanced at each other with raised eyebrows. Apparently, my brother didn't know what this was about either, and that was unusual.

"What's up, Pop?" Rowdy asked.

Dad didn't answer right away, looking between the two of us, as if trying to find the right words. That in itself was scary because our dad was never at a loss for words. He didn't use a lot of them, but he always knew what he was going to say.

"Dad?" I prodded. "What's going on?"

A few more seconds of silence, and my stomach started to do flips. Something was up, and I hated not knowing what that was.

"I got a phone call from Bill Irving about joining the ECHL."

It took a second for the news to process through my brain. Apparently, Rowdy's brain worked faster than mine.

"What was his pitch this time?"

My head snapped around to Rowdy, eyes narrowing. "This time? What do you mean, this time?"

Rowdy grimaced at the rising tone of my voice, flashing a look at Dad, who put up his hand, like he was stopping traffic.

"When was the first time?" My voice sounded screechy, and a little pissy. And that wasn't good. "What did they say? What did you say? When were you going to tell me?"

Dad waited a beat before asking, "Anything else you want to ask?"

I had the childish urge to stick out my tongue but settled instead for making a face. "I reserve the right to more questions later."

Now my dad grinned, and I knew it was because he was proud of me. And it just made me want to screech a little louder.

"Told your mom you should've been a lawyer."

"Lucky you, I decided to work for the *family* business."

I forced myself not to cross my arms over my chest and pout, because I wasn't twelve anymore.

Out of the corner of my eye, I saw Rowdy grimace. My dad's grin spread even more. I would throw up my hands and scream in frustration, but I knew it wouldn't get him to answer me any faster, so I started to silently chant, *I love my family, I love my family, I love my family.*

Finally, Dad said, "I didn't tell you the first time because it wasn't something I even considered. We were still building the league at that point. And I'd made a commitment to the other owners to give it ten years before we made any major changes or considered jumping ship. The ECHL put out feelers to two of our teams that year."

My brows arched. "And neither of you took the offer? Why?"

"Because neither of us felt it was a good fit. It would mean a whole hell of a lot more regulation that we don't have to worry about now. And there were logistical reasons. More travel. Longer travel. More expenses. We were doing well for ourselves. Why rock the boat?"

Because we were small potatoes in the grand scheme of all things hockey, and a larger professional league believed we could be more. Bigger league, more fans, more promotional opportunities. Fans from other areas coming to St. David for games. Eating at local restaurants. Shopping at local stores.

The business it would bring to the town would more than overcome any cons.

Unless it didn't. Unless we overstepped. Unless we overextended and—

"I can see your brain sparking, Rainy," Dad said. "And I know it sounds amazing. But there are other considerations. We're a big fish in a small pond right now. We'd be a small fish in a bigger pond, and there'd be a whole new learning curve." He exchanged a look with Rowdy that confirmed my sense that there was more going on than just a phone call. "Plus, I'm not sure it's what's best for you and your brothers."

And then I realized what this was all about.

"Wait. This is about you retiring, isn't it? I mean, I know you keep talking about it, but..."

I couldn't imagine this place without my dad. He was as much a fixture here as the aging popcorn machine we refused to replace because we'd had it since opening night. Dad had bought it from the Philadelphia Colonials, who'd had it in storage after they'd built their new arena years ago.

Now, little abstract pieces of information started to click together in my brain. Duties Rowdy had taken over. New responsibilities on my plate the past couple of seasons. It hadn't occurred to me at the time to think they were anything other than things Dad didn't want to do.

"Are you really considering retiring?"

He paused long enough for my eyes to widen completely. "Actually, your mom and I decided this season would be my last."

My head snapped around to Rowdy to find an almost comical dumbstruck expression on his face. I probably looked exactly the same. When he looked at me, he shook his head, reading my mind.

"I didn't know." Then he looked back at our dad. "Why so soon?"

Dad's expression was bemused. "Why do you two look so surprised? I never said I was going to work 'til I die."

"That's not—I mean—" I stumbled around for words. "I didn't— Well, shit, Dad."

"What she said." Rowdy shook his head. "Wait. Why isn't Rebel here?"

"Because I wanted to tell you two first. You're going to be the most affected. Rebel's never made any noise about a front office position, and he's been clear about the fact that he's not ready to leave the ice."

"And Rowdy is?" I shot my brother another look. "Is something wrong with you? Are you dying? Why didn't you tell me you wanted off the ice?"

Rowdy rolled his eyes and shook his head. "I'm not ready to give up playing completely, but I'm not getting any younger, and I don't want to play forever. But I'm not sure I'm ready to completely take over the team yet either."

"That's why I'm not retiring until the end of the season. I want you and Rain to get more involved with the day-to-day stuff. And Rainy, I want to know if you're okay with Rowdy getting the GM title and if you want more responsibilities."

My mouth opened in shock then shut with a snap.

"What do you mean, more responsibilities?"

"I mean, do you want more of a leadership role with the team? Obviously, I'm not looking for an answer now. Take some time. Think about it. We've got a few months to figure it out."

My brain sputtered, trying to get a handle on what my dad was proposing. I looked at Rowdy, wondering if he'd be pissed off at the possibility of having to share the team with me. And feeling fizzy excitement building at the thought.

Rowdy stared at me with raised eyebrows. Not angry, just curious.

"I don't know that I ever really gave any thought to who would run the team after you were gone," I said honestly. "I just assumed it'd be Rowdy."

"That would be kind of sexist, wouldn't it?" Rowdy gave me a challenging smirk. "I always considered this team as our team. A family team, and that includes you. No, you're not on the ice, but we wouldn't have butts in seats without you."

I didn't have a comeback to that. I mean, I could've said something snarky, but Rowdy was being serious. I didn't know how to deal with a serious Rowdy. So I just stared at him until he frowned.

"What?" He frowned at me. "Do I have something on my face or what?"

"No. I just...never considered that you..."

"That I what? Value what you do?"

"Well, maybe 'value' isn't the word I'd use."

Rowdy's brows rose, and he gave me a look I knew he'd learned from Dad. "So what word would you use?"

I huffed and rolled my eyes, not bothering to look at Dad for help. He was probably enjoying the show.

"I guess I just figured you were oblivious to what I did."

Rowdy rolled his eyes, making me think of Maddy. And then, of course, Brian. Which wasn't helpful right now.

"Or maybe," he said, "I just trusted you to do your job because I know you're good at it."

After a second, I stuck my tongue out at him, which wasn't very mature, I know. But it made him grin, which was what I wanted.

"Okay, maybe you're not *just* a brainless hockey player."

Rowdy's laughter busted out. "And you're not just a pain in my ass."

I pulled another face at him, which morphed into a smile. I did love my brothers, though they drove me to distraction much of the time and especially when they ganged up against me.

"So, Rainy, what are your initial thoughts?" Dad asked. "Right off the top of your head."

Like he'd flicked a switch, my brain started to churn again.

And words flowed out of my mouth.

"SO YOU HATED everything I said, didn't you?"

Rowdy shook his head as we walked down the hall to my office. "I didn't have time to digest half of what you said, so excuse me if I'm still trying to process it. And no, I didn't hate anything you said. Hell, I'm trying to decide if I'm pissed off because I didn't think of some of it."

I shrugged. "Our brains just work differently. I'm sure you'll come up with a whole bunch of stuff I would never think of."

He scrubbed a hand through his hair. "Hell, I'm still trying to get a handle on some of the shit Dad deals with on a daily basis. I mean, I know how trades work, but the fucking paperwork is gonna kill me, I swear."

"You'll figure it out. You always do."

He looked at me with a crooked smile. "Now, you're just trying to butter me up. You must want something."

We'd reached my office, and I motioned him inside with my hand. I knew he was going to be late for practice, but I said, "Just for a second. I want to run something by you."

His smile widened. "I knew you wanted something. But you know you don't have to ask my permission. If it's gonna cost money, you just need to ask Pop."

"I just want your opinion on something."

When he walked in, I shut the door behind him, earning a narrow-eyed look from my brother.

"Why does this conversation need a closed door?"

"Because I want it to be private, okay? Jeez, you sound scared."

"Not scared. Just rightly cautious. What's going on?"

I moved around my desk to sprawl in my chair, while Rowdy did the same across from me.

"Tell me honestly. How long have you known about the ECHL thing?"

Rowdy shook his head, his face screwing up in a frown. "Honestly, I didn't. But I got suspicious when I walked in on Pop talking to Joe McGinty at the Bigfoots. He couldn't get off the phone fast enough. But I heard him mention the ECHL commissioner's name before he knew I was there. It took me a day or two to realize who they were talking about. And when I did, I figured...I don't know, they were just shooting the shit."

Rowdy looked as perplexed as I felt, and he'd never been able to lie worth a damn, at least not to me. We sat in silence for a few long seconds, which was remarkable on both our parts.

"So what do you think?" I asked.

He didn't answer right away, and I could tell he was really giving some thought to what he wanted to say. For Rowdy, that was surprising. Usually, he opened his mouth first and considered his words second.

But since he and Tressy and her daughter, Krista, had started living together, he'd actually, dare I say, grown up.

Finally he sighed and ran a hand through his already messy hair, making it even more wild. "I think it's going to be a shit-ton of work and a metric fuck-ton of headaches. Part of me wants it. And part of me thinks it's the worst fucking idea ever."

I let out a relieved sigh. "Then we're on the same page."

"Thank fuck for that." Rowdy shook his head, blowing out a huge sigh. "So what the fuck are we going to do?"

"Luckily, we have a few weeks to think about it. And we're going to have to bring Rebel and Rocky in on this. Damn, I think that's why Dad told us first. So he didn't have to deal with Rebel. Boss move."

"I'm not sure that's enough time."

I took a harder look at Rowdy, at the worry lines on his forehead and the way he kept shaking his head.

"You know, if this is something you don't even want to consider, I'm with you."

His lips curved, and I swear he wanted to reach across the desk and ruffle my hair again, like he used to when we were kids. It'd always annoyed the ever-living fuck out of me, but I realized now it was his way of showing affection. I'd been a feral kid, definitely not a girly girl who loved sparkles and wanted to be a cheerleader. I'd grown up with three brothers. After I turned five, my mom didn't even bother buying me dresses because I'd end up in my denim overalls and sneakers anyway.

And to their credit, my brothers had never treated me like a weak, giggly idiot. But I wasn't an athlete. I loved our team, and I loved my job, but hockey wasn't my identity. I mean, this team meant the world to me, but for Rowdy and Rebel, it was who they were.

I loved the creative aspects of what I did. I loved seeing people have fun with the promotions or compliment me on the designs for the sweaters. I loved getting butts in seats for games and organizing events to raise money for the various charities in the area. The Devils allowed me to do that.

Rowdy loved to *play* hockey.

"I know," Rowdy finally said. "And I appreciate it. But it goes the other way too. If this is something you want to do, or don't want to do, I'm with you, Rainbow Brite."

Grinning, I threw a pen at him for using that nickname. He caught it out of the air like he was a ninja master. Damn him.

"Okay, we're on the same page. Let's circle back to this after Christmas. Rocky'll be home and maybe Rebel will be softened by the holiday spirit."

We looked at each other and simultaneously said, "Nah."

Laughing, I waved my hands at him, making a shooing noise. "Now go to practice so I can get some work done."

He chuckled and got up, heading for the door. But before he left, he turned. "Hey, thanks for helping Brian and his niece get settled. I knew you'd be able to handle that better than me. I appreciate it, and I know he does too."

For some stupid reason, my cheeks felt hot, but I nodded and smiled. "Of course. He's a member of the team."

Rowdy nodded, still staring at me like he could read my mind. And I really didn't want him to read my mind, because whenever I thought about Brian, my thoughts got x-rated. Which was both inconvenient and stupid, because that definitely wasn't happening.

When he opened his mouth again, I thought for sure he was going to tease me about Brian. Something stupid about me having a crush. I was ready to shut him down when he said, "If you and Brian are finally gonna do something about the fact that you both stare at each other like lovestruck teenagers, I don't need to know."

SEVEN

Brian

I LEFT the gym an hour early so I could go to the hotel, pack up our shit, and get to the school on time to pick up Maddy. She really didn't have all that much stuff, which made me a little angry and sad at the same time. She only packed a couple of duffel bags, one filled with clothes. The other one she'd never opened with me around. When I picked it up, I had to put a little effort into it, because it was heavy as hell.

The bell rang a couple minutes after I parked, and kids started streaming out of the building. Okay, more like sauntering. Most of the older kids headed for the parking lot, getting in their hand-me-down Chevy trucks and Honda Civics. No Beemers or Mercedes here, although there were a couple of classic muscle cars that made me smile. And a lot of the cars had Devils stickers on their bumpers or back windows.

Most of the younger kids headed for the buses lined up in

front of the building, but there were a few who aimed for the parking lot and the line of cars waiting for them. Surprisingly, Maddy walked out with another girl, dressed in ripped jeans and a black hoodie, whose mouth never stopped moving. Maddie didn't appear to say anything, though she nodded occasionally, red hair loose and falling around her face. Like she didn't want anyone to notice her. Made my heart hurt to see it. But she didn't look like she didn't want to talk to the other girl.

Maddy looked up at that moment and searched the parking lot. I was pretty sure I saw relief on her face when she saw my truck. But she didn't immediately make a run for it. She said something to the other girl, who smiled and nodded then turned in the other direction as Maddy made her way to my truck.

She grunted out a "Hey" as she got in, glancing at all our stuff piled in the back.

"Pretty sure I got everything," I said as I pulled away. "Checked all the drawers twice and the shower."

Maddy shrugged, like it didn't matter. "Thanks."

"Have a good day?"

Another shrug. "Okay, I guess. Just another school."

"Homework?"

That got a huff. "Of course. It's school."

And that was the extent of my small talk.

Surprisingly, Maddy asked, "How was practice?"

"Not bad. Didn't injure anything, so that's a good day."

A slight pause. "Do you get hurt a lot?"

I shrugged but took a few seconds to think about my answer. Because I realized Maddy had never seen me play.

"Not a lot, no, but I've had a couple of broken bones. And something always hurts."

"Mom isn't really into sports, so we don't really watch it." Another pause. "And we didn't have, like, regular TV."

Because they couldn't afford it, probably. *Shit.*

"Well, the game we play here is a little different than the NHL. It's a little, umm...more aggressive."

It occurred to me that Maddy might not like the game. And I was going to have to drag her to every damn home game. *Double shit.*

I had her full attention now as she turned to look at me, eyes narrowed. "What do you mean?"

Might as well lay it all on the table right away, so she wasn't surprised.

"Well, I play defense, and defensemen do a lot of checking."

"You mean you hit people."

"Well, yeah. I thought you don't watch hockey?"

She shrugged. "Doesn't mean Mom doesn't talk about you."

"So what'd she say?"

"She said you hit people for a living."

I opened my mouth to say, "Not exactly," but then shut it when I realized that's exactly what I did.

"I feel that needs a little context."

"I'm not stupid, Uncle Bri." I knew she'd just rolled her eyes even if I couldn't see her actually do it. "I get that you don't just go out and hit people. It's just the game."

"It's part of the game, yeah. I guess I just don't want you to be, uh, surprised at how...physical it can get."

She didn't say anything right away, and I figured she'd

decided the conversation was over. It wasn't until we were pulling into the driveway at our new apartment that she had something else to say.

"Are you going to get hurt?"

I parked and shut the engine off so I could turn to look at her. She wouldn't meet my eyes, but her lips quivered a little. Like she was scared. Hell, I didn't want her to be scared. I just didn't want her to freak out when I bled a little. Then again, I'd promised her no lying.

"Hey, Mads." I waited until she turned to me, trying so hard not to look worried. "Yeah, I can get hurt. It's a physical game, and I play hard. But I'm big, and I'm tough, and usually it's the other guy who goes down. But I don't want you to be afraid. Not for me...or of me."

Immediately, she rolled her eyes, and a little of that fear got pushed out by feminine exasperation. Now she looked so much like my sister that I just had to smile.

"I know *that*. It'll be fine, Uncle Bri."

I huffed out a laugh, and she smiled.

And that's when Mrs. Travers stomped out of her house, waving her cane like a sword.

"You two going to sit in that truck all night? Come out and get your keys before I freeze."

THE KNOCK on the door didn't surprise me. I figured it was Mrs. Travers with something else to throw at me.

First, it'd been freshly washed sheets followed by blankets. No idea what we were still missing because the kitchen was stocked with every kind of pot and pan I could think of and would never use, and the bathroom had towels that smelled like the sheets and blankets.

But it wasn't Mrs. Travers.

"Hey, man. Just checking in to see if you've got everything you need." Rowdy grinned at me then held up an insulated bag. "And we come bearing food, so I figure you'll be happy to see us."

The "us" part of that equation was a short, beautiful blonde whom Rowdy had somehow managed to convince to move from New York City to St. David with her young daughter, who bounced between her mom and Rowdy.

"Lucky for you, Rowdy cooked," Tressy said with a lopsided grin, which just made her daughter, Krista, laugh.

"Mommy, you don't cook that bad." Krista looked up at me with a glint in her eyes and whispered, "But Rowdy's definitely better."

With a smile, I waved my hand. "Come on in. We're just getting our stuff put away." I turned to yell toward Maddy's bedroom. "Hey, Mads, we've got guests."

I took the bag from Rowdy and headed toward the kitchen. "Thanks for this. I figured we'd head down to the diner for dinner, but this is better."

"Don't get too excited." Rowdy put his arm around Tressy, the move so natural, they looked like an old married couple. I figured that wedding would be happening pretty soon. "It's just baked rigatoni, a chicken casserole, and eggplant parmesan."

"Dude, you have way too much time on your hands."

Something crossed Rowdy's expression, so fast that I almost missed it.

"Yeah, not really. But we gotta eat too, and it's easy enough to make double."

"Well, I appreciate it." I turned to call for Maddy again just as she came out of her bedroom. She had a polite smile on her face, as if she figured she had to be on her best behavior or else. Or else what, I don't know.

"Hey, Mads, these are my friends, Rowdy, Tressy, and Krista. Rowdy's the captain of the Devils."

"Hi." Maddy nodded and raised a hand before dipping her head down, though her smile did seem a little more natural when she glanced at Krista.

"They brought us food, so we won't starve or rot away on fast food. At least for a few days."

Maddy stopped at my side, close enough that we were almost touching.

"Thanks."

"Can you put this in the fridge for me?"

"Sure." She took the bag, then glanced at Krista, whose bright smile made Maddy's smile a little more natural. "Do you wanna help?"

"Sure! Momma said you just moved here. We did too. Well, a little while ago. We moved here last Christmas. Christmas here is really fun. Did you know..."

The girls had moved out of earshot, and I turned back to see Tressy staring at the girls and Rowdy staring at me, still grinning.

"Sorry." I waved at the sitting area on the other side of the room from the kitchen. "Come on in. Sit down. You want something to drink?"

"Nah, we're not staying long," Rowdy said. "Just wanted to make sure you had some food."

"This is much nicer than I was expecting." Tressy's gaze swept around the place. "When Rain told me you were renting a garage, I didn't think it'd be this big."

"Yeah, me either. It's deceptive from the outside. And the two floors are nice."

It meant me and Maddy had separate rooms and baths. Yeah, they were small, but it'd been more than I was expecting, and I was grateful.

"Are you excited to be playing again?" Tressy asked.

Loaded question, especially with Rowdy watching me like a hawk.

I nodded. "I am. It just takes me a little longer to warm up than it used to. Don't want to embarrass myself with all the kids this weekend. I swear they get younger every year."

Rowdy snorted. "That's because we get older. Sprints get more exhausting, and the hits hurt a little more. Good thing you're here to give me a few weeks off."

"About that. You know I didn't expect you to give me your spot on the team."

Rowdy and Tressy exchanged a look that made my brain churn.

"Actually," Rowdy looked back at me, "there's some stuff going on behind the scenes that made this a good time for me to take some time off."

"Can you tell me?"

He exchanged another look with Tressy, her smile encouraging him to continue. "We're not broadcasting this, but I know you can keep your mouth shut. Only Dad, Mom, Rain, me, and Tressy know about this, but... We got an offer from the ECHL to join the league."

My mouth dropped open in surprise. That had not been anything I'd even thought about.

"Holy shit, Rowdy, that's...great?"

From his expression, I could tell he was torn. Rowdy couldn't hide what he was thinking for shit. And honestly, I didn't know what to think. The ECHL was a different level of play. More rules. More teams. More logistics. More headaches.

"We're not sure we're going to do it yet. Rain and I need to talk about it more. Rebel made it clear he's leaving management of the Devils up to us, so we're kicking it around. Right now, I'm stuck between 'Hey, we made it' and 'No fucking way.'"

"Sounds like you've got a lot on your plate."

"Understatement, man. Total understatement. And Rain's coming at this with a totally different perspective, which is great, but I need to bounce shit off another player, so you've been nominated."

"Gee, thanks. I think." I huffed, shaking my head. "You know I'm here for you, whatever you need."

"I know, man. And I appreciate the hell out of that. I know you're still getting settled, but we'd love for you and Maddy to come for dinner tomorrow at our place. Not gonna lie, I wanna pick your brain." He exchanged a quick look with Tressy, whose mouth curved into a smile. "We'll invite Rain too."

I blinked, my heart beating a little faster at the mention of her name.

"Uh, yeah, sure." Christ, I sounded like an idiot. "That sounds great. Thanks."

Rowdy's expression split in a shit-eating grin, which I chose to ignore.

"Then we'll see you tomorrow around six. Hey, Krista, we gotta go."

I looked over to see Krista pout, but it was the look on Maddy's face that made me want to smile. She looked happy, smiling down at Krista and taking her hand when the other girl reached out to pull her along with her.

Dinner tomorrow night would be good for her. Good for her to be around other people.

And being with Rain wouldn't hurt my mood either.

EIGHT

Rain

BLINKING, I thought about my words carefully before I gave Erin a response.

"Are you nuts? I mean, seriously. Because that's crazy."

Erin rolled her eyes and huffed out a sigh before flopping into the chair opposite mine in her café.

"So you think it's stupid?"

"No, that's not what I said. I said it's crazy. Not stupid. I actually think it's brilliant, but I also think you're nuts for wanting to add this to your plate. Don't you have enough to do? Seriously, you need to get laid."

Erin waved that thought away like it was a bad smell. "I don't have time to get laid. Besides, all the good guys around here are taken or they're hockey players."

And Erin wouldn't be caught dead dating a hockey player. Although, unlike me, she'd never actually dated one. I hadn't learned my lesson, apparently, since all I could think about was—

"And you've got dibs on the only one I'd even consider dating."

I wrinkled my nose at her. "What are you talking about?"

Except I was pretty sure I knew what she was talking about.

"Oh please," she said, "I know you've got a thing for Brian."

"Who says?"

"Your face, every time you talk about him."

I opened my mouth to deny it, then shut it before I said anything and incriminated myself. Erin grinned, indicating her victory, which made me want to give her the finger. Which would cement her victory in her mind.

"I still think you need to get laid more than you need to start a new business."

"But I already have the space, and it's not like we have a bookstore in town. It'd practically be a public service."

I rolled my eyes, but I could see how excited she was. And honestly...it wasn't a horrible idea. I loved books. I loved to read. Hell, more than once I'd lamented that the nearest book-store was almost an hour away. Of course, we had a library, but I couldn't own those books and horde them in my house...

"Don't you think you'd be biting off more than you can chew? I mean, you've already got the radio station and the newspaper and the café. There's just not that much time in the day."

"Granddad still runs the newspaper. Mostly. And Gil takes care of the radio station. I could do it." She paused, her eyes lighting up, and I knew exactly where she was going before she opened her mouth to finish. "If I had a partner."

"Uh..."

I should say no. I had so much on my plate already. I had a more-than-full-time job. I volunteered at no fewer than three local organizations. Christmas was around the corner and after that, the Winter Carnival in February, which was a part-time job in itself.

And yet...

I wanted to say yes. My mind already raced with ideas, and my gaze wandered around the space. There was more than enough room for bookshelves if she lost some of the tables. I'd always thought this space was too big for just the bakery. Too much empty space, too many tables. It made the business look uninviting. And I knew there were a few rooms on the other side of the wall with the radio station that could work as well.

"Rain?"

"Uh-huh."

Enough room for a children's area and a few cozy chairs and couches tucked into the shelves. The café could host book clubs and after-school reading groups and—

"Say yes, Rain."

I wanted to. Damn it, I really wanted to. This would be something just for me, and I couldn't help feeling that if I didn't say yes, I'd regret it. I also knew I usually jumped in with both feet before I truly thought things through. I always made it work out, no matter the cost, which was usually to my sanity.

I met Erin's gaze and saw the hope shining there.

You could do this. You'd have a partner, someone to split the work—

"Let me sleep on it, okay?"

Trying to rein in her smile, Erin nodded. "No problem. Of course. I know it's a big decision, but I *have* thought through a lot of the logistics. I've even put together a cost projection and business plan. And it'd be so much fun to do it together."

Digging into the pile of papers on the table, she grabbed a folder and put it into my outstretched hand.

"I know you're going to be busy getting ready for the carnival next month, so take your time." Her smile turned sly. "And maybe take a little time to have fun with, oh, I don't know, a hot hockey player."

Rolling my eyes and sighing, I put the folder in my bag and lifted my mug to my mouth so I couldn't stick my foot in my mouth. At least until I swallowed.

"I'm not looking to date anyone yet. Especially another player."

Except if Brian asked me out, I'd say yes so fast, he'd probably reconsider and run the other way. Not that he would ask because he had a lot on his plate at the moment, including caring for his twelve-year-old niece and getting back into hockey life.

"Right." Erin drew the word out to about five syllables. "But if you think I need to get laid, honey, you should take a look in the mirror."

I didn't need to. I knew exactly what I saw every morning. The bags under my eyes from restless sleep. Because I couldn't' stop thinking about a certain hockey player. "I'm perfectly fine being by myself right now."

Erin's brows rose. "Uh-huh. You should try saying that a few more times. Maybe you'll believe it then."

"RAINY! Can you shoot me those sweater designs for the games in March? Dad said I need to get them approved by the other teams before we send them to be made."

Closing my eyes, I took a breath and reached for calm, because this was the third time Rowdy had yelled from his office next door. I wanted to go next door and smack him on the head with the desk phone that he could use instead of yelling, then walk out again and not answer his goddamn question.

And since I refused to dignify his yelling with my own, when we had a perfectly working intercom system, I ignored him.

"Rain, you over there?"

I pulled up the file for the sweater designs then opened the program I used to create our social media posts and got to work on next week's posts. And waited.

"Rain? You know I can hear you typing."

I clenched my teeth together and flexed my fingers over the keyboard before I started to type again.

"Oh for fuck's sake," I barely heard Rowdy grumble, before he yelled, "Fine!"

I didn't bother to hide my grin when Rowdy walked into my office. I waited for him, leaning back in my chair, arms crossed over my chest.

"Yes, I know there's an intercom," he groused. "Don't start on me. Can you please send me the designs? Pretty please. Oh, and come to dinner tonight. I totally forgot to say something earlier."

"I sent the file as soon as I heard you get up to walk over here. And why are you inviting me to dinner? You never invite me to dinner."

He gave me a confused look. "Bullshit. You're just always too busy to come."

I had to give him that. "Okay, thanks, but why the sudden invite?"

"Brian and Maddy are coming. I told him about the ECHL thing, and I wanna pick his brain. I figured you'd want to be there too."

"You told him?"

"Yeah. He won't say anything. You know that. I want another player's perspective. You and I, we're too close to it. Be good to have an outsider's viewpoint."

Since I couldn't fault him for his logic, I gave him grudging props.

"Damn, look at you being all business-minded and shit."

He narrowed his eyes at me, which I had to say was a pretty damn good impression of our dad. "And look at you being a brat. Like always. Just come to dinner."

Since I didn't have plans, and my brother was a really good cook, damn him, I sighed dramatically and gave in. "Since you asked so nice..."

I thought he'd leave then, but he surprised me by falling into the chair in front of me. I looked at him expectantly, waiting for him to spit out what he wanted to say.

"So, I need to go to Harrisburg, and I was hoping you'd go with me."

"What? Why?" My brain still stuck in hockey mode, I

didn't realize the weird way he was looking at me meant—
"Oh. Oh! Rowdy, are you gonna—"

"Don't say it." He spoke in a low whisper. "I haven't told anyone else. But yeah, I am. And I want you to go with me to help pick out a, ah, well, you know."

My brother looked so adorably out of his depth that I couldn't help but squeal, just a little. I jumped up out of my chair and ran around my desk to wrap him in a big hug. Then I gave him a smack on the back of the head just because.

"Finally," I said. "I was beginning to think you were going to let this drag on too long. When do you wanna go?"

Rowdy's grin stretched from ear to ear when I pulled back to sit on the edge of my desk.

"I was thinking the first week in January. She and Krista are going to spend New Year's Eve in New York and stay for a few days to see her coworkers and her former neighbor. They'll be back late Wednesday night, so we could leave early Wednesday and be in Harrisburg by eleven. I'll even treat you to lunch. If you're busy—"

"Nope. Not busy." And if I were, I'd totally change my plans for this. "What about Mom?"

He shook his head. "She's gonna have her hands all over the wedding. If Tressy says yes. Which is great. I'm good with that. I just thought this was something you and I could do together."

Sometimes Rowdy made up for all the times he was a pain-in-the-ass big brother.

"I would love to," I said without a trace of snark. "I'm honored."

"Thanks, Rainy." Standing, he reached over and tapped

me on the chin. "I appreciate it. I know you won't let me buy anything stupid."

"Of course not. Plus, I know what all her favorite jewelry looks like, so I know what style we should be looking for."

"And this is why I asked you and not Rebel or Rocky. I'm gonna have other things for them to help me with."

"Sounds like you've got plans."

Rowdy just smiled. "I got a few things up my sleeves."

"I'm really happy for you. Tressy's great, and Krista's a sweetheart. I can't wait to be an official aunt."

"Hey, speaking of kids, thanks for helping Brian get his niece situated. I can tell he's feeling kinda overwhelmed."

"It's no problem." Were my cheeks getting hot? Why were they doing that? "I'd do it for any of the players, you know that."

"I know. Just wanted to let you know I appreciate it."

He got up then and moved to the door but before he left, he turned back.

"Don't forget dinner tonight."

Yeah, like that was gonna happen. I smiled and made a shooing motion with my hands toward the door. "Of course I won't. Now go, I've got actual work to do. And you have to deal with the other owners about the sweaters." Something I hated to do and was happy to let Rowdy handle this year. "Have fun with that."

"Love you too, Rainbow Brite. See you tonight."

I REFUSED to go through the whole "what to wear"

situation like I had the other night. I knew exactly what any of my friends would tell me.

"Wear something that makes you feel good."

Right now, I was seriously contemplating putting my pajamas on and crawling into bed with a new book, but I was an adult, for fuck's sake, and I had obligations.

Just admit it. You want to see him and you're acting like a teenager with a crush.

I gave my reflection in the mirror the finger and turned away with a huff. So far, I'd pulled on a pair of jeans that didn't have a baggy ass, so I figured I was off to a good start.

Most of my clothes had been chosen with comfort in mind. And warmth. Hockey arenas were cold in the winter. Duh. But that meant flannel and fleece comprised a big part of my wardrobe. Yeah, I had cute flannel shirts, but they were still flannel.

And no, I didn't want to wear flannel tonight. I wanted to look like a woman who might someday actually get laid again. Who actually wanted to get laid by the man I'd be seeing tonight. And who was totally out of reach due to circumstances beyond my control. Which sucked.

Brian had so much on his plate right now. And the fixer in me wanted to make everything better.

I have a problem. I know. Don't judge me.

Fuck it. I am who I am.

I grabbed a long-sleeved t-shirt in a pretty shade of blue that I never wore because it wasn't Devils' colors, but it was fitted and made my boobs look great. A little makeup and a loose braid that hung over my shoulder, and I looked presentable. Okay, maybe more than presentable.

Damn it, I looked good. Before I changed my mind and

tried to change into, oh, maybe a paper bag or something, I headed out the door.

Rowdy had built his home on part of the land our parents had owned. Mom and Dad had gifted all four kids with a couple of acres. Rowdy had built on his, a gorgeous house for the family he'd always wanted. And now had.

I hadn't decided what to do with my section yet. I hadn't been ready to build my own house when I decided to move out of my parents', and I wanted to be closer to town, so I'd bought my little house, which I adored. It was just the right size for me. But just for me. I couldn't imagine having to share it with anyone.

The drive took about ten minutes, and that's only because I hit the one stoplight in town, and I had to wait for a couple of deer to scoot out of the way before I could park in Rowdy's driveway.

So I was five minutes late. Brian was already there. Just seeing his truck parked out front made my heart pound. But I got out of my car and walked up to the door, reaching for the doorknob before reminding myself to knock. Before Tressy and Krista had moved in, I would've just walked in.

I'd barely rapped on the door before it flew open, making my eyes widen until I saw the reason why.

"Rainbow! You're here."

Krista wrapped her arms around my waist and squeezed. I reciprocated with a quick hug before she pulled back and started to bounce, her smile wide and her curls in two adorable ponytails above her ears.

"Hey there. What's got you all excited?"

I walked into the house, pretty sure I knew the answer to my question.

"Rain's here!" Krista shouted, making me wince at the decibel level, then she grabbed my hand and tugged me toward the back of the house.

I heard voices, one in particular that made it hard for me to breathe, but Krista kept up a running commentary all the way to the kitchen.

"Maddy and Brian are here. Maddy's gonna play games with me after dinner. She likes Candy Land and Hungry Hungry Hippos. And she said she'll watch *Blue's Clues* with me and then *Tangled* and *Zootopia*."

"Sounds like you've got your night all planned out."

"Well, you gotta have a plan, right?"

We'd just reached the kitchen and every single adult in the room laughed, because she'd absolutely picked that up from me.

"I think maybe Krista's been spending a little too much time with you," Rowdy said, his eyes crinkled with laughter.

"Don't mind him." Tressy smacked her hand against my brother's chest, her grin just as wide as his. "Krista, why don't you take Rain's coat to the chair with the others. Rainy, what can I get you to drink?"

I was about to say a beer but realized no one else was drinking alcohol. They all had what looked like soda.

"Ginger ale, please. With a lime, if you've got it."

Rowdy turned to get my drink, and I took a seat at the island, turning to smile at Maddy, who actually looked like she might smile for a second. Of course, she didn't. Then my gaze met Brian's, and my smile locked into place.

He looked lickable tonight. Not that he didn't most of the time, but tonight... I don't know what it was about a hot guy in a Henley shirt with the buttons open. I totally wanted to put my mouth on him and slide my tongue from his collar-bone to just below his ear and then I'd—

Shit. I blinked and looked away, anywhere but at Brian.

Way to make it awkward.

Luckily, Rowdy slid a glass in front of me and announced it was time to eat, saving me from any further ridiculous staring and grinning.

I was worried dinner would be uncomfortable, with me trying not to lust after my brother's best friend and all, but Krista saved the day. Chattering to everyone about school and even getting Maddy to engage. Tressy kept the conversation centered around the girls, and she even got Maddy to admit that school today hadn't been horrible, though she did have homework.

Rowdy, damn him, was a really good cook, and his pasta sauce was amazing. I concentrated on eating and not getting sauce all over my clothes, which I managed to do, just barely. And when the last plate had been put in the dishwasher, and the girls were settled in front of the fireplace with their games and the TV playing one of my favorite Disney movies, Rowdy sat across from me at the table and held my gaze.

"So. What do you think we should do?"

I'd hung my tote on the back of my chair because I knew I'd want the notebook I'd been jotting things down in since Dad had dropped his bombshell yesterday.

Ignoring Rowdy's smirk, I opened it to the first page.

"Where do you want me to start?"

Rowdy shrugged then tipped his chair back so he could reach the tablet I hadn't noticed on the island behind him.

"I don't have a fucking clue," he said.

Tressy and Brian both chuckled, which made me roll my eyes and mock-glare at them.

"You two are not helping."

"I'm just here for moral support." Tressy waved a hand at Brian. "He's the one with the hockey experience."

"And honestly, I just came for the food."

Brian's grin widened when Rowdy threw his pen at his chest, which Brian caught with amazing ease.

"Well, now it's time to pay for your supper." Rowdy caught the pen Brian threw back at him then pointed it at me. "Okay, Rain. You're up."

Forcing my brain to focus on something that wasn't Brian, I looked at my six pages of notes.

"Do we want to start with pros or cons?"

"Which do you have more of?"

Trust Rowdy to think of the one question that made my brain stumble around for a second.

I flipped through the pages. "Pros." By a lot, actually. But... "I think the cons are more important."

"Then you start with the pros," Brian said. "Get them out there first."

I smiled at him, and when he smiled back, I had to remind myself we had interested observers. Especially a nosy older brother who was looking at me like he knew exactly what I was thinking.

And he probably did.

Focus.

"Pro number one." I gave Rowdy the finger, just because I could. And it was totally worth it to hear Brian's low, raspy laughter. "Increased visibility for the team."

"We're filling seats now." Rowdy tapped his pen against

his pad. "But, yeah, we'd probably be able to pull in another thousand a game. But do we want to?"

"We won't ever be sold out every night, but more butts in seats means more money coming in."

"And more money going out," Brian chimed in. "More employees, more cleaning people, more food."

I nodded, giving Brian a quick smile before continuing. "Not to mention wear and tear on seats and the parking lot and the restrooms. The arena holds eight thousand. If we get five thousand for a game, it gets dicey with the concession lines."

Rowdy nodded. "Those aren't necessarily cons, but something to think about. Okay, pro number two?"

I didn't have to check my notes, I pretty much had them memorized. "It's a step up so it's a selling point. Not that we're not a professional league, but there's more name recognition with the ECHL. Plus, we'd presumably be affiliated with an AHL team, which could mean some financial and promotional aid with them.

"It also means we may get more players down from the AHL, if they're rehabbing or just need more playing time than they're getting in the AHL."

"And that could bring in more people."

"And bump our guys off the roster."

Rowdy went quiet, his attention inward for several seconds before he narrowed in on me again.

"And that's one of your cons, isn't it?"

I nodded. "Of course. Our team has always been a safe haven for our guys. Dad's made sure of that. The guys know they can come here to get their shit together."

"And when they need help keeping their shit together."

Brian's quiet comment drew everyone's attention, and I reached over to wrap my hand around his without a second thought. I would've done the same with anyone else, but the moment he turned his hand in mine and squeezed, everyone else disappeared. It was just him and me and the warmth in his eyes and the beating of my heart.

Then my idiot brother reached across the table and took Brian's other hand. "And when you need to get the shit beat out of you, I'll be here for you."

Brian's laughter made me ache deep inside as he tossed Rowdy's hand back across the table. But not before he squeezed my hand again before releasing me.

NINE

Brian

"HEY, man, you looked a little green at the start of the game, but you skated like the Mr. Whiskers who used to kick my ass. Nice to have you back."

Bobby "Bonesaw" Brassard sat next to me in the locker room Saturday night, unlacing his skates and grinning at me as I pulled my sweater off, wincing a little as my shoulder protested. I'd taken a hit into the boards late in the second period that was gonna require ice and a whole hell of a lot of ibuprofen.

"Thanks. It's good to be back." Another twinge as I dropped the sweater into the bin to be washed. "Mostly."

Bonesaw laughed, which sounded like tires on gravel. "Yeah, everything hurts a little more every year, doesn't it? Good thing I'm younger than you."

"By what? A year. Fuck you."

I couldn't stop grinning as I took off my gear and headed

for the showers. Half the team was already there, throwing good-natured insults back and forth. We'd won the game, which accounted for the laughter and smiles.

"Hey, Fiskers, you looked pretty damn good out there for not playing for more than a year."

Brennan Budgell wrapped a towel around his waist as he stepped away from the dripping showerhead, and I turned on the one next to him.

I sighed as hot water poured over my head and body, working on relaxing muscles I hadn't used in months. Fuck, that felt good.

"Thanks. Feels more like a decade, though."

The nerves I'd felt before hitting the ice for warm-ups had made my stomach flip and my jaw tighten. I'd tried to focus on my pregame routine, but for a few minutes, all my brain could focus on was making sure I didn't trip over anybody or my own damn feet.

The guys gave me space, though a few fans banged on the glass, calling my name and waving. Which helped make me feel more at home. Then I skated by the Zamboni entrance and caught sight of two familiar faces.

Maddy watched me with wide eyes and a smile, dressed in a Devils sweater with my number on the sleeve. Since I knew she hadn't owned one of those before we left the house, I assumed Rain was to thank for the gift.

I had a lot to thank the woman for already, not the least of which was the way she treated Maddy. Even though Maddy had still acted moody and distant a lot of the time this week, Rain continued to treat her like she did everyone else, with that smile and—

Fuck.

Not a good time to be thinking about Rain.

"Well, you didn't play like you've been off the ice for a year," Bren continued, thankfully forcing my thoughts away from a certain brunette. "You always stick-handled better than most of the guys in this league. Frankly, you were a pain in the ass when you played for the Animals."

The unexpected compliment made me huff out a laugh, which died when I heard Rebel say, "Still is a pain in the ass."

Rowdy's younger brother turned on the shower across from me, effectively cutting off anything I would've said in response. Probably a good thing, because I honestly didn't know what to say to him. He'd been icing me out since I returned. I knew we'd eventually have to settle our old shit, but that wasn't happening tonight.

We'd managed to stay out of each other's way since I'd returned, but we couldn't do it forever. And I don't know if Rowdy had talked to the coach or what, but Rebel and I hadn't had any shifts together all game.

"Hey, Jedi," Nolan Badini yelled at Rebel from the locker room, "nice fucking goal tonight."

Blowing out a breath, I shut off the water and toweled off as I headed back to the locker room to get dressed. The conversation in the showers had turned to Rebel's goal, allowing me to escape.

I fucking hated that Rebel and I were still not talking, but a lot of that had to do with Rebel's fucking stubborn-ass streak. I'd gotten over the damn fight years ago. Rebel held on to a grudge like a dog with a bone.

Problem for another day.

I'd just finished dressing and toweling my hair dry when I heard, "Brian. Good game, man."

Rowdy took a seat on the bench in front of my locker, dressed in a suit that made him look like a legit businessman, except for the hair to his shoulders.

"Thanks. Felt good to be out on the ice, though I think I'm gonna regret a few of those checks tomorrow morning."

Rowdy's smile widened. "You'll get used to it again. That pass you made to Weller was a beauty. You haven't lost your touch."

"Let's see how I play tomorrow. I'm kinda afraid I won't be able to get out of bed."

"You'll be fine. You're not *that* fucking old, Whiskers. You going out with the team?"

I shook my head. "I should probably get Maddy home. It's getting late."

"Dude, it's like nine-thirty." Rowdy laughed at me. "Besides, I think Maddy and my sister already made plans for tonight, so you might want to rethink that."

My brain couldn't compute that immediately. "Plans? What plans?"

"Rain told me you can pick up Maddy at her place. They headed out a few minutes ago, with Krista leading the way." Rowdy's grin softened. "Krista was saying something about a girls' night, but they were already out the door, so I didn't get all of it. Rain said to stop by on your way home to see if Maddy wanted to go home with you, but if I know Krista, she's gonna get her way."

I got Rain's address from Rowdy then headed out. I'd never been to Rain's home, and honestly, I was curious as hell. I'd imagined getting invited inside Rain's house at some point. Imagined what we could do all alone. I hadn't factored in two kids being there.

Probably better to have chaperones so I didn't make a fool out of myself and do something I couldn't take back.

When I pulled up to her house, I had to smile because this place looked like Rain. It was just fucking adorable. A small Cape Cod on a side street filled with other small homes, each one different in its own way.

Rain's house was stone, with a bright blue door and two large windows on the first floor, where light spilled out onto the small patch of yard. I pulled into the tiny driveway and parked in front of Rain's garage. I could barely hear music coming from the house and when I walked up to the door, I saw Maddy and Krista dancing around the living room.

Maddy actually looked happy. Carefree. Like the kid she was supposed to be.

I didn't want to walk in there and interrupt. Didn't want to disrupt Maddy's fun.

Dammit, I should've called before rushing over here.

Wind whipped down the street, the cold piercing my clothing and making me shiver. I couldn't stand out here all night. I just needed to make sure Maddy wanted to stay. And that Rain was okay with the company.

I knocked on the door and immediately heard someone running toward the door. I was smiling when Krista flung it open, curls a wild halo around her head and her smile so wide it had to hurt.

"Mr. Whiskers! Are you here to party too?"

I don't know how anyone could resist that smile. "I don't know. Am I allowed to join?"

"Of course. Everyone's allowed to join."

Then she grabbed my hand and pulled me inside. Maddy stood to the left, staring at me like I'd caught her doing something she shouldn't. I hated that she felt like she wasn't allowed to have fun.

"Hey, Mads. You have a good time at the game?"

I saw her gaze go to the bruise on my jaw, where I'd taken an errant stick to the face, before she nodded.

"You okay, Uncle Bri?"

"Ooh, you got a boo-boo, Mr. Whiskers. Rowdy gets those too sometimes."

"I'm fine. Doesn't even hurt." But it would tomorrow. I knew that from experience. The girls didn't need to know that though.

"I can get you some ice for that."

Rain spoke from somewhere behind me, and I turned to see her staring at me, her expression not giving anything away.

"Nah, I'm good. I'll go home and put some on."

"But Maddy can stay, right?"

Krista looked up at me with the biggest puppy-dog eyes I'd ever seen. The girl was good.

I looked at Rain. "Rowdy mentioned something about girls' night...?"

"We're gonna have cookies and hot chocolate and watch a movie." Krista started dancing around again. "Momma said it was okay if I could stay. But I want Maddy to stay too."

"Mads, you wanna stay?"

Shit, I knew as soon as the words were out of my mouth that they were the wrong ones. The look of guilt that flashed across my niece's face made my stomach roll. Dammit, I didn't want her to feel guilty for having fun.

"Brian, why don't you let me get that ice for you? Mr. Whiskers can hang out for a while with us girls, right?"

Was that going to help or hurt the situation here? I hadn't wanted Maddy to feel like I was pawning her off on Rain, but I wanted her to build friendships. That's why I'd moved us here.

Even though it wouldn't be permanent. But I had told myself I wasn't looking that far ahead. I just needed to focus on the now.

The growing smile on Maddy's face made up my mind. Krista started dancing again, which made me smile. Which made my jaw ache.

I raised a hand to rub at it while nodding at Rain.

"Sure, he can stay," Krista said. "He can be a princess for a night."

My brows rose as I watched Krista twirl in front of me. "And what do I have to do to be a princess?"

"Well, he definitely needs a tiara." This from Maddy, who looked like she was trying not to laugh.

"And a boa!" Krista shrieked at an ear-piercing level then shot off like a cannon up the stairs. Then from the top of the stairs, she shouted, "Maddy, come help."

When Maddy glanced in my direction, I gave her a quick nod and a wink, which made her lips curl in a true smile. And made me feel like I'd gotten this part right. But it left me alone with Rain, her expression making me wonder what I'd just agreed to.

"You're going to look good in a tiara and pink boa.."

I walked across the room to where she was leaning against the doorjamb that led to the kitchen.

"I'm more partial to purple. Do you think we can negotiate?"

"Yeah, I don't think that's going to happen. You've been

taken hostage for the night by a tiny benevolent dictator." She nodded her head toward the kitchen. "Why don't you sit. I'll get you that ice."

She turned and headed toward the fridge in the small kitchen at the back of the house. I followed because, well, I'd rather be with her. No-brainer. Looking over her shoulder, she didn't seem surprised to see me there. Actually, her smile widened.

I shrugged. "I figure if I stick with you, they can't gang up on me. I'm afraid I'm going to end up with pink fingernails tonight."

As she grabbed a reusable bag out of a drawer and filled it with ice, she said, "Oh, I'm sure you'll look lovely in pink."

"How do you know what color my underwear is?"

Her eyes flashed up to mine, wide and startled, and I cursed my malformed sense of humor.

Christ, I was an idiot.

Then she laughed, one of those deep belly laughs that made me want to kiss her so I could feel her lips tremble against mine with the force of it and drink in some of her joy. Instead, I forced myself to stay where I was and return her smile.

Overhead, I heard the girls running around then I heard pounding on the stairs, and finally, they appeared in the kitchen. Krista held a mound of things with feathers and bows and sequins. And Maddy held a delicate tiara with a smile on her face that I'd never be able to refuse.

Yeah, I was gonna wear the damn tiara.

AN HOUR LATER, the girls had fallen asleep in a pillow fort in front of the fireplace and the TV, leaving Rain and I sitting on the couch, exhausted.

I held a fresh bag of ice to my jaw and a can of soda in the other hand. Rain held a mug of hot chocolate with enough sugar in it to keep her up all night. Then again, both the girls had had the same hot chocolate, and they were out cold.

"Did you secretly spike their cocoa with something to make them sleep? I didn't think they'd ever shut off."

Rain chuckled and took another sip. "You sure you don't want some? I make a killer hot cocoa. Just ask the girls."

"I'm not sure I'd be able to fall asleep tonight if I drank that. And I've got a game tomorrow. You sure it's okay they stay tonight?"

"Of course." She waved my doubts away. "Krista spends nights here all the time. Unless you're worried about—"

"No." I shook my head. "Not worried. Not at all. I just know you have to work tomorrow too."

She shrugged. "I like having them here. Krista is like a little ball of bright light. Always glowing. I'll take them into town for breakfast at the bakery then drop Maddy off after that. If that works for you?"

"That's fine. I'm just surprised."

Honestly, I was kind of shocked Maddy had wanted to stay. Then again, maybe she needed a break from me. It'd been an intense week, with moving and starting a new school and all the shit that went with that. I couldn't blame her for wanting a night off.

"She seemed to have a good time at the game," Rain said, then covered a yawn with her hand. "Sorry. It's not the company."

"I should go."

I didn't want to though. I wanted to stay and talk to Rain. Hell, we didn't even have to talk. I'd be happy to just sit and stare at her. But that would be creepy and weird, wouldn't it?

"No. Please stay. Just for a little."

She reached across the cushion and touched my arm, her fingers sweeping across the bare skin on the inside of my wrist. Heat spread from that point of contact, traveling through my body like quicksilver, and my gaze fixated on her hand. And then I started to imagine what her hand would feel like on the rest of my body.

Several long seconds passed before her fingers twitched, and she pulled her hand away.

"I know there are a couple of games on. My Leafs are playing tonight in Calgary."

Our gazes met again, and I grinned. "Still hoping for a miracle, huh?"

"It's gonna be their year," she said, optimism in her smile. "I can feel it."

I laughed because the Leafs hadn't won a Stanley Cup since 1967. But Leafs' fans began every year with the same hope.

"Said like a true fan. At least Ovechkin got a ring so I'm good for a few years."

"Still a Caps fan, huh?"

"Always and forever." Her smile made me nod. "Yeah, I can watch the Leafs get their asses kicked."

Her nose wrinkled just before she threw her napkin at me. It barely made it halfway across the cushion. "Like to make a little wager on that?"

"Sure."

"If the Leafs win, you owe me dinner."

"And when they lose?"

She shrugged. "I'll buy you dinner."

"You're on."

No way in hell I was turning down that bet. I won either way.

TEN

Rain

I COULDN'T BELIEVE I'd gotten Brian to agree to the bet so easily.

I mean, I'd gotten exactly what I wanted, which was dinner with him. But the fact that he'd agreed so fast made my heart race. And I couldn't stop smiling and staring into his eyes like some lovestruck idiot.

Enough of that.

Breaking the mesmerizing hold of his gaze, I stood.

"Just let me clean up this stuff," I said as I gathered the plates and bowls from dinner, "and we can watch the game."

"I'll give you a hand."

I waved him off, needing a few minutes to get my hormones under control.

"Why don't you go find the game and sit down. You want something else to drink?"

"Sure, just some water. Thanks."

It took me two minutes to get the table cleaned off, and when I came back out, I saw the game on the TV in the front corner of the room and Brian rearranging the covers over the girls. They'd built their pillow fort in front of the fireplace along the side wall, which left the couch in front of the TV open.

Brian had closed the doors to the fireplace, as the logs were basically ash, and turned off the only lights in the room, I assume because they were on the tables closest to the girls. But that left only the TV and the faint glow from the kitchen. It made the room seem way more romantic than it should.

Get a grip.

There were still two girls in the room. Romance was probably far from Brian's mind, anyway.

I handed Brian his glass of water as he sat on one end of the couch, and I set my glass on the side table as I sank onto the other end. My couch was an L-shaped sectional, which allowed Brian to stretch out his long legs. He looked completely relaxed, one arm behind his head as he watched the game.

"Not looking good for your guys tonight," Brian said as the second period ended. He'd sunk even deeper into the cushions, practically lying full out. I'd lain on my side, head on a pillow that was nearly touching his leg. Only inches separated us, and it took all my self-control not to scoot even closer.

"They could still come back." Though the 6-2 score in favor of Calgary didn't bode well. A yawn caught me off guard, and I lifted a hand to cover my mouth.

"I guess miracles do happen." Amusement laced his voice. "Damn, this couch is comfortable. Don't let me fall asleep, okay?"

I made a noncommittal noise because, honestly, I didn't think he should drive home. And yeah, my couch was comfortable and long enough to accommodate his body.

"I like your house."

Smiling because he sounded completely relaxed, I said, "Thanks. I bought it from an older lady who moved to a retirement community after her husband died. They were season ticket holders since the beginning. She still is. I fell in love with it the first time I saw it. Before her husband died, I told them I'd buy it if they ever decided they wanted to sell. Harry died about five months after that, and Kathy decided she didn't want to live here without him. They were so close. They did everything together. And then he was just gone. Massive heart attack."

I still got sad thinking about it. Next to me, I felt Brian shift just before his hand gripped my shoulder. The warmth of it felt like a drug seeping into my blood. Every muscle in my body went liquid, and I stilled, not wanting him to move.

"Sounds like you knew them well."

"I did. They were the sweetest people. And Harry loved the Devils."

"So you had a lot in common."

Did he think I was sweet? Or just that I loved my team?

Great, something new to obsess over.

"They were members of the booster squad, and Kathy would make gingerbread cookies of the players every year."

"Wait, I think I remember them. She gave them to the team. Small-town hockey. Can't beat it."

I sighed, the idea that we could screw up our team by moving to the ECHL pushing its way back into my brain. I'd managed not to let it take up space there for a few hours, but now it was back.

"You're worried about switching leagues."

His quiet voice made my breath hitch. I told myself it was because of the decision we would have to make about the team, but some of it was definitely just the thrill I got every time he spoke to me.

"Yeah, I am."

"You know it's okay to not want things to change."

"But isn't that just being stagnant?"

"Why fix what ain't broke?"

"But what if we turn down a really great opportunity?"

"If the league wants you that badly, they'll wait for you."

We fell silent for a few seconds as I let those words roll around my head a little.

Then he said, "Anything worth having is worth waiting for."

My breath caught in my throat. It almost sounded like he wasn't talking about hockey now. Could he possibly be talking about me?

We hadn't said a word about the incident between him and my ex. The incident where he punched out the asshole who had been a dick to me. It's almost like it'd never happened.

But it had, and right now, it was sticking in my brain. What should I say? Should I say anything? If I said the wrong thing, it'd be so completely awkward, and I didn't want it to be awkward between us. This was nice. Friends talking.

But wouldn't it be so much better if you were more than friends and there was kissing?

Yes. Yes, it would.

"Brian?"

"Hmm?"

"I'm glad you're back."

"Yeah, me too."

Okay, now what, smart girl?

I didn't have a clue what to say next. My tongue was tied. For the next few minutes, there was silence. The TV volume was barely audible because we hadn't wanted to wake the girls and then I realized Brian's breathing had become rhythmic and deep.

Lifting myself onto one elbow, I turned to look at him.

Sound asleep. His head was turned a little away from me, but I could see his eyes were closed, his lips slightly parted, his chest rising and falling slowly. I couldn't look away. He just looked so damn...handsome. I wanted to run a finger along his lips. I wanted to lean over and press my lips against his, then curl up against his side and fall asleep, warm and cozy.

Instead, I got up as slowly as I could, not wanting to wake him or the girls. Reaching for the crocheted blanket on top of the sofa, I laid it over him as gently as I could.

Unfortunately, that meant covering up the slightest bit of skin I could see where his shirt had ridden up from the waistband of his track pants. I had the insane urge to run my fingers along that exposed skin.

You have seriously got to stop.

Sighing, I crossed my arms over my chest and considered my options.

Then I did the only thing that made any sense. I got my own blanket from another chair and lay back down on the couch, watching the Leafs come back to within one goal before losing. Then I put on the sleep music channel and closed my eyes.

———

I WOKE to whispers I couldn't quite hear. Muted giggles. Then the low rumble of a male voice.

My eyes flew open, my heart racing. For a split second, I didn't know where I was.

Then last night came back in a flood of images. The girls asleep on the floor. Brian asleep on the couch. And a bet on a hockey game, that no matter who won, I was going to dinner with Brian.

Sitting up, I realized I was the only one in the room. The giggles and whispers seemed to be coming from my kitchen. And I probably looked like a hot mess.

Glancing toward the kitchen at the back of the house, I caught a glimpse of Maddy leaning against the counter, but I couldn't see anyone else. I snuck off the couch and tiptoed up the stairs to the bathroom, so I could at least make sure I didn't look like a homeless person and swish some mouthwash so I didn't offend anyone with my morning breath.

Back downstairs, I walked into the kitchen to find both girls clustered around Brian at the cooktop in the island, dropping chocolate chips on pancakes.

"Rainy, look what Brian made." Krista grinned as she bounced up and down, pointing at the skillet, her hair a halo of curls around her head. "Hockey player pancakes."

Brian looked up and caught my gaze with a grin of his own.

"Hope you don't mind. Girls were hungry and you were out cold. We thought we'd let you sleep."

"I don't mind at all, unless you're not going to feed me. Then we have a problem."

"I think Uncle Brian made enough for the entire team." Maddy rolled her eyes but her curved lips gave away a smile.

"Hey, I'm hungry," He sounded offended. "Don't worry, they won't go to waste."

"Did you find everything you needed?"

Brian's mouth quirked. "Apparently, someone else has made pancakes in your kitchen before."

"I knew where everything was, Rainy."

Krista's smile radiated joy.

"The girls have been a big help," he said. "So all you have to do is sit and eat."

Yeah, that wasn't going to happen. "Let me just make some coffee and anyone want hot chocolate? Or chocolate milk?"

Maddy's eyes lit up. "Ooh, I'll have some of that." Then she seemed to think twice as she looked at Brian, as if he had to agree. "Please."

Brian just smiled and said, "I'll have one of those too."

Behind me, I heard Krista telling Maddy where to find the right glasses and telling everyone she'd get the forks, because I didn't put them in the right spot and only she'd be able to find them.

I bit back a laugh because she wasn't wrong. The utensils weren't in any of the drawers. They were in a pullout bin in the cabinet next to the dishwasher because it was easier just to throw them in there after they'd been washed.

My laughter hitched to a stop when Brian leaned closer and said, "That little girl'll be running the team in no time."

He was close enough that I could smell the lingering scent of clean soap and the warmth of his skin.

"She's so damn cute, no one can tell her no, so she pretty much gets away with anything. She's a character."

Maddy smiled as she let Krista order her around, following the other girl's directions, and soon we all had plates of pancakes and glasses of chocolate milk that I made with Hershey's Syrup, and coffee for me because if I didn't have my coffee… Well, no one wanted that.

When Krista asked if she and Maddy could watch cartoons while they ate, I said of course and the girls made a beeline for the front room, leaving Brian and me alone and staring at each other across the island.

"Sorry for falling asleep last night," he said. "Totally didn't mean for that to happen."

Nodding my head toward the small table in front of the window that looked out on the back yard, we sat and started on the mountain of pancakes Brian had made. Some had chocolate chips. Some had blueberries. I hadn't even known I had blueberries. Must have been in the freezer.

"No problem. I'm sorry you had to sleep on my couch, though."

"Honestly, that couch is pretty damn comfortable. Beats the one in our apartment, though it's not that bad. I'm just sorry we're interrupting your morning."

"Brian, you're not interrupting anything."

"So no big plans today?"

"Nope, just going over to the café to talk to Erin about some plans. I'll probably take Krista with me. She loves to help stock the pastry case and talk to everyone who comes in."

"That girl just loves to talk. Reminds me of someone."

I laughed, because I knew exactly who he was talking about. "Yeah, with her and Rowdy in the same room, you can't get a word in edgewise. You'd think he raised her."

"He and Tressy make a good couple."

"Yeah, they do. The perfect little family." I paused because I didn't want that to seem bitchy. "And I mean that sincerely."

Brian huffed out a laugh between bites. "I know what you mean. He got lucky. Tressy and Krista are great."

"They are. And I love that they're so happy. Sometimes, it just points out the, um, deficits in my own life."

"So...you're not seeing anyone?"

He held my gaze, waiting for my answer.

I shook my head. "No. Been too busy lately to even care about dating. What about you?"

"Hadn't found the right girl."

Did he say "hadn't" or "haven't"? The two held very different meanings in the context of this conversation, and my brain began to spin in circles. But if the way he was looking at me was any indication, "hadn't" was definitely the word he'd used. Because he stared at me with an intensity that made heat skitter through my body.

I knew I should say something, let him know that I would date him in a heartbeat. That I would've dated him if he'd stuck around last year. That I'd be open to a hell of a lot more than just dating, including but not limited to kissing, touching, and definitely—

"Uncle Brian, we need more pancakes."

And the bubble we'd been in popped when Brian turned to smile at Maddy.

"Good thing I always make too many."

Then he reached for the door to the wall oven and pulled out another plate of stacked pancakes.

"Thanks, Uncle Bri," Maddy called over her shoulder as she made off with the plate.

"How was she last night?" he asked, still staring at the door, though Maddy had disappeared.

"She seemed to have a good time. Though she did get tense when you took that hit and got in that fight."

He sighed heavily. "Yeah, I was afraid of that."

"But she seemed fine the rest of the night. I actually caught her cheering a few times."

"She seems to be fitting in. She's made it seem almost weirdly easy. And that worries me. Because I don't like that it's so easy for her. Like she does it all the time. Hell, I don't know what the hell I'm trying to say."

"No, I get it. Most kids would be nervous in a new school, new environment. It's probably just how she copes with a new situation."

"So you don't think I should be worried?"

"I think you should talk to her about it. Ask her how she's doing."

"I've tried. She just says she's fine and changes the subject."

"I think you just need to be there for her when she wants to talk. I—"

"Hey, Rainy—Krista! How's it going, kid? And you're Maddy, right? Brian's niece? I'm Rebel. Rain's brother."

I looked at Brian as we realized at the same time that my next eldest brother was about to be a problem.

I still didn't know what had happened between Brian and Rebel. Neither of them had ever talked to me about their cold war. Maybe I didn't want to know. But Rebel was about to realize Brian had spent the night. And he was gonna be pissed. Not that he had any right to be, but if Rebel wasn't grumpy about something, he was either asleep or buzzed. And even when he was buzzed, he was pissy.

So him finding Brian here this early... Yeah, not gonna go well.

Then again, maybe he'd behave himself with the girls here.

Of course, no one could resist Krista's charm and when Rebel appeared in the doorway to the kitchen, he had Krista on his back, her arms around his neck. Kids loved Rebel. Maybe because he still acted like one most of the time, even though he was twenty-eight.

He took one look at Brian then turned to me and said, "We need to talk."

I sat back in my chair and crossed my arms over my chest. I can be just as pissy when I need to be.

"Actually, I can't think of a single thing we need to talk about right now. As you can see, I'm busy."

Rebel's jaw tightened, and I knew he wanted to order me around, like he had when we were kids. Back then, I'd idolized my older brothers and had trailed them like a puppy. Until hockey took over their lives, and Rocky, my youngest brother, and I had been left to our own devices.

Rebel looked like he was grinding his back teeth into dust while he decided what he would say with two children in the vicinity.

Turns out, there wasn't really anything he could say, which made my smile widen.

"You want some pancakes?" I asked, all innocence. "Brian's are great."

Okay, maybe I was being a little bit of a brat, rubbing it in Rebel's face, but goddammit, I didn't want my brother to ruin my morning. And right now, he was totally bringing down the mood.

Then I saw Maddy glance between Brian and Rebel, saw the slight stiffening of her shoulders. And I'd had enough.

"But I'm pretty sure you already ate, didn't you, Reb?" I looked at Maddy and rolled my eyes, trying to lighten the mood a little. "He's kind of anal about his feeding habits."

Then I looked back at Rebel and arched my eyebrows, making sure Rebel knew exactly what I was telling him without actually saying words. He should get his pissy mood out of my house, like now.

His brows rose in surprise, like he hadn't expected me to stand up to him. I had no idea what was going on with him, but damn it, he needed an attitude adjustment, and it was coming soon. Just not now with the girls here. Especially Maddy, who was sensitive enough to be picking up the vibes.

And then, because my brother wasn't always a complete asshole, he realized why I was disinviting him from visiting this morning. I saw him glance at Maddy and grimace. My mom had not raised any of us to be insensitive, and Rebel, though he had a thicker skull than the rest of us, almost always realized when he needed to cut and run.

"Uh, yeah, I did. But thanks for the invite." He turned his rare smile on Krista then made sure to include Maddy, because he wasn't a complete Neanderthal. "I can't stay anyway. Just thought I'd stop to talk."

No, he'd seen a strange car in my driveway, and he was nosy, or he'd recognized that car as Brian's, and he'd wanted to read me the riot act. Either way, he was being a dick and totally invasive. And I was totally going to rake his ass over the coals. Later.

"Then I guess I'll see you at the arena later tonight. Okay bye."

Yes, I sounded like a complete brat, but no younger sister with two or more older brothers would convict me in a court of law.

Out of the corner of my eye I saw Brian's mouth twitch, like he was trying to squash a smile. So I gave Rebel the Frenchie smile, the one she gives to Sandy during "Summer Nights." Which reminded me that if I was going to open a bookstore with Erin, we would need to include "Grease" in the store playlist.

Rebel rolled his eyes and sighed long and hard, but turned toward the door, Krista still clinging to his back.

"Talk to you later, Rainy." Then he nailed Brian with a look. "See you on the ice."

I huffed out a sigh as he walked to the front door, Krista chatting away.

"We should probably be going too," Brian said when we heard the front door close. "Game tonight."

He said that like it answered every question I might have about why he was leaving. And yeah, I got it. Players had their pregame routines. Eating schedules, naps, rituals. So many rituals. Even though our league and our players were a little...unconventional, they still had their rituals.

"I'd be happy to keep Maddy. If she wants to stay. I could drop her by your place later. I've got some things I have to do, and I planned to take Krista too."

I saw him working through the pros and cons. Saw the hesitation, saw him look at Maddy, who just happened to look over at that time and caught him staring at her. Almost as if she'd read his mind, she started to frown then made her way back to us.

"What's wrong?"

Immediately, Brian's mouth twisted into a grin. "Not a damn thing. Chill, little girl. I need to get back to the apartment to get ready for the game tonight, and Rain wanted to know if you wanted to stay with her and Krista so you're spared the tedious rituals of a hockey player. Anyway, I need to get going."

My lips twitched, but I just barely held back a smile.

"But it's, like, morning." The look on Maddy's face was almost comical. "The game isn't until tonight."

"You're welcome to come to the rink with me. I want to get some ice time this morning. After last night, I think I need a little extra warm-up time. You can hang out in the stands, do some homework."

Maddy's eyes widened. "Uh, I think I'll stay with Rain." She glanced my way for a bare second. "If it's okay with her."

I kept my smile calm. "Yep, that's perfectly okay with me, if you don't mind being busy. I've got to make a stop at the bakery to talk to Erin, then we're going to help my mom bake cookies, and we can always use more hands. She makes hundreds to give out to practically everyone in town."

I wasn't even kidding. My mom baked Christmas cookies for an army.

"I like Erin." Krista started to bounce with all the enthusiasm of a seven-year-old hopped up on hot chocolate and pancakes. "She makes yummy scones. Can we get scones? I love scones!"

"Yes, we can get scones, and we can have them after lunch. But only if you eat lunch. Deal?"

Krista whooped, shouted, "Scones!" and took off to take a lap around the living room.

Brian watched her with a wary amusement, shaking his head. Even Maddy seemed to be a little exhausted at her energy. But she didn't change her mind about staying.

"Then if Maddy's okay with helping you out today, I need to leave so I can get to the arena."

I wondered if he realized that Rebel was probably heading to the arena too, hoping to catch him there. And since I couldn't do a damn thing about that, I tried not to think about it. They were both big boys. They needed to figure their shit out. But I really, really wanted to know what the hell their deal was.

"Brian?"

"Yeah?"

His eyes met mine and I couldn't think of anything I wanted to say to him other than, "Kiss me, please," which totally wasn't going to happen. Even I knew there were limits to my appeal, and asking him to kiss me while his niece and my almost-niece discussed the various types of scones available at the bakery was one of those limits.

But I really wanted to kiss him. To stand on my toes and put my hands on his cheeks and feel that dark red stubble on his cheeks against my palms and press my lips against his. Hard.

And for someone who *usually* got what I wanted, I felt more than a little frustrated.

Yes, I was spoiled, but I knew it, and I tried not to let it dictate my attitude. Meaning, I recognized that I was and tried my damnedest not to be a bitch when I didn't get my way. And right now, I knew I wasn't going to get my way.

"If I don't see you before the game, have a good one."

His lips curved in a quick smile, there and gone almost before I realized it.

"Thanks." Then he turned to Maddy and grinned at her. "Try not to have too much fun without me."

Maddy rolled her eyes, but she had a smile lurking around the corners of her lips, which quickly disappeared when she glanced at me. Still, she didn't look at me like she only tolerated me, so I figured that was a win.

"I'll see you after the game, Uncle Brian."

A twinge of jealousy caught me in the midsection, but I shut that shit down fast because it was so damn stupid.

Brian looked at me again and nodded his head toward the front of the house. "Walk me to the door?"

My brows arched, but I followed him to the door as the girls turned on music from *Descendants*, currently Krista's favorite movie.

"Thanks again for keeping Maddy busy. I think...she needs the distraction."

"Of course."

"And I'm sorry about falling asleep here last night. I don't want to cause you any issues with your brother."

I shrugged. "Rebel can be an asshole. You know that. Just ignore him. He doesn't control my life."

He didn't respond to that, but he held my gaze for a few seconds before turning and walking out the door. I wanted to go to the window and watch him walk away, but I knew I had an audience of two young girls.

So I turned with a grin.

"Who wants to get a sugar high?"

ELEVEN

Brian

I GOT to the arena and, no surprise, Rebel's Bronco sat in the players' parking lot.

Guess we were finally going to confront the elephant in the arena.

Grabbing my gear out of the back of my truck, I headed through the service entrance, expecting him to be waiting for me in the locker room. Except he wasn't. Guess we were going to settle this on the ice.

Five minutes later, I skated onto the ice, where Rebel was taking shots at the net from center ice. I knew from the parking lot that no one else was here.

I skated over to him, sticking a puck from the pile and getting off a wrister before Rebel turned his attention back to me.

The Lawrence brothers all had the same color hair, but while Rowdy let his grow, Rebel kept his short. And all the siblings had the Colonel's blue eyes, but Rebel's were a shade lighter, which made them seem colder. Or maybe that cold stare was just for me.

"We gonna talk this out?" I figured why beat around the bush. "Or are you just going to continue to freeze me out?"

Rebel didn't say anything immediately, just kept staring until I thought he was going to continue to hate me for the rest of our lives. And that would fucking suck. Because at one point in our lives, we'd been good friends.

"I don't trust you," he finally said. "I don't think I'm ever going to trust you again. And I don't want you anywhere near my sister."

Yep, that's pretty much what I'd expected, right down to the reference to Rain.

I shook my head, leaning on my stick. "You were out of control, Reb. You needed help."

His jaw clenched, the muscles shifting under his skin. "You went behind my back. After I specifically asked you to keep my issues between us. I was handling it."

"No, you weren't. You needed help, Reb. You wouldn't talk to anyone. I was fucking worried about you. I saw you heading down a hole I have fucking intimate knowledge of, and I didn't want you to disappear down it."

"You should have fucking talked to me first before you went to my dad."

"I fucking tried talking to you! You wouldn't fucking listen. You had your fucking head in a bottle. The only reason you managed to hide it from everyone else is because you were at college. And your default personality is grumpy, moody bitch so even the people who thought they were your friends didn't notice. And the ones who did were right there with you, fucking their futures to hell. I could see you getting farther and farther out of reach, and I couldn't fucking stand it. I could see the goddamn wall you were about to hit. Was I just supposed to let you crash and burn?"

Rebel's eyes had gotten narrower the longer I ranted, but he kept his mouth shut and let me go. When I finally stopped, sucking in air, I waited for him to hit back.

And waited.

"You didn't trust me."

No, I hadn't, because I knew from experience that people didn't just get through or get over a drinking problem.

"You needed help." I wasn't backing down on this. "I wasn't going to wait until you were in too deep to get back out."

"You didn't fucking trust me to figure it out for myself. You went to my dad. To the one person you knew I wouldn't want to know."

"Because he was the only one I thought would be able to help."

"You went to him because you wanted him to think you cared."

Okay, that was a fucking low blow, and I was getting pissed. "I *did* fucking care. I *do* care. Don't give me that shit. I know you're pissed at me, and I get it. But I know how hard it is to dig out of that hole. I know most people who fall down that hole can't get themselves out of it. They need help."

"Did you even stop to think that I was getting help in my own way? You never even gave me the benefit of the doubt that I could turn myself around."

"You were gonna lose your place on the team. You know that, right?"

Rebel's chin lifted in defiance. "I wouldn't have let that happen."

I wanted to throw my stick on the ice, grab him by the shoulders, and shake him. "Jesus, you're still so damn stubborn. You know what? I don't give a shit if you still hate me. You're still fucking here and that's all I fucking care about. You can hold your fucking grudge, Reb. Because it doesn't matter. You're still here. You didn't fucking end up dead in a ditch somewhere. Hate me all you want."

He shook his head, eyes still so cold. "I don't hate you. I just don't fucking trust you. And I don't want my sister to get burned by you next. So whatever relationship you think you're going to have with her, you're not."

It stung. It shouldn't have, because I'd known exactly what he was going to say about me and Rain. But it still felt like he'd stuck a knife in my side. And my anger continued to rise.

"There's nothing going on with me and Rain. She's been great with Maddy, and Maddy seems to like her. Maddy's my focus right now. You know her mom's in rehab, right? She's gonna be there for weeks. Maddy won't have her mom for more than a month. She needs all the help she can get. Every friend she can find. Your sister's amazing with her."

Rebel's expression finally showed cracks, but only for a couple seconds. "Rain doesn't need you fucking up her life like you fucked up mine."

Okay, now I was fucking pissed. "Your life doesn't seem very fucked up. In fact, you've got a pretty fucking sweet deal here. You don't have to worry if you're going to be traded or get a contract for the next season. You have a safety net a lot of people don't."

"So you were jealous? That's why you ratted me out to my dad?"

I wanted to scream in his face but managed, just barely, to keep it together. "I didn't fucking rat you out."

"No, you betrayed my trust."

"Are you sober?"

His expression didn't change. "I didn't have a problem with alcohol, asshole. But you didn't see anything other than what you wanted to see."

"Reb, I was there. You were practically drinking yourself into a coma every night."

"No, you weren't there. You were already gone. You had no idea what was really going on."

"We were friends. I fucking cared about what happened to you."

"I wasn't fucking drinking myself to death! I had a nervous fucking breakdown, which you would've known if you'd been able to see past your own damn drama!"

The words rang out across the empty arena, almost slapping me in the face. Rebel's cheeks burned with an angry red tinge, and his eyes blazed. And the knot in my gut twisted until I could barely breathe.

"I was drowning," he continued, "but not for the reasons you thought. And I was getting help, but when you went to my dad, everything blew up again."

A strange buzz sounded in my ears. "Jesus, Reb, why didn't you—"

"Say anything to you? Because you'd already fucked me over. I didn't think you deserved anything else that I could say. I had my own shit going on. So no, I didn't fucking explain myself. And when it was my turn to join this team, you fucking left."

"Because you wouldn't want me to be here. You would've frozen me out, it would've affected everyone else around us."

"Again, maybe you should've fucking asked."

We were both breathing hard, but Rebel's last statement hadn't been shouted. It'd been said so calmly, it felt like another knife in my gut. I didn't know what to say. Because he was right. I'd been blinded by my own shit, and I hadn't seen the situation as I should have.

Jesus, I *was* the asshole.

"I'm—"

"Don't."

Rebel stopped me with a hand held out in front of him, which I guess I should be glad wasn't connecting hard with my face. My world had been rocked once again, but this one felt more like a kick to the head instead of the gut.

"Just fucking don't. I'm trying my damnedest not to combust every time you're around. But it's fucking hard. And yeah, I know the reason you're here. And..." he took a deep breath, "I'm working on getting over my shit with you. My therapist told me you're a trigger I could never deal with because you weren't around. I didn't want to fucking deal with you. And I still don't. But I'm not that much of an asshole to not know that that little girl needs a safe space right now and this is it. So I'm going to put my shit away and deal with you being here. But we're not friends. Not anymore. And I'm not sure we can ever be."

Those words dug into my gut and made them twist until I thought I wouldn't be able to breathe. He sounded so final. In the back of my mind, I'd hoped, *believed*, we could clear this shit out between us. But once again, I'd been mistaken about what that shit had been.

So I didn't say anything, because I didn't want to make it worse.

Except, "I'm sorry. Jesus, Reb, I'm sorry, and I know it's not enough—"

"It isn't." Reb shook his head and took a deep breath. "At least, not now. We just need to steer clear of each other off the ice. And don't insert yourself into my sister's life and then think you're just gonna say 'see you' and leave at the end of the season or whenever you don't need us anymore. Ice is all yours."

He turned his back on me and skated to the open gate to the locker room.

And I shot pucks at an empty net until my shoulders ached.

TWELVE

Rain

"HEY, Erin! I got some hungry, sleep-deprived kids here who want sugar!"

Herding the kids through the back door of Crack One Open and into the kitchen, I made sure the door was shut tightly. I'd promised to fix that for Erin for months, but the season had started and, well... "Chaos Reigned" wasn't the Devils' motto for nothing.

Erin popped her head through the swinging door to the café, and I could tell by the look on her face that she was more than a little happy to see me.

"Oh, thank god. I thought I was going to have to close. Can you please grab those trays and bring them out here? Game mornings are always insane, and Davi called off sick, and Mary's car wouldn't start so she's going to be late."

Then she disappeared back into the front room, the tail of

her thick braid the last thing I saw before the door flapped closed.

Maddy looked at me like a deer in the headlights. Krista had already disappeared through the door into the café. She'd become a fixture here and knew her way around. Maddy, of course, had no idea that Erin ran on caffeine and sugar and this place hung together by a very thin thread that any little deviation in routine could break. Apparently that thread had been snipped sometime this morning.

The kitchen looked like it'd been caught between two ravening packs of dogs. Sugar and flour coated every surface. The scent of cinnamon hung heavy in the air and the scent of warm yeasty rolls made my stomach rumble.

But first things first.

"Maddy, can you grab that tray over there? I'll take these two. Sorry, I know you didn't sign up to work for your breakfast, but I promise it will be worth it."

Without a word, Maddy grabbed the tray I'd pointed to, loaded with cinnamon rolls, while I picked up the two holding donuts and spinach-cheese croissants. And opened the door to a mob scene.

Since we'd come in the back, I hadn't realized how utterly chaotic the café was. Most of the opposing team loafed around at tables, drinking coffee and shoving various pastries in their mouths. Several people, who I recognized as the other team's booster club, huddled in a group near the door, while the line at the register wound all the way around the room.

Erin looked more than a little frazzled, her usually perfect braid nearly undone while she took orders from multiple people at the same time.

Right.

"Maddy, hon, put that tray on the counter for me. I need to..." I sighed. I didn't know what I needed to do first. Even for me, this was a mountain to climb.

"I can take that bucket with the dirty dishes into the back." Maddy shrugged. "If you want."

I wanted to hug her, but I was pretty sure she wouldn't appreciate that. "You are a lifesaver. Thank you."

Without another word, Maddy grabbed the bin and took it into the kitchen, leaving room for me to put the other trays down before I started combining trays in the display counter.

The next half hour flew by in a rush of fulfilling orders for Erin, who ran the register. Maddy, bless her, took several bins of dirty dishes back to the kitchen and filled the utensil trays and napkin holders a few times, while Krista entertained the line with her bubbly personality.

When the last of the line had finally been dealt with, and there were only a few people left at the tables, Erin threw her arms around my shoulders and squealed just a little. Then she turned to Maddy and, before I could say anything, gave the girl a quick squeeze.

"Oh my god, *thank you* so much." Erin's fair complexion was flushed and her hair had escaped most of her braid. "I think my head would've exploded if you hadn't walked in when you did. It's like everyone decided they needed a cinnamon roll and coffee this morning. Maddy, you and Krista take whatever you want and have a seat. I'm going to make you two some of my special hot chocolate."

While Krista whooped and made a beeline for the scones, Maddy grabbed a cinnamon roll and sat with Krista at one of the tables that was relatively clean.

"You *need* to hire more staff." I crossed my arms over my

chest and gave Erin the look I usually reserved for my brothers when they didn't listen to me. "Are you ready to let me help you with that?"

Erin and I had been discussing this for a couple of months. But between her schedule and mine, we hadn't been able to find time to talk about it in depth.

"I will if you say yes to the bookstore."

The look she gave me while she dropped huge dollops of whipped cream on top of two mugs of her homemade hot chocolate was a challenge, as if she knew she had me. And she probably did.

Oh hell, I should just admit right now that I wanted to go in with her on the bookstore. Because I did. I really did.

"Just think what we can do when with this space when we tear down that wall."

She gestured to the wall dividing the café with the empty storefront next door. It wouldn't be such a huge project because at one time, these two spaces had been one big space. The building had been split into smaller spaces in the fifties, with half going to the radio station and the paper and half going to the bakery and café. The radio station and news-paper took up the second floor of the building, but the front space held remnants of the history of the building. I could already imagine that area filled with bookcases and cozy little nooks to read.

I sighed as she took the mugs to the girls, who were munching away on more sugar than they should reasonably consume during one morning, but they'd earned it.

And I'd earned the double-shot latte I'd been trying to avoid because I'd already had more than enough caffeine today. So I took the one Erin made for me before we took seats at the counter, far enough away from the girls that they couldn't hear our conversation. Not that they were listening anyway. They'd raided the stash of books Erin kept for kids by the door, and Maddy and Krista were paging through a Christmas book.

"So," Erin said when she sat down next to me. "You ready to say yes?"

"*If* we do this," I looked Erin in the eyes, holding back a smile, "I'm going to handle staffing."

The smile Erin gave me acknowledged the fact that she'd won me over. It was broad and toothy and so freaking excited, I couldn't help but smile back.

"Whatever you say."

I shook my head but couldn't hold back my smile anymore. "Okay. I'm in."

Erin squealed again and started to do a little seat jig. "We're going to have so much fun."

"But... you know I can't really give any time to this until after the winter carnival. And neither can you. You promised you'd help wrangle food stands this year."

"And I'm definitely keeping my promise. But this is so exciting!"

The bell over the door chimed, and Erin's attention flashed away. Her eyes narrowed and her mouth tightened, and I sighed, because I only knew one person who put that look on her face.

Shit.

I turned to find Rebel talking to Maddy and Krista, and the guy even had a smile on his face. But I knew where he'd been and who he'd been with, and I wanted to know what had happened between him and Brian.

He and Erin had had a rocky relationship since she'd moved here. Her relentlessly sunny outlook on life had rubbed up against his perpetual grump since the moment they'd met. But this was not the relationship of romance novels. They genuinely didn't like each other.

Which was hard for me because I loved both of them. Erin was the sister I'd never had. And Rebel was the brother I had to love harder because he was harder to love.

"Hey, would you keep the girls occupied for like ten minutes out here? And can I use your back room?"

"Sure, but only if you're gonna rip him a new asshole, and you tell me all about it later."

I smiled and nodded. "Thanks. I appreciate it."

Then I walked over to Rebel, smacked him on the shoulder, and said, "Follow me."

Rowdy and Rocky let me get away with a lot most of the time. Rebel, not so much. But he waved a hand at the girls and trailed along after me to the tiny office off the kitchen.

I rounded on him as soon as the door was closed.

"I want to know what the hell is going on with you and Brian. You're acting like more of an ass than normal and..." I sighed. "You'd been acting more like a normal human lately. But then Brian arrives, and you become a dick again. What the hell's going on with you?"

My brother sat his ass on the edge of the desk, both hands gripping the edge, knuckles going white

"You telling me he hasn't told you?"

"He hasn't told me shit about this," I waved my hand in the air, "situation. Whatever the hell this situation is. You're my brother. You fucking tell me."

Reb's mouth flattened and he shook his head. "It's still

none of your business, Rainy. It's my business. And he stuck his nose in where he shouldn't have. But you know what, I got it off my chest, and we're done."

I crossed my arms over my chest. "Did you do it with your fists?"

He looked me in the eyes. "The guy doesn't have a scratch on him."

"Then why do I think you punched the shit out of each other?"

"Maybe because you can do that with words. And once you get it out of your system, it's done. At least, it is for me. But you should know you can't trust him. Not with anything that matters."

I shook my head. "Reb, you're my brother, and I love you. But you're pissing me the fuck off. Just tell me what the hell happened."

His head tilted back, and he looked me in the eyes. "And if I'm not ready to tell you? Are you gonna give me the benefit of the doubt?"

I groaned, just a little. "Jesus, it's been nearly a decade. Don't you think it's time to bury the hatchet? And I don't mean in his head."

"Trust is a hard thing to restore." He shook his head. "Look, I know I can't tell you what to do with your life—"

"Not that you don't try."

"—but I just don't want you to get hurt. That's all. And I don't trust him not to do that."

Rebel had a look on his face I didn't normally see. Usually, he sneered or grimaced. I rarely saw the guy smile anymore. Very rarely was it anger. I think that would be easier to handle sometimes.

This made my heart ache, because Rebel was hurt. He was covering it under a hell of a lot of angst, but whatever was going on with Brian, it hurt.

"Don't you think I can take care of myself?"

He actually cracked a little bit of a grin. "You're my little sister. Of course, I don't think you can take care of yourself. I think it's why I was born before you. It's my fucking life's mission to make sure you're safe and happy."

And here was the Rebel that made me laugh, the one I wanted to strangle with my own hands and give him a wedgie and hug him until he wasn't always so fucking miserable.

"Jesus, Reb. What the hell am I supposed to do with you?"

"Make my life fucking easier until he's gone."

I couldn't do that. I wasn't going to *not* be friends, or more, with a man I'd had a crush on forever just because it would make my brother's life easier. Because Rebel was going to make it his mission in life to make sure Brian left as soon as possible.

And I wanted him to stay.

THIRTEEN

Brian

I STOOD under a hot shower for as long as I could stand it, trying to clear the shit out of my head.

Fuck. I'd been wrong. And not just a little wrong. Really fucking wrong.

Because I'd been wrapped up in my own shit. No wonder Rebel thought I was an asshole. I'd never told him about my sister or father back then. I'd only ever told Rowdy and then, not a lot. Rebel had been younger, and I didn't want him to think less of me. To think I was as weak as they were.

Yeah, I'd been that asshole.

I'd only ever thought I was doing what I needed to do to keep things on track. Lin and Maddy were living with my parents at the time and Lin and my parents fought twenty-four-seven.

Jesus, that'd been a fucked-up few months. I'd kept my mouth closed way too much, when I should've been talking to my mom, talking to my sister, getting her the help she needed. But I'd had plans. I was going to play professional hockey. Except the only team that wanted me was the Devils. And while they were professional, they weren't exactly where I wanted to be.

AHL. Then NHL. And then... that plan just exploded spectacularly when I had to play and deal with a drunk dad and my alcoholic sister and a toddler.

Fuck.

With a sigh, I got out, dried off, got dressed, and headed out to pick up Maddy before I had to play tonight. But I didn't get all the way out the door.

"Hey, Brian, you got a minute?"

The Colonel's voice stopped me in my tracks, and I turned with my hand still on the door, forcing my mouth to smile.

"Didn't think anyone else was here," I said as I walked back down the hall to where the Colonel was standing. He was dressed down, something you didn't usually see in the arena. Track pants and a Penn State sweatshirt. He looked pretty damn good for his age, which was seventy-five, only a few years older than my dad, who looked like he was at least ten years older.

Not going there.

"Stopped in to do a little paperwork and heard you on the ice. Wanted to check in. See how things are going."

More likely, he'd seen Rebel and I having it out on the ice and wanted to be sure we weren't going to beat the shit out of each other.

"They're going. Maddy's settling in at school and the apartment is pretty great actually."

Reston nodded, his gaze never leaving mine. "Good to hear it. And you and Rebel? Everything okay there?"

What the hell could I say? That I'd fucked up my relationship with his son by ratting him out to his father for the wrong reasons? That I'd been a complete fuck-up and didn't deserve to be here?

"Honestly," I shook my head, "I don't think he's ever going to forgive me. But we won't let it spill out onto the ice."

The Colonel sighed. "You know me well enough to know that's not what I'm worried about. Rebel looked up to you just as much as he did his brother. Maybe more so because you weren't his brother. I know you were just looking out for him back then. I think you two will find your way back to that friendship again. It's just going to take some time."

I didn't want to disillusion the man whose name was on my checks so I just nodded. I wouldn't be here all season, a fact that I was actively ignoring, so I didn't think we had enough time to get back to our old relationship.

Pretty sure the Colonel didn't believe that nod. I certainly didn't. But he just nodded. "Okay, glad I caught you here. I know Maddy's at the house to help with cookie making."

I'd completely forgotten that's what Maddy was doing with Rain this afternoon. So that I could get ready for the game.

"Reb and me," the Colonel shook his head, "we're not much for all the Christmas stuff. Left to his own devices, I think Reb would hibernate for the month of December except for hockey. Sometimes, I think I might join him, but that's just between you and me. My wife and daughter love it, so..."

He let out a long-suffering sigh that made me grin.

"I haven't really been around my family much to cele-brate in the past few years, sir," which made me either a shitty son or too wrapped up in myself to care. "But I think Maddy will enjoy it all, so thank you for including her."

"Having young kids around has brought a little of the magic back to the season for me, I've got to admit. That Krista could make the Grinch cry tears of joy, I swear. And she's been making a little headway with Rebel. We're thrilled to have Maddy spend as much time with us as she wants."

"I can't thank you enough for that. I want to make sure Christmas is as good for her as it can be without her mom."

"Will she be able to see her mom at all over the holidays? We always have an open house on Christmas day all after-noon and night. You're welcome to join us."

"No, the facility won't allow us to see Lindsay until after we've done a mandatory group session. The next one isn't until after the holiday. Don't know what Maddy will want to do that day, but we'll talk about it. Thank you."

And I meant for everything, but I couldn't continue to slobber all over the guy for taking us in.

"Of course." The Colonel smiled, his face transforming. "Now, I've got a few more papers to sign, so I'll see you later. And Brian...don't beat yourself up too much. Work some of that shit out at the game tonight."

"HEY, HOW'S IT GOING?"

I could practically hear Maddy shrug through the phone line as I sat in the parking lot of the arena in my truck, letting it idle. "It's all good. We're in the kitchen making like a million cookies. This place is huge. I think they have more decorations than those places in the movies Mom makes me watch. It's kinda a lot."

I huffed out a laugh. "Yeah, I've been there at Christmas a few times. It's like Whoville, just not as tacky. You having a good time?"

"It's...different. I mean, everyone's really nice and all, it just seems like a lot of work to make all these cookies and just give them away to random people."

Damn, this girl was way too jaded for twelve. It's probably exactly what I would've said at her age, though, too. But damn it, that's not what I wanted for Maddy.

"The Lawrences go all out for Christmas. They have a lot of events at their house, for the team and the town. Besides, Miss Raffi and Rain love all that stuff."

"Yeah, they seem pretty into it. I mean, it's really pretty, and I'm having a good time, so...yeah."

I couldn't be completely sure because I couldn't see her face, but she sounded sincere. "Good. That's...great, Maddy. So, I'll see you at the game tonight."

"Aren't you coming here before the game?"

"No, I'm going to take a nap then shovel some food in my stomach so I don't bonk at tonight's game."

Maddy's laughter made me smile. "Yeah, we wouldn't want the old man to bonk."

"Hey, who are you calling old, little girl?"

"If the skate fits, Uncle Bri."

We hung up after we both said see ya later, because she'd picked up on the fact that I didn't like to say goodbye. Kid was smart. Way smarter than me and Linny combined, I swear.

I drove back to our little house and had just pulled some pasta out of the fridge to reheat when my phone rang.

Rain.

I swiped that call open so fast, the phone nearly slid out of my hands.

"Hey, everything okay? I just spoke to Maddy but—"

"Yeah, everything's fine here. Sorry, didn't mean to worry you. I was just checking to make sure *you're* okay."

With a sigh, I wondered how much to say. And exactly what to tell her. How much did she know about what had happened with Rebel? If I had to guess, exactly nothing. He wouldn't have wanted her to know.

"I'm fine. And yeah, Reb was there, but we talked a little. That was it."

A slight pause. "Talked about what? Did you work out all your man stuff?"

I huffed out a laugh. "Man stuff? Really?"

"Yeah, you know, the touchy-feely stuff men don't like to talk about but that they really should. The stuff women talk about all the time."

"We talked, Rain. Can we just leave it at that? You know your brother. If he wants to tell you something, he'll let you know."

A slightly longer pause this time. "Okay. I just...I'm worried about you, Brian."

That feeling I shouldn't be having about her flooded through me. I wanted her. And right now, even though I knew I shouldn't say one more damn thing, my defenses were down.

"I appreciate that. More than you know."

"Oh." Another pause. "I, um... I care about you, Brian. I hope you know that."

Oh hell. Every nerve ending in my body lit up like a fucking Christmas tree.

"Yeah, I do. You care about a lot of people. That makes you the person you are."

"No, I mean, I *care* about *you*. Damn, I really don't want to have this conversation by phone. Maybe we could have lunch tomorrow when Maddy's in school. Talk a little."

This is exactly what I shouldn't do. What Rebel didn't want me to do. Spend time with Rain. Talk to Rain.

And it's exactly what I wanted.

"Sure. I can do lunch tomorrow."

"Would you...I mean, why don't you come to my house? We can have a little privacy. You know what this town's like. The fact that we sat at the same table will be all over town before we finish eating."

Warning lights should be flashing over my head. We'd be alone. All alone.

Bad move. Very bad move.

"Sure. Sounds like a plan. What time?"

"How about twelve-thirty?

"Want me to bring anything?"

"No. But thanks. I got it covered."

"Okay, then, I'll see you at the game. Maddy still okay?"

Rain chuckled just a little. "She's currently being bossed around by Krista, and my mom's in her element with all the help. She seems to be having fun."

Good. "Thanks again, Rain. She deserves to have some fun."

"You're good for her, Brian. And she obviously loves you."

Since I was still working over the accusations Reb had thrown at me, I didn't know how to answer that. Because I wasn't so sure I was good for anyone.

"Thanks. I gotta go."

"See you tonight."

"HEY, Mr. Whiskers! Can't believe you were able to get your skates on today. I've heard it's harder for old guys like you to keep up with the younger players. Not as much stamina as you used to have."

The chirping had been relentless since the first period when I'd whiffed on a shot. But the doubt monster that'd been gnawing at my confidence since this morning had convinced me to pass the puck to another player, who'd had a much tougher angle and had missed the goal. To make things worse, the other team had gobbled up the rebound and taken it down the ice to score.

Which made the score 5-2. And not in our favor.

Fuck me. I thought about telling Coach to fucking bench me so I didn't do any more damage, but I'd kept my mouth shut because I knew he would do it himself if he wanted. But here I was, out for another shift.

We were in the offensive zone, and the other team was all over our players. Mostly Reid Weller, a second-year, twenty-year-old who could skate like the wind but didn't have the bulk of some of the other guys. And the kid had a temper, but there was something about him, something that had made the Colonel sign him right out of juniors.

Tonight, though, it was like the other team's defense had made it their mission to push him over the edge. And I could see the kid's nerves shredding with every shove, every jab that was almost but not quite a penalty.

Since I was pretty much over this day and not really feeling in a generous mood, I decided to make the other team's day unenjoyable. Even though I knew I'd pay the price when it was over. Hell, it'd be worth it.

So the next shift, when they started in on Weller, I invited one of the defensemen to dance.

In our league, that means something a little different than in other professional leagues. It means that if we fight, we dance. But I'd deal with that later.

So I smacked the hell out the puck and sent it into the offensive corner. And when dickwad got there before me, I got up nice and close and pinned him to boards, tying the puck up with my skates and stick.

Then I whispered in his ear, "Hey, asshole, you wanna go? Give me your best shot."

Now, I knew the fans at the boards would be able to read my lips or, at the very least, get the gist of what I was saying and, apparently, they wholeheartedly approved because they banged on the glass and cheered me with a whole range of profanity-laden comments. Which, honestly, warmed my heart.

They must really hate this guy because soon the entire arena was chanting, "Fight, fight, fight!" and I was happy to oblige. Apparently, so was my dance partner.

The rest of the teams had clumped together, holding each

other back like they wanted to join in the fight. Total bullshit. They were waiting for me and the asshole to square off. Finally, the guy got tired of my taunting—and the way I kept giving him a just a little love tap across the numbers with my stick—and turned with a smile.

"You wanna fucking take me on? Let's do it."

He dropped his stick and got the first shot in, a solid hit against my helmet that made my ears ring. But it didn't make me second-guess my intentions. I was up for this. After the day I'd had... Hell, I was going to fucking love this.

I went for an uppercut and connected with his jaw, snapping his head back. But by this time, he'd grabbed the shoulder of my sweater, trying to hinder my ability to throw punches. Fuck that bullshit.

Ripping myself away from him, I put up my fists and winked at him. And yeah, that just pissed him off, which was totally the point. And the crowd went wild.

Then we had a fight. I don't know how long it lasted. We both got a few good ones in, especially one that left me with a bloody lip. But he had a cut above his eye, so we were pretty even when we got done beating the shit out of each other and finally wound down to the point where the linesmen could come in and break us apart safely.

Now, the fans roared, making the entire arena deafening loud and possibly causing the rafters to ring, or that might have been my ears.

When we pulled apart, we nodded and skated to our respective sin bins to serve our penalties. Knowing that in five minutes we had another penance to serve. And this one was the real ball-buster.

FOURTEEN

Rain

"HE'S NOT HURT, is he? He's bleeding."

I smiled at Maddy, making sure it was my "everything's fine" smile, and nodded. "I've seen your uncle take on much harder hitters than this guy. Trust me. He's fine. And after they've served their penalty, then comes the fun part."

"The fun part?"

"Just wait. You'll be teasing him about it for days. Trust me."

I smiled and nodded and made sure my face didn't express the fear I felt. Brian had taken a few hard hits and, yeah, he was bleeding. But it wasn't the bleeding that was making me worry. It was the couple of hits to the head. He'd been out of the game for months, and I don't think he was in the habit of punching his coworkers at his previous job.

From the box where I was sitting with the girls, I watched him shake his head a few times, like he was shaking hair out of his eyes. Then I watched him blink a few times and roll his shoulder.

I breathed a sigh of relief. He looked okay. Like he didn't have a head injury, or a concussion or had broken anything. It'd just been a fight. And our guys fought all the time. It was part of the game. I didn't really enjoy the fighting aspect of it. It always made me cringe, whether it was my brothers or any of the other players.

But we had our own ways of dealing with fights that I did enjoy. And Maddy would get to see her uncle in a new light. Now I was smiling.

The game had been pretty uneventful up until this point. It was Sunday, the stands were half full because it was the weekend before Christmas and people had shopping to do and meals to prep. The next few months of hockey would be better, attendance-wise. But the crowd would remember this and talk and maybe there'd be a few more people at the next game. Because we hadn't really had an instigator on this team since a couple seasons ago. That player had been a walking hair trigger. Just touch him, and he went off. The crowd had loved him.

He'd gotten poached by one of the other teams after that season and then had moved back to Canada and gotten picked up by one of the western leagues.

The game continued for another five minutes, the fans' smiles getting bigger because they knew what was coming. And when the whistle blew for a stoppage, my grin couldn't be contained.

Maddy looked at me then looked down at the ice.

"What's—"

The other player's music began to play as he stepped

onto the ice. Each player picked their own song at the beginning of the season and was required to do a fifteen-second "performative apology." Yes, they were required to literally dance back to the bench.

"For our first apology of the night," our in-arena announcer's voice sounded like a late-night DJ on some old '70s R&B station, smoky and smooth, "Kenny Duncan from the Fitchfeld Feenoms has chosen that tried-and-true classic that we all know and love."

While our fans booed, Duncan skated to center ice, where a few teammates joined him. The music was perfectly timed for them to begin the arm motions for "YMCA." A lot of the guys used this one because they claimed to be unable to dance. Which had always seemed funny to me because they could balance on two blades of steel and fly up and down a sheet of ice like they'd been born with the ability. And yet they claimed to have no rhythm.

When our league claimed to be the most fun you'd have at a game, we weren't kidding. We took our fun seriously. But I wasn't watching their team. I watched Brian. He didn't look nervous, just leaned back on the bench and watched the other team perform with a slight smirk on his face. Like he was waiting to show them up. And if I remembered correctly, he would.

"Next up, let's welcome Mr. Whiskers back to the ice for his rendition of ABBA's 'Gimme! Gimme! Gimme!'"

I glanced at Maddy, just to make sure she was watching. Not surprisingly, her mouth dropped open as she watched Brian skate to center ice.

If I hadn't seen his performance before, my mouth would've been hanging open too. Now, I just couldn't stop smiling. I'd asked him once if he'd had help coming up with his dance, and he'd nodded. "Kinda," he'd said. "My sister loved this song, and she made me dance with her when we were younger. I already had the moves down. No-brainer."

It was only fifteen seconds long, but it was the best fifteen seconds of my day, maybe the week.

With his arms in the air, he skated in a circle to the music, making complicated patterns, like he was vogueing. And when he came to a stop, he did the best Magic Mike body roll I'd ever seen.

The audience went wild. Maddy started to laugh uncontrollably. I whooped and clapped. Even my mom, who'd agreed to come to the game today because Krista had flashed doe eyes at her and said please, whistled through her teeth before dissolving in laughter.

When it was over, Brian skated to the bench, where his teammates slapped him on the back and tapped their sticks against his leg pads. Except for Reb, of course, who'd already skated to the blue dot for face-off.

Brian's grin held my attention. He looked lighter than he had the whole time he'd been here so far. I was mesmerized. And when he looked up into the box where we sat and winked... Well, I just about combusted. I knew it was for me. I knew that because when he waved, Maddy waved back.

The game was pretty uneventful after that. No more fights. Just a few minor penalties. And we won the game in overtime.

This was turning out to be our winningest season ever.

"SO," Tressy drew the word out to about five syllables, "is there something you wanna talk about?"

I looked at my almost-sister-in-law with true consternation and a little bit of fear. Rowdy and I were still planning our trip to Harrisburg to get Tressy a ring. Had I inadvertently said something that had made her suspicious? Shit, I couldn't remember that I had, but... "I don't have a clue what you're talking about."

"Uh-huh. Okay."

Nodding, Tressy arched her brows and made a face as we waited in the green room on the lower level. Maddy and Krista were playing some complicated hand game in the corner with a few of the other players' kids, while the rest of the WAGs mingled and chatted with the Devils' Angels dance team. Most of the WAGs were girlfriends. Not a lot of the team members were married, although that could change in any given year.

I gave Tressy a look. "What does that mean?"

Her wide-eyed innocent look just made my gaze narrow.

"I don't know what you're talking about." She shrugged. "I just said okay."

I was about to question her again when Brian walked into the room. He caught sight of Maddy, who rolled her eyes in professional preteen fashion but crossed the room to give her uncle a quick hug. I couldn't hear what they said above the rest of the conversations in the room, but Maddy was apparently giving her uncle shit for that dance.

While I wouldn't be giving him shit, I'd tell him I'd want to see it in a room with just the two of us, while he was naked. I'm sure Tressy would want to know this. I totally wasn't going to tell her.

Brian gave Maddy his complete attention while she spoke to him, but finally she turned away to get the backpack she'd left across the room, and he walked over to me.

My smile widened with every inch he came closer.

"Still got your moves." I arched my brows. "Maddy seemed amused by them."

Brian's grin made me burn from the inside out. "Nice to see her smile like that. If it means I gotta take a few punches and shake my ass a few times, I'll do it."

Out of the corner of my eye, I saw Tressy give a little wave and walk away, probably to meet Rowdy.

When she was out of earshot, Brian said, "Hey, while we've got a sec, I just want to make sure we're still on for tomorrow."

Heat bubbled inside, making me wish tomorrow wasn't so far away.

"Yeah. We are."

"Good." His smile disappeared but now his gaze was heated. "I'm really— I'm looking forward to it."

"Me too."

After a few seconds of staring at each other, I blinked and let my gaze fall to his mouth. "Did you get that looked at?"

I pointed to his lip, which he reached up to touch, making a face when he did.

"Yeah, needed a couple stitches. No biggie."

In some people's worlds, a wound requiring stitches would be a big deal. Not in ours.

"Um, you ready, Uncle Bri?"

Well, damn. I'd been so wrapped up in Brian, I hadn't noticed Maddy coming up behind me.

"Yeah, kid." His gaze slid to the side and his grin turned soft. "You hungry? Let's get something to eat."

Maddy's head tilted to the side, her gaze bouncing between Brian and me, before she nodded. "Sure. I can eat."

"Good, 'cause I'm starving. See you later, Rain."

I almost said, "See you tomorrow," but stopped myself just in time. Instead, I waved and tried to contain the smile that wanted to hijack my expression.

"Sooo, there's nothing going on between you and Brian, right?"

"That's right." I didn't even bother to turn around to see Tressy, who must be in stealth mode. "We were just talking."

"Uh-huh. Well, when that just talking turns to not just talking, you know you can trust me if you need to discuss."

"Nothing to discuss." I grabbed my tote, gave Krista a hug, patted Tressy on the shoulder, and headed for the door

---

I'D TOLD Dad I was working at home this morning, which wasn't unusual on the Monday after a game.

The team had the day off from practice, though they were encouraged to work out or take a yoga class at the only gym in town. Some of them even opted for ballet, which I thought was amazing for flexibility.

And while I did do a few work-related things, including updating our socials and banking a few posts for the rest of the week because I didn't want to have to work Wednesday or Thursday, mostly I got ready for my not-a-date with Brian. We were just two friends meeting for lunch to discuss...something. Not sure what that something was, but I didn't really care. Brian and I would be alone to discuss anything we wanted.

I'd have him all to myself. No brothers, no niece, no prying neighbors or landlords or friends or townspeople who loved to gossip or would tell my brothers I was having lunch with a man. It was part of the reason I'd bought this house across town. I loved my family, but growing up as a girl with three brothers, I also loved my space.

I'm not a great cook, not like my mom or Rowdy. Damn him, he'd inherited the good-cook gene from my mom. But I'd spent enough time in the kitchen with my mom, and I was pretty... Well, I was decent.

And I liked to cook. When I had the time. Which wasn't often. I had a few signature dishes that I could pull out when I had friends over, but this was just lunch.

So, a good hearty soup and thick roast beef sandwiches were on the menu. I whipped up a potato soup loaded with cheese and bacon and chives, because really, who didn't like bacon and cheese and potatoes. And the roast I'd put in the crockpot last night before bed was now fall-apart soft and going to be yummy. I even made homemade rolls, although I cheated with the bread machine.

When Brian knocked on the door at twelve-thirty, the house smelled amazing, and I couldn't stop smiling when I saw him standing there.

"Hi." I waved him in and shut the door against the cold wind whipping through the valley today. "It's bitter out there."

"Yeah. Forgot how cold it can get here." He shuffled his

feet across the welcome mat as I shut the door behind him. "Damn, Rain, what's that smell? It's amazing."

My face was going to hurt if I kept smiling like this. "Lunch. I hope you're hungry."

"I'm starving, so I hope you made a lot."

I motioned for him to follow me back to the kitchen, where I'd set us up at the table by the window.

"I'm used to making much more than I should because my brothers almost always drop by for some reason, and they're always hungry. Especially Reb—"

Dammit, I hadn't wanted to bring him up, not already, even though I knew I was going to ask Brian about what had happened between him and my brother. But first I wanted a little bit of time to just talk.

"You can say his name." Brian gave a wry huff. "It's not like we're mortal enemies or anything."

"I know that. I just didn't want to start off on that note."

"So what do you want to talk about?"

Now that he was here and watching me with those intense eyes with his arms crossed over his broad chest, I was lucky we didn't have an audience. Because anyone with eyes would be able to read my emotions.

"Why don't we get lunch first?"

He didn't answer right away, just stared at me, like he was trying to read my mind. If he could, would he run? Was this attraction one-sided? Was I seeing something that wasn't there?

Then I thought back to the other night when we'd fallen asleep on the couch and the way he'd looked at me. No, I wasn't wrong. I knew what I'd seen, and I wasn't wrong.

He wanted me, hopefully as much as I wanted him. And I was done waiting for the right time. This was the time, right or not.

"Sure, lunch sounds good."

He stood on the other side of the island from me, taking dishes and plates that I filled with food, making small talk. We settled at the table, talked a little about the game last night, laughing about the intermission games with fans and discussing the league standings, in which we were solidly second place.

"Denny and Reid have been on a tear this year," I said. "They're our top goal-scorers, and they're playing like two guys who don't want to stay in this league very long."

"Yeah, they're young and hungry. And they're good. I noticed Coach working them hard during practice this week."

"It just seems like everyone is stepping up their game this year. Might be why the ECHL is giving us another look."

"I know you said your dad's leaving the decision up to you and your brothers, but what do you think he wants to do?"

I shrugged. "I honestly don't know. He's really not said a lot, which for Dad is odd. Dad aways has an opinion."

And honestly, that had me worried, but we weren't here to discuss my dad, or any other member of my family for that matter. I asked him if he wanted more food, but he declined and I rose to take our dishes to the dishwasher, but he rose and followed me, slotting his plate and dish next to mine. And, as ridiculous as it sounded, it was the sexiest thing he could've done at the moment. Which was stupid, I know. And yet...

"Brian?"

He leaned against the island, close enough for me to be able to reach out and touch him if I wanted. And I wanted.

"I really hope I'm not overstepping any boundaries right now, but," I took a deep breath, "I like you, and I'd like to see you in a context outside of work. If that's not what you want, you just have to tell me."

He didn't move right away, just continued to stare at me until I could feel my cheeks getting red from embarrassment. Had I made a mistake? Did he not feel the same way about me? Oh my god, I was an idi—

I barely realized what he was doing when he reached for me, curving his hand around my neck, the warmth of it seeping into my skin like a drug. He tugged, and I closed the few steps between us as he moved his hand from my neck to frame my face with both hands.

Oh wow.

My lips parted, though I wasn't sure if I was going to say something or just as an invitation. I have no idea what I would've said because my brain stopped working as soon as his lips touched mine. At first, he kissed me like I was breakable, like I'd run if he got too close.

So I wrapped my arms around his waist and lifted up onto my toes so our lips could more completely align, and then I pressed my body against his and kissed him with all the pent-up longing I'd been storing for years.

I felt like I'd won the lottery after a decade of playing, my yearning for him dissolving every line of defense I'd erected since last year. My desire for him burned like sparks in my blood, making me tingle all over, while my core clenched with need.

For a few brief seconds, he let me control the pace, let me kiss him like I'd dreamed about, our lips pressed together, and our bodies smashed up against each other like we were trying to melt into one another.

And then it was like a switch flipped. His fingers flexed against my cheeks, drawing me even closer, until my lips parted. The tip of his tongue swiped against my bottom lip, and I moaned and welcomed him in.

Excitement jangled through me like a drug, and that's what it was. One I couldn't get enough of. I rose onto my toes to get even closer as we melded together into a kiss that felt like the start of something amazing, not just an amazing thing in itself. But his height, which I loved by the way, had become a hindrance. Yes, I wanted to climb him like a tree, but that would seem kind of desperate, right?

So I craned my neck, and he bent his as our kiss settled into this long-term agreement of pleasure. My hands spread across his back, pressing into him, until I needed more than the promise of feeling his skin. Before I realized I'd made the decision to do it, my hands slipped beneath the warm cotton and hit pay dirt.

He groaned into my mouth as my fingers flexed into his skin, kneading the muscles I could feel beneath. His hands, up until now still cupped around my face, began to act on their own instead of as a pair. One stilled around my neck again, holding my head up so he could kiss me harder, deeper.

His other hand slid to my shoulder then around to my back, pressing and sliding, pressing and sliding, until he reached my waist. I thought for a split second that he was going to stop there, like, oh, I don't know, a gentleman out of a Victorian novel or something.

But I should've known better, because, yeah, Brian definitely had plans of his own. And I was all in on whatever he wanted. Because he wanted me. I could tell it in the way he held me and the way he kissed me. The way his entire body tensed against mine and, yeah, by the bulge between his thighs.

He'd worn jeans today, but they weren't loose enough to hide his erection. A shiver of desire ran down my spine and made my thigh quiver. And made me wet.

Too fast? Fuck no, not fast enough.

He spread that one hand across my ass and molded me through the thin cotton pants I wore. Just the thought that those long thick fingers were that close to my center made me make an embarrassingly needy sound. I had just enough self-control not to hoist my leg around his waist and force him to take my weight.

Or maybe he read my mind because he slid his other hand down my back to my other side and squeezed both cheeks, a split second before he lifted me off my feet. He moved away from the island so I could wrap both legs around his waist, my arms moving up to circle his shoulders and hold on while he adjusted me in his arms.

Our lips separated as he looked down at me, a question in his eyes that I could tell he didn't want to speak aloud.

I nodded immediately, not wanting to break the spell. Thankfully my house wasn't that big, and he carried me into the living room in a matter of seconds, not even long enough for me to worry that he wasn't sure what he wanted to do.

Those thoughts scattered the second he laid me out on

the couch we'd slept on together the other night and spread out over me. I sucked in a deep breath at the sheer size of him hovering, blocking out the light from the front windows.

Brian must have thought I couldn't breathe because in the next second, he flipped our positions. I scrambled up to put a knee on either side of his hips, my hands braced on his chest while I stared down at him. My braid fell over my shoulder, and when I bent closer, it fell forward and brushed against his cheek.

He reached up and caught it between two fingers, wrapping it between them and tugging me down so our lips met again. This time, our kiss was a little slower and a whole hell of a lot hotter. And I'd thought it wouldn't be able to get hotter. But the slow, sensual lick of his tongue in my mouth revved my libido, the muscles of my pussy contracting until I wanted to push one of his hands resting on my hip between my legs.

Brian didn't seem in a hurry to do much more than kiss, and damn, the man did it so well, I could go along with the plan. For a little while, at least. But the heat between my legs continued to build until my hips needed to move.

I pressed my core down until I could grind against his erection, relieving at least a little of the ache. His breath hitched when we connected, the seam of my pants rubbing against my clit as I arched my back and slid up and down his length.

Fuck, I wished we were naked. I also knew we'd gone from zero to sixty in record time. The only excuse I could give for that was because it was Brian. I'd lusted after this man for way too long.

And I didn't care what had changed since yesterday.

Whatever had gone on between him and Rebel. I knew I should. Knew I should at least find out how this, Brian and me, was going to affect the dynamic between Reb and me.

But frankly, right now, I couldn't care less. It was only me and him right here and now. That's all that mattered.

His hands on my hips held me tightly but didn't hinder the rhythm I'd started. He let me take over again, but I knew now that if he wanted something different, he would do it. Take it. And I'd gladly give it.

Slowly, I found myself sinking lower until I was laid out flat above him, our bodies perfectly aligned. If only we were naked.

Pushing up, I braced my hands on his chest until I could get into a seated position, his cock still between my thighs and pressing against my clit. I was loath to give up that sensation, but I needed to see his face when I moved my hands under his shirt and tugged it up. I couldn't stop my gaze from flipping down to see what I'd uncovered, and the dark trail of hair that started around his belly button and continued beneath his jeans was well worth it. The man didn't have a perfectly carved six-pack, but he was solid. And he definitely didn't manscape. As I pushed his shirt up farther, I uncovered a thin mat of dark hair across his chest that made me want to pet him.

No sooner had I thought the words than he reached behind his shoulders and drew his shirt over his head with one hand. I mean, I'd read the books where they described it, and how the woman nearly fainted from lust. The writers weren't that far off on that. Oh my god, I needed to suck in a whole lot of air and then make sure I didn't drool because, holy hell, was that hot!

And it left him shirtless, which was amazing too. Okay, more than amazing because now I could touch him.

I slid one hand from his stomach to his left pec, letting my fingers glide through the soft hair to the nipple that was hard and tempting. I wanted to lean down and bite it, but I was a little afraid I might scare him off if I started to use my teeth already. So instead, I pinched it between my thumb and forefinger, watching his eyes narrow and his lips part as I did.

The intensity in his gaze gave me more confidence, and I slid my remaining hand up to do the same to his other nipple.

"I won't break, you know." His voice rumbled beneath my hands, making my pussy clench and my thighs tighten.

"Do you want me to do it harder?"

"Yeah, I do."

My hands actually trembled for a second before I gave him what he wanted. His expression didn't change, except that his eyes narrowed even more. So I did it even harder. His hips jerked beneath mine. His fingers squeezed into my hips and held me tighter against him. I wanted to move, but he held me so tightly, I couldn't. And I really liked that.

I played with him for several seconds before I noticed his jaw working. I leaned forward to press a kiss against the stubble then rubbed my cheek against his, enjoying the sensation against my skin.

"Fuck, Rain. I don't want to stop."

"Who said anything about stopping?" I spoke directly into his ear then bit the lobe, making him groan again. Damn, I really liked that.

"There're things we should talk about."

I flicked my tongue behind his ear, and he breathed out

heavily. "Do those things have anything to do with us right here and now?"

I pulled up so I could see his expression when he answered. He paused just long enough for me to worry that maybe there was before he shook his head.

"No."

And then he flipped me onto my back.

FIFTEEN

Brian

THE EXPANDING smile on Rain's face made every part of my body tighten with anticipation.

And yeah, there was still that voice in the back of my head that said this was going to cause problems, but I was going to ignore that voice because Rain wanted me.

She'd made that crystal clear. And who was I to turn her down for anything? Not happening. Hell no.

The smile she gave me now was all the proof I needed to continue. And I had all sorts of ideas on where to start.

Lowering my mouth to her neck, I put my lips against her warm skin and drew in her scent, which was clean and just a little floral. It wasn't perfume. It wasn't strong enough to be perfume, but whatever it was, it held me in thrall. I wanted to put my lips all over her body and check to see if that scent was everywhere.

Her sharp little inhale made my cock twitch as her fingers

dug into the muscles of my back. I wanted to suck her skin into my mouth, but I didn't want to leave a mark. At least, not where anyone could see it.

This was a small town, and no one would mind their own damn business. I didn't want Rain to have to deal with that kind of attention. Right now, the only attention I wanted her to worry about was mine.

I kissed my way down her neck but was stopped by the neckline of her shirt.

"Am I allowed to even the score here?"

"What do you mean?"

She looked a little dazed, midnight-blue eyes blinking up at me. My ego swelled, along with other parts of my body.

"I mean, I'm missing my shirt. It seems only fair..."

Her smile made my blood chug like lava.

"Oh yes, definitely. Let's make this fair."

Sitting up on my knees, I put my hands on the hem of her shirt and tugged it up slowly, revealing inches of golden skin and finally a hint of pink lace. Sucking in air, I kept lifting her shirt until I could pull it over her head. Her hair fell back around her shoulders, dark and silky. Her braid had lost its tie at some point. I wanted to feel it brush against the skin of my thighs while she sucked my cock into her mouth.

Yeah, I was jumping ahead a few steps and assuming a whole hell of a lot, but I couldn't force the image away, now that it was stuck there. I dropped her shirt to the floor, my attention stuck on her hair. I reached out to run a thick rope of it through my fingers and had the urge to bury my nose in it and just breathe her in. Then again, I'd uncovered other areas I wanted to explore during this stolen time.

And it was stolen. There'd be a price to pay later. There always was.

Letting my gaze roam, I stopped at that little pink bra I'd uncovered. It was lace but the fabric had hearts sewn into it. Little white hearts that made me want to play connect the dots with my mouth and tongue.

Since I had the caveman urge to just rip it off, I put my hands around her waist and said, "Take it off for me."

I thought she'd reach behind her to unsnap it. Instead, she reached for the band around her chest with both hands and drew it over her head. Her breasts jiggled when she set them free, and I nearly swallowed my tongue.

"Fuck, you're pretty, Rainy."

Her lips held a sweet curve that made me bend forward to taste it, to kiss it off her lips and make her groan. That kiss got hot and hard, our tongues tangled, and my hands slid up from her waist to cup her tits. They weren't big, but they were the perfect fit for my hands. Her flesh warm and soft, her nipples tiny and pebbled. Her eyes closed as I rolled the tips between my fingers. I watched her throat ripple as she swallowed, her lips part as she drew in air, and then I bent and put my lips around one perfect little nub. I sucked it into my mouth, let my teeth graze the skin and heard her gasp, her fingers sliding into my hair and tugging. I wanted her to tug harder, but I didn't want to release her, so I squeezed, just a little harder.

I got what I wanted. She wrapped her fingers in my hair and pulled. And that bite of pain felt so fucking good.

Switching my attention to her other breast, I played with her for long minutes, using my tongue and my teeth together to learn what she liked. And discovered that Rain liked a little bite with her pleasure. She arched into me, offering more of herself to me.

I took it all. She felt so damn good and tasted even better. I lost myself in making her squirm against me.

One of her hands fell from my hair to glide down my arm then diverted to my waist. Her fingers slid beneath the waistband of my jeans, leaving a wake of goosebumps as she slowly made her way to the button on my jeans. But she didn't stop there. The little tease then drew one finger up my stomach to pinch one of my nipples. Hard. It felt so fucking amazing, I released her with a loud sucking noise that filled the silence of the room. Didn't want to accidentally hurt her.

Our eyes met as I sat back on my heels. Her teeth caught in her bottom lip before she said, "Why'd you stop?"

"I don't plan on stopping. Unless you tell me to."

I watched her closely for any hint that I was moving too fast for her. But I'd wanted her for years, lusted after her for years, and I finally had her exactly where I wanted her. Beneath me. And even though I knew this could cause issues later, I didn't give one fuck at the moment. Because Rain was staring up at me with a smile.

"I don't plan on telling you to stop. In fact, if you don't continue right this second, I'm going to order you to continue."

"I didn't realize you were so bossy."

Her smile spread. "You like it, though, don't you?"

"I like you however I can get you, Rain."

She put a hand on my shoulder and gripped me tight. "Then come back down here and kiss me again."

I leaned forward and did what she wanted, melded our lips together and drove my tongue between her teeth. I couldn't get enough of her. With one arm holding me steady, I used the other to caress her from neck to waist, loving the way her skin heated for me.

Now she rewarded me with a long scratch of her nails down my back with one hand while her other grabbed the waistband of my jeans. Her fingers slid between my skin and my boxer briefs, just far enough to almost, but not quite, graze the tip of my cock.

I drew back far enough to say, "You gonna be a tease?"

I felt her smile against my cheek. "Yeah, I am. But don't worry, I think you'll like it."

She slid her hand free then brought it to the button on my jeans, working it free while our lips met again, our breath coming harsh and fast as our mouths became greedier.

Then I felt her release the zipper, my cock practically leaping out of my pants and into her hands, like it had a mind of its own. I bit back a groan, cupping a breast tight as my hips thrust forward. I needed pressure, my cock begging to be fondled, squeezed, and pumped hard.

She pulled back, pressing a hand against my chest to make me give her some room. I didn't want to give her room, and I didn't want to give her mouth up. For right now, she was mine. And I wasn't going to give up any part of her willingly.

For a few seconds, she let me take what I wanted, getting to know her body and what she liked. What made her moan and what made her twist in my hands and what made her arch into me.

When I released her mouth to kiss my way down her body, she lay there, just breathing hard for several seconds.

Until I dipped my tongue into her belly button before pressing kisses down her stomach to her pants.

They had a drawstring waist, and I used my teeth to pull the string until it loosened.

"Lift up."

I heard her swallow, but she arched her back and lifted her ass off the couch so I could pull her pants off. Just her pants. I wanted to see her in her underwear. I wasn't disappointed.

The underwear matched the bra. Pink lace with little white hearts all over them. They looked sexy as all hell, and I wanted to put my mouth on them right over her clit.

Her legs were already spread, my knees holding them open. I could tell she was wet from the darker material between her legs.

"Fuck, Rain. You're so pretty, baby."

Without warning, I put one hand on her mound, the heel of my palm directly over her clit, and pressed. She moaned and circled her hips. I let her grind on my hand for a few seconds, watching her face as she did. Eyes closed, lips slightly parted.

When I took my hand away, her eyes flew open, and she made a sexy little sound in the back of her throat, her lips turned down in a pout.

"Hey."

I grinned. "Don't worry. I won't leave you hanging. Put your feet on my chest."

Her brows drew down in a frown, but she followed my direction, which I didn't realize would be such a fucking turn-on. My impatience took over, and I yanked her panties down her legs, pulling them off one foot at a time.

Then I gripped a knee in each hand and spread her open.

I heard her suck in a deep breath, felt the slight resistance in her legs, but she held my gaze with her own, not moving to cover her nudity. And why should she? She was fucking beautiful. Curvy and soft and golden, with dark short hair on her mound and pink folds between her legs that looked slick.

I thought about telling her what I was going to do but decided she had to know already.

Gripping her under her knees, I pulled her close enough that I could drape her legs over my shoulders.

Her little gasp became a moan when I bent my head to flick her clit with the tip of my tongue.

"Oh my—"

She cut off as I settled my mouth over her sex, my eyes closing as I licked and sucked and tasted her. The sounds coming from her mouth made me want more. I'd been lusting after this woman for years and now I had her exactly where I wanted her. In my hands. And against my mouth.

She squirmed against me as my tongue slid into her channel, licking deep. Her taste flooded my senses, and I wanted to keep her here with me until I could make her come on command. Until she just needed to look at me, and she'd be wet.

Because all I needed to do was think about her and I got hard. And I was so fucking hard right now. My cock throbbed and ached, but I didn't want to just take her and fuck her like a Neanderthal. I wanted to get her off at least twice before I got her to ride me.

I didn't have to wait long for her to get off the first time, because in just a couple of minutes of tongue-fucking her, I felt her stiffen, her heels digging into my back as she moaned.

I felt her pussy ripple around my tongue, her thighs quivering when I pulled back and licked her clit once more, then took her legs and settled them on either side of my thighs.

Her eyes opened, her heavy-lidded gaze connecting with mine, making me grin. I felt like a fucking conquering hero. But I wasn't done. I was still wearing my jeans for a reason. Which she noticed.

"Are you going to take those off now?"

"Not just yet."

"Why—"

She gasped when I dragged a hand up her thigh and worked one finger between her pussy lips. Her inner muscles clamped around me immediately, and she reached for my wrist with one hand.

"Brian."

Her little panting breaths made me more and more determined to see her come again, this time with my hand. I was being greedy, but I didn't give a shit at that moment. Because her flushed cheeks and rapidly rising and falling chest were a drug to my libido.

Planting one hand into the cushion next to her head, I held her gaze as I leaned over, my finger starting a slow rhythm of plunge and retreat. She groaned, her eyes fluttering closed, but I pulled my finger out completely and they flew open.

"Don't stop." I barely heard her, her voice a whisper.

"Then make sure you keep watching me. Because I think I just found my new favorite pastime. Watching you when I make you come."

"Oh fuck, Brian."

The sound she made when I worked two fingers inside her made me smile, and the twist of her hips let me know she wanted even more. I spread my fingers inside as my thumb made contact with her clit. I circled it a few times, pressed hard and rubbed, finding what she liked and then giving her more.

My own breath rasped in and out, like I'd just done wind sprints. But I clamped down on the urge to rip off my jeans and fuck her right now.

No, I needed to watch her come again. Needed that dopamine hit I got when she clamped around my fingers. It took less than a minute before she made that amazing sound deep in her throat, her head digging back into the cushions and her body tightening until she broke again.

When she'd relaxed back into the couch after I slid my fingers free, I watched her breathe, watched her slowly blink back to full awareness. I loved that I'd made her boneless. That she trusted me enough. That she wanted *me*.

Her lips curved in a smile that revved my lust even higher, made my jaw clench and my fingers curl so I didn't grab her and turn her onto her knees so I could fuck her from behind. My body wanted that, just so I could get off. My brain wanted to watch her ride me.

She startled me by pushing up and maneuvering around onto her knees in front of me. I held my breath, the voice in the back of my head telling me she was going to tell me to get the hell out.

Instead, she reached for my jeans, and this time I let her.

"My turn," I heard her say under her breath as she worked the button open and shoved the fabric down my hips.

Luckily, my cock had escaped the waistband of my boxer briefs, and they went down with the jeans.

The cooler air of the room made my balls tighten. Or maybe it was the way she looked at my body. Like a woman with a mission.

"Take them off, then lie down on the couch."

I huffed out a short laugh that died the second she wrapped her hand around my cock and squeezed.

"Holy fuck, Rainy. Do that again."

She looked up at me from beneath her lashes, her lips curved in a wicked little smile. Then she squeezed me even tighter and did a slow pump up my shaft. I tried not to groan too loudly, but my body was pleading with me to stay right here so she couldn't stop.

"Now lie down," she said. "And I'll return the favor."

"I didn't make you come for a favor. That was all for you."

"And I appreciate it." Her voice had dipped into a quiet, low register that raised gooseflesh and made my stomach clench. "But it's my turn to do what I've been dreaming about doing for years."

Her words made me go still, blood pounding in my ears. "Years."

"You have no idea how detailed my dreams can be."

"And you don't have a clue how hungry I am for you."

Her smile widened until I could see her teeth, exactly what I wanted to feel on my cock.

"I look forward to finding out. On your back, Mr. Whiskers. Let's see how you purr."

Her words were so ridiculous, I burst out laughing, which

made her smile become a grin, as if she'd said that just to make me laugh.

"Yes, Miss Lawrence. I can't wait to feel your claws in my skin."

Rain scrambled off the couch so we could trade positions after I ditched my jeans, socks, and sneakers, swinging one leg over my hips before my back even hit the cushion. Her hands hit my chest a split second later, and she leaned over, hair spilling across my chest and tickling my cheeks.

Leaning all the way down, she brushed her lips across mine in a tease of a kiss. Whisper-light and so fucking enticing, my entire body broke out in goosebumps. Combined with that, she let her nails dig into my skin, just like I'd dreamed about.

Finally, our lips met and melded, our tongues tangling again, as her pussy hovered tantalizingly close above my cock. My hands fastened around her hips in a flash, but some instinct made me stop just before I ground her down against my erection.

"No rushing in this game." She spoke against my lips, then dragged them along my cheek to my ear. "But there will be full-body contact. And some deep penetration in the zone."

She smiled against my ear, just before she bit the lobe and made me huff out a groan.

"You're gonna fucking stop my heart before we score, Rainy."

"I already came twice. Thank you, by the way. I figure I owe you the same."

"When I come, I want to be deep inside you."

I wasn't fucking kidding. I wanted to pump hard and fast inside her until I felt her body pump mine for everything it had.

She didn't seem to have a response for that, mainly because she was kissing her way from my ear down my neck to my chest. I heard her labored breathing, felt her body take in deep breaths. When her lips circled one of my nipples then nibbled at it with her teeth, my back arched to give her more. But after she did the same to the other, she continued her way down my body. When her mouth reached my cock, without touching it, she looked up at me and smiled again. Then she bent her head, her hair trailing along my stomach, and licked a path down my shaft.

I grabbed the back of the couch with one hand and the side with the other and hung on as she licked back up to the tip then swirled her tongue around it. I didn't want to force myself down her throat so I made my hips stay flat on the cushion, but it was a tight battle. I was rewarded for my patience when she took me in her mouth and sucked me hard.

Her mouth felt like heaven, like every dream I'd had. But so much fucking better. Heat when she encased me completely and cool when she lifted off and blew a cool stream of air across the tip.

Staring up at the ceiling, I found myself panting, barely getting enough air with every breath. All my nerve endings felt like they were on fire, but it was the best goddamn sensation ever.

She sucked me for several long minutes, like I was her favorite treat. And when she finally released me, and I could draw in a deep breath, she gave me a look that let me know she had even more plans.

With the most sensual look I'd ever seen a woman give me, Rain released me with an audible pop then moved farther down my legs, her hair trailing along my thighs. A fucking fantasy come true. Her fingers followed, nails in my skin raking fire.

Every muscle in my body tightened, and I had to close my eyes and will myself not to blow right there. But I'd told her I wanted to be inside her when I did.

"Condom." My voice sounded like I hadn't spoken in years. "In my wallet."

Her gaze met mine again as she slowly rose to her knees then slid to the side where my jeans lay on the floor. Reaching over, she pulled my wallet from the back pocket, flipped it open and extracted the condom. Then she dropped my wallet to the floor and opened the condom packet. As the foil followed the wallet to the floor, she leaned forward and rolled it down my erection with gentle fingers.

I had the almost unbearable urge to flip her back under me, but I knew it would be better for both of us if she was on top. For me, because I could watch her every move, and for her, because she wouldn't be crushed under me.

Our height difference wouldn't matter with her riding me. And it gave me the best fucking view possible.

I was about to beg her to move faster because she just sat there, her gaze making a slow route from my groin up my abs to my chest and, finally, to my eyes. Holding out her hands, she waited for me to weave our fingers together and steady her as she moved her body until her sex aligned with mine.

Releasing one hand, she gripped my cock and tilted it at

the perfect angle for her to sink down onto me. Her eyes fluttered closed as I breached her tight, slick pussy. She let gravity bring her down, taking each inch of me into her wet warmth until we were totally meshed together.

Sitting there like a queen, looking like my absolute best wet dream, she smiled right before she began to rock back and forth and blow my fucking mind.

Holding on to my hands for balance, she rose just a little before gliding back down, each time going a little higher and dropping back down a little slower. Holding my gaze the whole time.

Her cheeks flushed, her eyes heavy-lidded, she rode me slow and steady, like she was trying to draw it out. With her every movement, I tried my best not to blow. But it got harder with every second not to just let go. I could tell she was getting closer to another orgasm. Chasing it while pushing me.

Long seconds played out as she rode me, time suspended for this small window of time. And then her pussy clenched around me, and she bit her lip, moaning just a little. Her rhythm changed, became less smooth, a little harder, like she was chasing that O, or trying to force me over the cliff. I was determined to hold on as long as I could, but I could tell I was reaching the end of my rope.

Releasing her hands, I grabbed her hips and held her steady for my thrusts. I couldn't keep still anymore. I needed to move. My first thrust made her eyes close as she arched over me, her hands flat against my chest. We rocked together, working toward a mutual goal, in perfect sync. I'd never experienced this with anyone else.

Finally, with a breathy moan, she tensed, her pussy

pulsing around my cock. And when she fell forward and lay against my chest, boneless, I held her hips and thrust until I couldn't hold back anymore.

My release pumped into her, and I groaned as my eyes closed. Everything went black and my arms wrapped around her, holding her tight.

SIXTEEN

Rain

FEELING like I'd just inhaled a couple of Red Bulls and a horse tranquilizer, I lay spread across Brian's overheated body like a slug.

My bare ass was going to be cold in a few minutes but right now, I wanted to stay here forever, or at least until I needed water, which would be soon. I also felt like I had enough inspiration to write two hundred promo posts about why you should come see live hockey. And it didn't have much to do with the game itself.

"Rain?"

"Hmm."

"We really need to talk about this."

I ignored the little squiggle of unease in my tummy. "About what? How amazing we are in bed together?"

He huffed out a laugh and his hand petted me from my shoulder to just above my ass. "Well, yeah, we are."

"Then what do we need to talk about except when we're going to do this again?"

"This, you and me, this is complicated."

My immediate thought was, *It doesn't have to be*, but I bit my tongue on that one, the logical half of my brain kicking in. Because he wasn't wrong.

I hated the logical half of my brain right now.

Taking a deep breath, I pulled up my metaphorical big-girl panties, which I still consider to be silk and lace and sexy.

"I know that." I lifted my head so I could look him in the eyes. "But I also know I don't want to stop what we started. I've been lusting after you for years, Brian. Did you know that?"

His eyes widened in surprise before he could get his expression under control. "Years?"

He sounded stunned, which made me smile. Guys could be so clueless.

"I've had a crush on you since Rowdy first brought you home. I was a teenager and girl teenage hormones rage just as much as boys. You had to know."

He shook his head. "You were completely off limits then, so no, I didn't notice. If I had even glanced in your direction, your brothers would've pulverized me. And with good cause."

"I get that. But later? Why did you never ask me out?"

"Because you were always dating other guys. When I started with the team, you were away at college. When you got home, you were dating that kid, Chisholm. Then you announced you weren't dating hockey players. And then..."

I grimaced. "Then I went out with Zelinsky."

Brian's body tensed, like he wanted to say something but didn't know how.

"For the record, he wasn't a dick to me," I said. "I mean, he was self-centered, but he never was intentionally mean to me. Probably because he knew my brothers would obliterate him if he was. I honestly thought he cared for me, and..." I sighed. "Okay, I'm not proud of this, but he was nice to look at and he had a good body. And my brothers hated him, and yes, I know that makes me a brat, but— You know what? I don't have to explain myself to you."

With a huff, I sat up, ignoring the amazing view of Brian's naked body on display, and scrambled off the couch. Which probably didn't look as elegant as I would've hoped. Grabbing his shirt, because it was right there, and I wanted him to see me in it, I tugged it over my head, sighing just a little when it drowned me. And covered me in his scent.

Rolling my eyes, I plopped into the chair across from him and crossed my arms over my chest.

"So what are we going to do about this?"

"You mean us?" Brian's voice sounded rough and sexy, and I liked it so much, it just pissed me off.

"Okay, first off. Is there an 'us'?"

"Do you want there to be?"

I gave him a look that would've made my brothers wince and slink off like kicked puppies. Or at least, that's what I hoped they'd do most of the time.

"Brian. We just fucked our brains out on my couch. It was my couch's first time, so maybe be gentle with it. I can count on one finger how many guys have been invited into my house to fool around. That one finger is you."

A smile twitched around the corners of his lips. "I hope it's not the middle finger."

Now he wanted to be cute and funny.

"I guess you'll just have to hang around a little and find out. I acknowledge the fact that this situation is fraught with—"

"Did you just use 'fraught' in a sentence?"

Now I did give him the finger, which made him laugh, drawing my gaze down to the tight muscles of his abs. Which made the muscles between my thighs clench. And dampen. Dammit, I could go again.

Don't look at his dick. Don't look at his dick. Don't look at his dick.

Biting my tongue, I swung my gaze around the room, getting caught on the open curtains on my window. Which meant anyone walking up to my door could've seen us having sex. Lucky for us, it was the middle of the day, and all my neighbors were at work. And amazingly, none of my brothers had decided to visit. Particularly Rebel.

Which brought me back to the discussion we were having, while in the back of my head I was thinking that I should buy shades for those windows.

"Are you trying to change the subject?"

He shook his head. "Just giving you props for your word usage."

"Here's another word for you. Avoidance."

"I'm not trying to avoid talking about the situation. And yeah, this situation is *fraught*," he placed an extra emphasis on the word, "with pitfalls.

"Then maybe we just need to get everything out in the open and talk about it like adults."

"If you want to know what happened between Reb and me, you need to talk to him first. It's not my story to tell."

So obviously, it was something that Rebel had done. What a shock.

"Then what are you suggesting? You just want to forget this happened and never speak of it again?"

It'd been a bitchy jab, and I wanted him to tell me to stop being a brat, but he didn't answer right away, his gaze boring into mine. And my stomach curled in on itself.

"No, I'm not."

Sitting up with an impressive display of shifting muscles under warm skin, he put his feet on the floor and his elbows on his knees. Luckily for me, he was still totally naked.

"But," he sighed, "we both have other people we've got to think about in this situation."

He was right. Although I really, really wanted to keep this about us, we couldn't. We didn't live in a vacuum. We had to consider my family and the team.

"So," I drew the word out a little, "you don't want anyone to know? About us."

I couldn't help it. My gaze slipped down his naked body then snapped back up to find his eyes crinkled at the corners.

"For now, yeah. That doesn't mean I don't want to see you." His gaze wandered my body, which made me burn from my sex to my nipples. "It just means we need to be... circumspect."

"Ooh, that's even longer than 'fraught.'"

"Longer, huh? You trying to tell me something?"

My cheeks flushed, my core clenched, and I wanted to jump back on the couch and ride him again. Hello, new obsession.

"I think I've already told you everything you need to know."

He looked into my eyes, nodding. "This doesn't mean I'm ashamed of you or of us. You know that, right?"

I nodded solemnly, because I could see he was serious. "Yes."

"Then you also know I want to pull you back on the couch and fuck you wearing my shirt. Right?"

I had to swallow before I could respond. "I was hoping, yes."

He reached out his hand, and I took it because I wasn't about to say no.

"Then don't let me disappoint you."

———

"WHY DO you look all glowy and shit? It's only six in the morning. No one should look this happy when the sun is barely up." Erin yawned. "And you're smiling weird."

"No, I'm not. You're just delirious from lack of sleep."

It was Wednesday, the day before Christmas, and I'd promised to give Erin a hand in the bakery. It was all-hands-on-deck today because everyone in town and in what seemed like a fifty-mile radius had ordered their pies, rolls, bread, cookies, muffins, and cupcakes for the holiday to be picked up today.

Besides the regular staff, Erin had recruited a few of the Angels to help as well. Luckily, they hadn't arrived yet to hear Erin's way-too-loud pronouncement.

Eyes narrowed as she slugged down scalding-hot coffee, Erin stared at me like I was an exhibit at a science fair that she couldn't figure out. I didn't meet her gaze because I was dropping cupcake liners into pans before I filled them with batter. I already had ten pans ready to go and would start on the roll tins next.

"You got laid, didn't you?"

I felt my cheeks burn and turned away to grab more cupcake liners that I really didn't need.

"You need to make more cake batter. I'm pretty sure we don't have enough."

"We have more than enough. And now you're avoiding me. Damn, girl. Good for you. Who— Oh my god, did you finally nail Brian?" Her squeal had to be able to be heard all the way to Philly and Pittsburgh. "Finally. I'm so proud of you."

I rolled my eyes as I shoved balls of dough into the tins. "Jesus, Erin, why not just announce it to the world. Which you can't do, by the way. And I can neither confirm or deny what exactly happened Monday afternoon."

"Then I'm right." I couldn't see her smile because she'd turned to take out another two trays of rolls from the ovens then immediately shoved in another two trays of bread. "You and Brian got it on. Good for you. Glad to know one of us is getting laid."

Erin had been in the bakery for two hours already and probably wouldn't stop for another four, at least. So I was going to give her the benefit of being nearly completely without a filter because of exhaustion.

But I'd been dying to talk to someone about what had happened, and I knew if I told Erin, she could be trusted to keep her mouth shut. Because Brian was right. We couldn't afford the knowledge that we were sleeping together to get out. Just too many complications.

"Look, I promised Brian we would keep this just between the two of us." I expertly filled this tray and started another. This wasn't my first holiday helping Erin. "You have to promise me you won't tell anyone."

Erin threw me a look that let me know exactly what she thought of that. "That seems like a recipe for disaster."

"Only if anyone finds out before we decide to spill the tea."

Erin walked over to the stand mixer and threw some ingredients in for what looked like chocolate chip cookies. Or maybe muffins.

"Rainy, we live in a small town. Gossip is like currency. You know I would never sell you out, but someone's gonna find out. And then what are you going to do? I mean, why aren't you telling anyone anyway?"

"You mean, besides the fact that my brother Rebel hates him, and he's Rowdy's best friend? That my dad signs his paychecks? That he's only here because he needed a place where his niece will be taken care of when he's not around?"

"And why do you think your dad or Rowdy will care if you're dating him? And Rebel can go fuck himself, seriously. He's a dick if he thinks he can dictate your love life."

"I know that." I sighed, pushing the trays down the huge stainless prep table in the middle of the room. "But something major went down between the two of them, and I still don't know what happened. Reb won't talk about it, and Brian won't tell me because he says it's Rebel's story to tell. Whatever the hell that means."

"Just sounds like another one of Rebel's dickhead moves.

Why should your brother get to dictate who you sleep with? Maybe he's just pissed because he's not getting any. That man is the most uptight asshole I've ever known. And you just want to please everyone. You know you can't do that all the time, right? You can't make everyone happy."

Erin turned back to add more ingredients to the oversize mixer, and I stuck my tongue out at her while she couldn't see me. But she wasn't wrong.

The problem was, that was me. That was my fucking job. Make everyone happy. And I was damn good at it. Brian had certainly left with a smile on his face Monday when he'd gone to pick up Maddy from school. We hadn't seen each other yesterday because we'd both had to work and Brian couldn't exactly tell his twelve-year-old niece that he was going out for a few hours in the evening and leave her alone, especially not two nights before Christmas.

He'd told me they'd been planning to spend all day Wednesday cocooned in their apartment watching movies and eating junk food because school was on break and so were the Devils. Brian had told me Maddy didn't want a Christmas tree. She didn't want to make a big deal about the holiday. And I got that. I did. Her mom wasn't there. I couldn't imagine what she was feeling.

And I hated that I couldn't really do anything to help her through this. She'd probably hate me if I tried.

I hated when anyone—my brothers excluded—were unhappy or even mad at me. Everyone loved me. Well, almost everyone. I knew there was one ex who definitely did not love me.

"I'm not kidding, Erin. I need you to promise me you

won't say anything. When we're ready, we'll be the ones to break the news."

Erin turned from the mixer to give me a raised eyebrow. "You know I would never rat you out. Especially to your brothers. But isn't Miss Raffi gonna take one look at the two of you and know exactly what's going on? I swear your mom can read minds. And you're all going to be at the same table tomorrow. How's that gonna work? Because that face of yours," she waved her finger in front of my nose, "is not designed to hide secrets. Especially from your mom. Your brothers are clueless, most of the time, but Rowdy's smarter than the average bear. Sometimes. Then again, he's got his own females to worry about now, so maybe he won't notice that you're fucking his best friend."

I stared at Erin for a second, wondering if the steady stream of words coming out of her mouth had finally stopped, before I said, "Exactly how much caffeine have you had this morning?"

"Not nearly enough." Erin suddenly and tightly wrapped her arms around my shoulders and hugged me, making me laugh and hug her back. "Rainy, you're the best friend a girl could have, but you spread yourself too thin. One of these days you're gonna snap."

"Well, you better hope it's not until after the holidays or who's going to help you fill these muffin tins?"

The back door flew open as we were pulling apart and Caity shouted, "The calvary has arrived!" as five members of the Angels' dance team filed through the door.

Erin winked to let me know my secret was safe. And I made sure my face didn't scream, "I got laid last night," when

I turned to greet the other girls. Even though I wanted to shout it to the rooftops.

"RAIN, baby, grab that pan. And the lid. Oh, and the potatoes. Rowdy, make sure that cranberry sauce doesn't boil over. Reb, uh..."

Our mom trailed off, looking round the kitchen, and Rowdy and I exchanged a grin. Rebel wasn't usually allowed in my mom's kitchen. First, because he had no interest in learning how to cook. Second, because he was a disaster in the kitchen. Appliances had been known to burst into spontaneous flames when Rebel touched them.

"Why don't you go ask our guests if they need anything?"

"Why don't you have him start the fire, Mom?" Rowdy said. "He's good at making things burn."

I huffed out a laugh that I didn't bother to hide. Rebel rolled his eyes from where he leaned against the counter in Mom's huge kitchen, where we were in full Christmas feast mode, and it was all-hands-on-deck.

"Obviously, there's a story behind that," Tressy said from her station in front of the wall ovens, where she was taking out the rolls. Krista stood on a stool beside her mom, putting the rolls from an already cooled pan into a basket and covering them with a towel. Maddy was on shuttle duty, taking baskets and bowls to the buffet table so Rocky could arrange everything on warming plates.

The rest of the guests, including Brian and several members of the team, either didn't want to go or couldn't get home for the holiday. I couldn't remember a Christmas when we didn't have at least twenty people around the dinner table.

And I'd never wanted it any different.

Rowdy snorted. "Oh, there definitely is—"

"And you're not going to hear about it now."

Rebel pushed away from the counter and headed toward the great room, which had at one time been the dining room that seated at least a hundred when this had been a working inn. Mom and Dad only ever used it for gatherings of more than the family, which included all holidays, Winter Carnival get-togethers, team parties, sewing club meetings, book club meetings, and ... Well, it got used a lot more than you might think.

"He nearly burned down the house making toast." I winked at Krista, wide-eyed and bouncing on her toes. "We usually don't even let him in the kitchen at holidays. Safer that way."

To be fair, it'd been an ancient toaster that Mom had set on the counter to be put in the trash. Rebel had mistakenly thought he was supposed to use that instead of the shiny new one still in the box. He'd plugged it in, put his bread in to toast, and left for another room.

By the time he got back, the toaster was in flames and the fire department had already been dispatched by the security system. Rebel saw flames and grabbed a tablecloth to smother the fire. Not a big deal, but he would never live down starting a fire by making toast.

Rowdy and I brought it up almost every year, mostly because Rebel could barely boil water. Our mom had tried and failed to teach Rebel and Rocky how to fend for them-selves. Rebel lived off takeout and Mom's leftovers.

At least Rocky was still at college and got decent meals in the cafeterias.

"Hey, Miss Raffi, can I give you a hand with anything?"

Just the sound of Brian's voice was enough to make me flush all over. Luckily it was warm in the kitchen and no one was looking at me directly.

"Actually, can you help Rain with those mashed pota-toes? You're almost done with them, aren't you, Rainy?"

Except my mom, who gave me the most innocent look, which was totally false. Either she knew, with her scary mind-reading-mom abilities, the thoughts I was having about getting Brian alone again, or she was taking a shot in the dark putting us together to see what we would do.

"Yep." I scraped the potatoes into a serving tray, which I handed to Brian with a smile when he crossed the room. Which just happened to be the exact moment Rebel walked back into the room.

He couldn't quite hide the immediate scowl on his face, but he got it somewhat under control before my mom turned to him.

"Pop says he needs an extension cord."

"In the closet in the basket on the top of the shelf."

Brian's and Rebel's gazes met and held for a second before Rebel headed for the closet Mom had indicated. Anyone in the room who was paying attention could tell there was something brewing between the two of them. And my mom was paying attention.

"And Rebel, make sure your dad doesn't trip the breaker like he did last year, please."

"Sure, Mom."

Flashing a smile that looked more like a grimace, Reb turned and headed back out. Brian watched him go, Mom watched Brian, and I watched Mom.

SEVENTEEN

Brian

"HEY, MADS, I GOT YOU SOMETHING."

We'd gotten home from the Lawrences' Christmas dinner about an hour ago. Maddy had been quiet but not withdrawn, like I thought she might be.

I'd asked her again this morning if she'd wanted to go to dinner, and she had assured me she had. So we'd gone.

"I'm sure the food'll be good. And we won't have to worry about cooking," was all she'd said.

Which was true. The food had been amazing. And it hadn't just been us and the Lawrences. Five other teammates had been there as well, so it wasn't like we'd crashed a family event. The minute we'd walked in the door, Krista had attached herself to Maddy's side, and Maddy had seemed happy to let her. The girls had even exchanged gifts. Maddy had brought home a book for Krista from the small holiday store at school. No idea where she'd gotten the money, but that was a question for another time.

Krista had given Maddy a necklace with a heart charm. Tressy had told me later that Krista had insisted they go shopping specifically for Maddy Monday night, and Krista had picked out the necklace at the small pop-up store on Main Street that catered to kids shopping for parents and siblings.

"She's really fallen in love with your niece," Tressy had said, her hand on Brian's arm as she watched the girls exchange gifts next to the massive tree in the corner of the family room. "And Maddy's just amazing with her. She's a sweet kid."

I couldn't agree more. Now it was my turn to show her how much I loved her.

"I told you I didn't want a gift this year." Maddy barely turned her head away from the television playing *The Muppet Christmas Carol*. It was the one movie we'd agreed to save for tonight before bed. Apparently *The Muppet Christmas Carol* was the best holiday film ever according to a majority of Fiskers.

"Yeah, well, I didn't listen to you. And neither did your mom."

Her head swiveled around so fast, I thought she'd give herself whiplash.

"What?"

I pulled out two gifts from beneath the pillow next to me. I'd stuffed them there when she'd been in her room changing. Linny had given me the present before she'd gone to rehab, telling me to give it to Maddy Christmas night. She explained that they always saved one gift to open Christmas night to extend the excitement of the day.

"This one's from me." I held out a gift bag, because I was a guy. "And this one's from your mom."

The small box was wrapped in shiny paper and had a bow on it.

Maddy stared at the gifts for a few long seconds before she took them. She opened mine first, flashing me a smile with a hint of tears in her eyes as she pulled out the fluffy pajamas with cats wearing sunglasses. I'd seen her eyeing them online the night we'd moved in here.

"Thank you, Uncle Bri."

"They're washed and everything. Ready to wear."

Her smile grew even wider. "I love them."

"I'm glad." I paused, glancing at the box from her mom. "You don't have to open that now. You can do it when you're alone."

I didn't want her to feel she had to share her mom's gift with me. The look she gave me was grateful, but she set the box on the couch and said, "Be right back."

When she returned from her second-floor room, she handed me a bag.

"I got you something too."

"So neither of us listened, huh?"

"Guess I take after you."

Her smirk made me laugh and give a mental sigh of relief. No tears. I wasn't equipped to handle tears tonight. And I didn't want her to cry on Christmas. She'd had enough fucking upheaval. I didn't want this night to be filled with tears and angst. But she still hadn't opened her mom's gift.

"Let's open them together," she said.

"Sure."

I immediately dumped the bag on the cushion next to me

and laughed at the small stuffed toy that dropped out. The vaguely human-shaped toy had an Elvis pompadour, an evil grin, red eyes, and wore a Devils' sweater. The team mascot, Tony.

"Thanks, sweetheart. I'll sleep with it every night."

Maddy's smile wavered a little as she tore the paper from her mom's gift and lifted the lid on the small box. Then it widened as she lifted out a small key on a long chain.

I waited for her to explain as she slid it over her head. Until I realized she didn't have to.

"I gave that to your mom."

Maddy smiled up at me. "She told me you gave it to her when you got your driver's license.. She said you told her that if she ever needed you, she should text you a pic of the key, and you would come. She didn't need to tell you why. You'd just come get her."

Linny had used that key a few times, once when I'd had to drag her out of a party because she'd gotten too drunk to walk. I'd been in high school then.

"She told me one day she'd give it to me when she didn't need to be rescued by her little brother anymore."

Yeah, I got the symbolism. And Maddy was smart enough to understand what it meant.

"She's gonna be okay this time." Maddy nodded, her smile tempering just a little, becoming a little more sure. "She will."

"Absolutely, kid."

For the first time, I had hope that she would.

RAIN

Hey, you wanna grab lunch today?

THE TEXT CAME AROUND nine-thirty Monday morning, just after I'd dropped Maddy off at the local YMCA.

The team had left the day after Christmas for two overnight away games. Maddy had stayed with Raffi, who had also entertained Krista and another kid from Krista's school, whose parents had needed a last-minute caregiver for their son. The woman was a saint. Or a soft touch with a huge heart who rarely said no to anyone. Not that she was a pushover. Miss Raffi had raised four amazing humans. Including the woman who'd just invited me to lunch.

BRIAN

Yes where?

RAIN

My place? Working there this afternoon

BRIAN

1230?

RAIN

See you then

FUCK, I'd missed her this weekend. I'd thought about her almost all the time I didn't spend worrying about Maddy. How the fuck did real parents do this every fucking day?

I hadn't seen Rain since Christmas dinner, which had been an exercise in self-control. I felt like every time I tried to talk to her, ten people watched us. Which was ridiculous. There'd been nearly twenty people at dinner and at least eight conversations going on at the same time. We'd been seated at the same table, but on opposite ends. Rebel had been at the other table but directly in my line of sight so I couldn't easily ignore him. And he wasn't about to be ignored.

I knew we needed to talk, but that wasn't going to happen at practice or on the way to a game. And my downtime from hockey centered around Maddy after school, helping her with homework and getting her fed and doing dishes and cleaning up and making sure she had everything she needed for school the next day.

Maddy had been quiet when I'd dropped her off at Miss Raffi's the day after Christmas. She'd given me a hug, her hand wrapped around the key her mom had given her. Then she'd disappeared into the kitchen where I could hear Krista chattering away.

When I'd picked her up Sunday, after a couple of grueling games that we'd split, and a busted lip from a high stick, we'd had to go to the mandatory intake session at the rehab. If we wanted to see Linny at all during her six-week stay at the center, we had to attend a meeting at the center, which was an hour and a half away.

Naturally, she'd been silent the entire drive, and I'd been anxious about what exactly this was going to be. Luckily, the session had been geared toward the kids, who ranged in age from two to seventeen. And the therapists had been amazing. They'd split the group into two by age. Maddy's group leader hadn't sugarcoated anything but had explained the process then let the kids talk and ask questions. Meanwhile, the adults had their own session in the next room.

On the drive home, she seemed a little more like herself, telling me about what she'd done this weekend, which had involved a lot of movies, cookies, and a couple pizzas, including one with broccoli that she'd actually liked.

We didn't talk about the session. I figured if she wanted to, she'd let me know. We did talk about her plans for the week, since school was still out until after New Year's. I'd been worried about leaving her alone in the apartment while I went to practice and workouts, but apparently, Miss Raffi had taken care of that too.

The local YMCA ran a program for kids during the day throughout the break. Swimming, art classes, songwriting workshops, video game programming. Hell, I wanted to sign up. Maddy seemed excited to go. And it kept her mind off other things.

I'd dropped Maddy off at nine that morning. She'd waved once then disappeared inside. And I'd gone to practice.

With a smile on my face because I knew I'd get to see Rain at lunch.

I was the first guy at the arena, but only until Rowdy walked into the locker room, dressed in track pants and a Devils' sweatshirt. I expected a greeting but not a conversation. Instead, he motioned for me to follow him into the deserted coaching office, next to the locker room.

"Hey, everything okay with you? I know you got a lot going on, but is there something I can help with?"

I grimaced. "That first game was pretty shitty, wasn't it?"

I'd fumbled a couple of passes that might have cost us goals in both games. And the fact that we'd lost one of the games hadn't helped.

Rowdy shrugged that off. "We all have shitty games sometimes. I wasn't talking about your ice time. How'd the rehab meeting go?"

"Not as bad as I thought. I think...we'll get through this."

"Good. I'm glad to hear it. I just need you to know that if you need anything, I'm here. No matter what. We're friends first."

A friend whose sister I was looking forward to getting naked in a few hours. And whose brother would have my head if he knew. Reb and I absolutely needed to figure our shit out before Rain and I got caught. And we would. It was a matter of time.

I'm not sure Rowdy would be too thrilled with me messing around with his sister either.

"I know. And I appreciate it. Hell, I couldn't do this with Maddy without you and your family."

"Jesus, Brian, I'm not looking for gratitude. I'm just," Rowdy huffed, "I'm worried about you. You look fucking exhausted. Are you getting enough sleep?"

My lips quirked into a grin. "No, actually, I'm not getting enough sleep. And you still have my undying gratitude forever and always."

Rowdy's grin eclipsed mine. "Fuck you, asshole. Fine. I'll shut the fuck up. But maybe you need a nap."

"What the hell? Am I two?"

"Nah, man, you're at least fifty, right?"

Bonesaw slapped me on the back after delivering his one-liner, all wide smile and gleaming teeth. He'd snuck up behind me like a stealth jet. He was so big and so damn quiet.

"Nah, man, I thought that was your IQ."

The comeback slipped out without thought, making Rowdy snort, while Bonesaw gave me the finger as he left the room and disappeared into the locker room.

Through the door, I saw most of the team had arrived now and was getting changed. I spied Rebel on the other side of the room, back to me while he pulled on his gear.

Rowdy watched me for a second before he shook his head, and we both headed into the locker room. "I'll see you on the ice."

"You're taking practice?" My brows arched. "Thought you were too good for us now."

"I can still kick your ass in sprints."

"Wait, is that a challenge?" Wellar called out from across the room. "Are the ol—uh, the *seasoned* players gonna duel it out on the ice?"

Rowdy looked at me. I looked at him. We both said, "No," in perfect unison, which made me snort and Rowdy laugh.

"Must be getting soft in your old age."

Rebel's quiet taunt floated through the locker room, eliciting a collective "ooh" from the team. Since I couldn't tell if Rebel was ribbing me or his brother, I kept my mouth shut.

Rowdy, on the other hand, took the bait. He crossed his arms over his chest.

"You wanna test that theory, little brother?"

"Who says I was talking to you?"

Rebel's gaze snapped to mine, his brows arching. If I'd

been smart, I would've let it slide. Would've ignored the challenge. But with the frustration eating at my gut, and the entire team watching, I met his gaze.

"I'm not that much older than you." I stripped off my shirt. "And I was always faster."

Which was true. Reb's strength on the ice wasn't his speed. It was his defensive skill and his ability to read a developing play. I had decent stick-handling skills and, yeah, I had speed.

Our now-silent teammates watched our interaction like they were at a tennis match, their heads on a swivel. Even Rowdy had fallen silent.

"Wanna put that to the test?" Rebel said.

"You throwing down a challenge?"

The words fell out of my mouth before I realized what I'd done.

Rowdy winced. Reb's grin turned sharp. And Bonesaw whistled under his breath, shaking his head. The atmosphere in the room felt charged, and I wanted to kick myself. Unless...this could be the answer.

"Yeah." Reb crossed his arms over his chest. "I guess I am."

"Gentlemen, we have a Challenge."

Kane Ness stepped into the center of the room, standing on the team logo. He had most of his gear and his skates on, dark skin gleaming in the fluorescent light.

Behind me, I heard Denny Hollowell say, "Uh, what's going on?"

"Fiskers," Kane said, "do you accept the challenge?"

I rolled my eyes at Ness, who was playing this for all it was worth. But I'd practically dug my own grave.

"Yeah, I guess I do. Let's get this over with."

Fuck. This was going to hurt.

"YOU BOTH KNOW THE RULES. The loser must wear the Tutu of Shame for the next warm-up and do the Dance of Contrition."

The team was lined up along the boards, expressions ranging from outright glee from the veterans to utter confusion from the new guys. Obviously, the Devils hadn't had a Challenge issued for at least two years.

Even the coaches sat on the benches grinning like they'd won the championship and sucking down coffee.

I'd fucking walked right into Rebel's plan of utter humiliation. Of course, there was still a chance I'd win. I'd always been a faster skater than Rebel. But I wasn't in great shape. I mean, I hadn't completely let myself rot away. But Rebel looked like he'd been working out every day for the past twenty years. He was sleek, lean, and staring at me like I was a bug he was about to crush.

Shit.

"For those of you who haven't been here since the last Challenge, which Rebel won, by the way," Kane smirked at me, "when a challenge is thrown down and accepted, the challengers have to complete an agreed-upon task. So what's it gonna be, boys? Shots? Obstacle course? Or sprints?"

Since I'd been the one to accept the Challenge, I got to pick it. And none of them were a good fit right now. So I chose the task with the best chance of survival. Not necessarily the best chance of winning.

"Sprints."

Out of the corner of my eye, I saw a couple of guys wince, but I kept my attention on Reb. He didn't look surprised by my choice. Actually, he looked kinda smug. Good. I needed all the incentive I could get to pull through this without killing myself.

How fucking embarrassing would it be to hyperventilate and pass out in front of the whole team?

Rowdy skated over to me while Kane and a few of the other guys skated to the opposite end of the ice. Rebel waited with his arms crossed over his chest at the closest goal line.

"Sprints?" Rowdy looked at me with raised eyebrows. "You know he's younger than you, right?"

"By two fucking years. Don't be an asshole. Don't you think I can keep up?"

"Do you?"

I gave Rowdy a look, which he correctly interpreted. Shaking his head, he waved a hand at me to line up with Rebel on the goal line. "Just don't kill yourself to prove a point."

I skated over to line up with Rebel.

"You know I'm gonna kick your ass, right?" Rebel glanced at me.

"I know you're gonna try."

"You two ready?" Kane called from the other end of the ice.

I took a deep breath and nodded, wondering how bad I was going to hurt after this.

"Skate!"

"BRIAN? ARE YOU OKAY?"

Rain had opened the door to her home seconds after I knocked, almost as if she'd been waiting for me.

I held out the pizza I'd brought, biting back a wince at the ache in my thighs.

"Yeah. I'm fine. Why?"

Taking the pizza, she gave me a wry look. "Because you look like you're in pain. Did something happen at practice?"

I followed her through the house to the kitchen, where she put the pizza on the table then turned to examine me through narrowed eyes. Crossing her arms over her chest, she let her gaze travel up and down my body. And even though I knew she wasn't looking at me with lust, my body responded like she was.

"Just a few sprints before practice."

"Before practice?" Now her brows arched, and her gaze met mine. "Why were you doing sprints *before* practice?"

Sighing, I shook my head. I knew she was going to find out eventually. And I knew it was better she hear it from me. Still...

"Rebel and I dealt with some of our issues."

She looked me up and down again. "I don't see any visible bruising."

"We didn't fight." I sighed again. "We Challenged."

I could practically feel the exasperation rolling off her in waves. "You Challenged. As in one of you has to wear the tutu and do the dance."

"Basically, yeah."

"Oh, for—" She rolled her eyes. "You lost, didn't you?"

I eased myself into a chair at the table, biting my tongue against a grimace.

"What makes you say that?"

She huffed out a sigh, probably trying to think of a diplomatic way to say, *"because you look like shit."*

Instead of answering, she went to a cabinet and got paper plates and glasses then to the fridge for bottles of Coke. She put everything on the table then sat across from me.

"Because you let him win."

"Not exactly."

Her expression held a whole lot of *I call bullshit.* "Really?"

I lifted my arm to reach for the soda and winced as it pulled something in my back.

When I looked at her, her eyes had narrowed even further. "Guess it's good we don't have a game until the weekend. How much pain are you in?"

"It's not that bad."

Her lips twitched as if she were holding back a smile. "Uh-huh. You want a piece? And I should I get the ibuprofen?"

She flipped open the pizza box and put a slice on a plate. When she looked up and noticed my grin, she laughed, a husky sound that made my cock twitch. "Down, boy. I'm not sure you're in any shape for, um, extracurricular activities."

"I'm not that old."

I had to admit, at least to myself, that maybe I wasn't exactly in shape for what I wanted to do to her. Then again, there were all sorts of positions we hadn't explored, and a bed we hadn't made it to last time.

"I didn't mention your age, big guy. Just that you seem a little worse for wear. Because you challenged my brother to a freaking sprint duel."

"For the record, he challenged me."

While we ate, I gave her the rundown. How I'd chosen the sprints because I knew I'd have a fighting chance to actually beat Rebel.

"But yeah," I said with a shrug, "I planned to throw it even if I felt I could win. Which, trust me, I couldn't. Your brother's a freaking machine. Maybe if he sees me humiliate myself, he'll finally give me a break."

She snorted gently. "Until he finds out about us."

Yeah, there was that.

"There hasn't been much of an us to talk about." I watched her carefully. "I'm sorry about that."

She shrugged, her lips in a slight smile. "We've both been busy and the holiday…"

"I'm not upset that we haven't been alone much lately." Or at all. My mood got serious fast. "I don't just want an occasional hookup, Rain. Eventually, I'd like to take you on an actual date."

"That's not what I want either." She shook her head. "I mean the hookup. I would like to go on a date. But I understand why we can't right now. We both have a lot going on."

We did. Not just me. She had the Winter Carnival coming up, in addition to her full-time job with the Devils and her new bookstore venture with Erin.

"I heard you had good games this weekend," she continued, "even if we didn't win both games."

I let her change the subject to the games this past weekend then let her fill me on how Maddy had spent her weekend with Miss Raffi.

"And what'd you do all weekend?"

I asked before I finished the last swallow of my soda,

gathered up the plates and threw them in the trash, while Rain put the glasses in the dishwasher. Just as she turned, I made my move, putting my hands on either side of her hips on the counter, trapping her between my arms.

I loved that little hitch in her breathing as I towered over her.

"I spent time at my mom's. Spent some time with Erin working on a business plan for the bookstore and cleaning out part of the shop. Caught up on my reading."

I lowered my head to rub my nose along the side of her neck, feeling her shiver in response.

"What are you reading?"

She sucked in a breath and put her hands on my hips, which, I had to admit, were pretty fucking sore. I hadn't been kidding when I'd said I'd given Reb a run for his money. I just hadn't won.

"A new romance." Her voice held a hint of a smile. "About hockey players."

I pulled back a little so I could look in her eyes.

"Seriously?"

She nodded. "Seriously. They're really popular these days."

"And why is that?"

Her lips curved in a smile that made my heart race.

"Well," she trailed one hand from my waist up my stomach to lay it flat on the center of my chest. "Hockey players are tall."

"A lot of them, yes."

"And muscular." She patted my chest. "But underneath it all, they're just big teddy bears."

I huffed out a laugh. "Teddy bears, huh?"

"Romances are fantasies, of course."

She was being a brat again. And I was here for it.

"So, you don't think hockey players can be soft and cuddly?"

She shrugged, her gaze dropping before she looked up at me through her lashes. "I don't know. I guess some of them are. I like my players with a few rough edges."

Taking my hands off the counter, I wrapped them around her waist, giving her a squeeze before sliding them around her back and pressing her against me. Her smile widened.

"How rough?"

Biting her bottom lip, she slid sideways, taking one of my hands and tugging me along with her.

"I guess you'll just have to find that out on your own."

She led me up the stairs and down a short hallway to an open door. I had a few seconds to take in the dark wood frame of the queen bed on the far wall, the warm green paint, and the couple of pieces of furniture that matched the bed.

Then she turned me around, pointed one finger on my chest, and gave me a little push. But I wasn't a pushover.

Grinning, I grabbed her around the waist and tossed her on the bed. She gave a little yelp that dissolved into laughter as she propped herself up on her elbows.

"You still look a little stiff," she said. "Maybe I can help you with that."

I huffed, amused. "I'm sure you can. But first you need to be naked."

Grabbing the waistband of her soft cotton pants, I tugged them down her legs with a little more force than normal. She laughed as I dropped them on the floor, flopping onto her back as she pulled her shirt over her head. I'd already taken off my shirt.

Now I paused to admire the absolutely stunning vision of Rain sprawled in front of me, her hair spread out on the pale pink comforter, matching cream silk bra and panties gleaming against her skin.

"I think I want you to keep those on."

"I think I want you to take these off." She lifted one slim little foot and rubbed her big toe along my thigh to the edge of my boxer briefs, almost but not quite close to my cock.

"Condoms?"

She nodded toward the head of the bed, at the bedside table. I reached over and pulled out the drawer, grabbing a foil packet from the stash there.

My back twinged slightly at the movement, but I refused to let my earlier stupidity affect my precious time with this woman. I tossed the condom on the bed, shoved my jeans down my legs, and kicked them off while I ran my hands up her smooth thighs.

"Pretty."

My voice sounded like I'd swallowed gravel, which made her shiver and bite that bottom lip again.

I skimmed over her hips then dragged my hands back down to her knees. So fucking soft. I couldn't stop stroking her while she watched me with those midnight blue eyes. But on my next pass, I hooked my fingers in the strings of her panties and dragged them down her legs.

Her breasts rose and fell in a faster rhythm, her breathing and mine the only sound in the room. Her skin warmed beneath mine, a flush spreading across her chest and into her cheeks. I wanted to know how much hotter her pussy was.

My gaze dropped to her center, and I pushed her thighs apart as I pulled her closer. Standing between her legs, I trailed my fingertips up the inside of her thighs, feeling her muscles quiver beneath the skin.

I spent long seconds watching her as I stroked her, getting closer and closer to the place I wanted to bury myself. When I brushed one fingertip against the soft lips of her sex, she made a little sound that made my cock bob. Her gaze dropped for hot seconds before she lifted it back to mine.

I barely noticed the strain in my thighs as I stood, rolling the condom down my shaft. Barely noticed the twinge in my back when I moved closer, stopping when my thighs hit the mattress. My cock was so hard it jutted almost straight up. I pushed it down until I was aligned with her opening, then slid inside.

The heat of her body hit me like a drug, and I groaned as it seeped through my blood, making me want to thrust hard and fast. Her back arched as I breached her, sinking deep. My fingers bit into her thighs then I forced myself to loosen my hold so I didn't hurt her. Then I remembered her comment about being rough.

Tightening my hold again, I yanked her closer, my cock sinking deeper. She sucked in a breath, eyes fluttering closed as her hands reached for mine. Then she gripped me tight and opened her eyes. And nodded.

And I took her.

EIGHTEEN

Rain

"HEY, RAINY DAY." Rowdy nodded at me as I walked into the small sitting room in our parents' house, where we were all gathered for New Year's dinner.

Mom had made pork and sauerkraut, of course, and once again they had a full house. However, a few people were missing.

Tressy and Krista had gone to New York City to visit her agent friends. Since the team had had a game yesterday and a game tomorrow, Rowdy had stayed home. I'm pretty sure he was cool with that. For all that Rowdy loved a good party, he was still a small-town boy. He'd been happy to have an excuse not to go.

And Brian and Maddy had gone to visit Maddy's mom at rehab. I'd been thinking about them all day, hoping everything was okay. Hating that this was something I couldn't help them with. It made me twitchy.

Mom had given me one of her looks in the kitchen and asked if I was okay. Of course, I said yes. And then she'd just looked at me until I'd said I needed to get something and retreated to this room. Yes, I was hiding.

Apparently so was Rowdy.

"What are you doing in here?"

"Same thing as you. Hiding."

I made a face at him and sat on the chair opposite his.

Rowdy grinned at half the wattage of his normal smiles. "We need to figure out what we're going to do about that offer."

Making a noncommittal grunt that must be passed down in the family, I stared out the window at the snow-covered hills in the distance. We'd gotten a few inches the previous night and our little valley looked like a Hallmark movie. More snow was forecast for next week, and some-times that meant low attendance at the games. It was weird that people freaked out about a few inches of snow, when we could deal with feet later in the season, if it was a bad year.

I'd decided to increase my social media posts and add another email to the regular lists. Tomorrow. I'd planned to take today off. Like, do nothing related to work at all. But I'd probably break that plan tonight when I got home because I wasn't going to see Brian.

Which sucked. And I probably wouldn't see him tomorrow either.

"Hey, Rainy Day." Rowdy snapped his fingers, and I snapped back to reality. "Earth to Flower Child."

I blinked and refocused my gaze on Rowdy, his mouth curved in a slight grin.

"What?" Ooh, that sounded kinda bitchy. "Sorry. Things on my mind."

"I said, I think we should meet with Rebel and Rocky for lunch next week and talk about this."

My brain immediately said no to a lunch date. I didn't want to give up the time with Brian. But I also didn't want to tell my brother no because he'd know something was up. Because I never said no.

"Sure." I nodded, smiling a little for good measure. "What day?"

Rowdy didn't respond right away, like he was thinking it over. Then he crossed his arms over his chest as he leaned back in his chair.

"Whatever day you don't want to meet up with Brian."

Shock made my eyes widen and my mouth drop open before I could control my expression. But I'm pretty sure my cheeks had burst into flames, and the fact that I couldn't hold his gaze laid my secret wide open.

"I don't know what you're talking about."

His grin was lopsided. "Neither did I until just now."

I rolled my eyes and shook my head. "Then you still don't know what you're talking about. I can do any day next week—"

"Except for Monday through Thursday, but you *can* do Friday because he'll be getting ready for the game."

"And you still don't know what you're talking about."

Rowdy's grin grew. "Get it straight, Rainy. Either you don't know what I'm talking about, or I don't. Either way, it's odd that you've been working at home so much. And that Brian doesn't get to the gym to work out until after you get back to work."

I didn't want to lie to my brother, but I would if I had to. And I wasn't adverse to a little bodily harm either. Like my boot toe against his shin. "Pick a day, whatever day, and I'll be there."

"Hey, no judgment from me." Brian held up his hands. "I think the man's great. Hell, I'd date him if I wasn't in love with the most amazing woman in the world. And I want you to know he hasn't said anything to me. But if I can figure out what's going on, Rebel's not gonna be far behind. He's more intuitive than he lets on, and he can be a judgmental prick."

I saw an opening, and I took it. "Do you know why Rebel hates him?"

Rowdy gave me a look that said he knew I was deflecting. "I think hate is a strong word. Majorly pissed off is probably better. And no, Reb never told me."

He paused, and I could tell he was mulling something over.

"But you suspect...what?"

Rowdy shook his head. "I don't wanna make wild guesses about our brother's life, because he's a scary fucker. I love him, but I don't think he'd second-guess cutting my brake lines."

I rolled my eyes, because even for Reb, that was going too far. "But you obviously think you know something."

"No, I honestly don't. What I do know is Reb had a rough senior year in college. You probably don't remember because you were a sophomore and involved in practically everything on campus."

He wasn't wrong. I'd rushed a sorority, wrote for the school paper, played intermural volleyball (yes, volleyball, not hockey), and maintained a 4.0 grade point average that year.

And I hadn't gone to Penn State, like Reb and Rowdy and Brian. I'd gone to Villanova.

"Reb majored in hockey and partying," Rowdy continued. "I know Dad took a trip to see him. Alone. Like, without Mom."

Holy. Shit.

No, I hadn't known that. When it came to their kids, Mom and Dad were a team, but Mom always took the lead. For Dad to do a solo parenting gig... Hell, I didn't even know what to think about that. It was just so foreign.

"What the hell did Reb do? And do you think that has something to do with Brian and Rebel's feud?"

Rowdy sighed, like I was busting his balls. "Look, you didn't hear this from me, but...yeah. I think it's got everything to do with that."

My brain spun like a hamster in a wheel, trying to piece together what Rebel could've done to make Dad go solo.

"Honestly," Rowdy continued, drawing my attention back to him, his worried expression one I rarely saw on his face, "I'm worried about Rebel, and I'm not sure what to do about it."

"Worried how? You think there's something going on with Reb he doesn't want us to know about?"

"If Rebel had his way, I think he'd be perfectly happy to stay in his own little bubble of hockey, only leaving his cabin when he needs to forage for food."

Okay, that might be extreme, but probably not far off. Still, I'd always considered us a team, me and my brothers. Yeah, Rebel was a loner, but I'd always figured I could count on him when it really mattered. I knew he'd be there if I needed him. I'd just have to ask. But maybe I'd overlooked the fact that he needed us and couldn't figure out how to ask.

Dad had said Rebel had made it clear he wanted nothing to do with the running of the team. He only wanted to play. I'd just assumed that'd change when Dad handed over the reins to the team to us.

Apparently, Rowdy was thinking along the same lines.

"Dad wants to retire at the end of the season," he said, "and leaving this decision up to us is a huge deal for him. He's not getting any younger, and I think he and Mom don't want to always be tied down to St. David for nine months out of the year."

I did know that, though I really didn't like to think about it. It meant Dad was getting old. And yeah, I knew he was almost twenty years older than Mom, but he'd always seemed so...not old. Seventy-five wasn't that old-old. Not anymore.

Nodding, I sighed. "I know. I just thought... I don't know, that he'd be around forever. I don't want to let him down."

Rowdy winced, like I'd actually kicked him. "Neither do I. But I can't play and run the team if we're going to move up another league. This could be a huge deal for us., but just thinking about the mechanics of that move are making me twitch."

Grinning, I couldn't resist the urge to rib my big brother. "Wow, that's a big word. Mechanics. Like you actually know what it means."

Rowdy took it the way it was intended. With sisterly love. He gave me the finger.

"Yeah, well, the deal is, we're all on board with this, or we don't do it. But if we do, it's gonna be a hell of a lot more work for all of us. Rebel included, whether he wants to be involved or not." He held up a hand to stop whatever I was going to say. "That's not a question. This is a family business. I'm not going to be the only one making decisions."

I appreciated the fact that Rowdy had stated clearly that this was "our" decision. Not just his. Of course, it would mean more work. For all of us. And it wasn't that I didn't like to work. I loved to be busy. I loved to have my fingers in all the things. I loved our team. But maybe I'd realized recently that there was more to life than work. And maybe I liked to have my fingers all over a certain player.

Rowdy must have read my expression because he shook his head. "I'm not going to be sole owner/operator of the Devils, Rain. No way in hell will I take this on alone. It's going to be a team effort. Even if we don't decide to join the ECHL, when Pop retires, this is going to be a family-run business. And family means all of us. Even Rebel, because if he's going to play, he's going to pitch in on the backside too. And I don't care if he's a fucking pain in the ass about it, he's still going to do it."

That was definitely going to be interesting to watch, but I was on board with everything Rowdy had said. It would be less work with the three of us.

"And if he doesn't?" I asked.

"That's when it could get interesting."

I looked out the window again, tracing the pretty, snow-covered hills. "How? It's not like you can beat him into submitting to your will."

"Interesting solution, but yeah, not gonna happen." He paused, his gaze turning sharp. "I'm considering asking Brian to come on as an assistant coach."

Oh. Oh wow. My brain snapped, crackled, and popped

with that information, ideas pinging all through my brain, but all of them leading to one constant refrain: If Brian took the job, he'd be here all the time.

Is that what I want?

Is it what Brian would want?

"I'd hoped having Brian here would let him and Rebel work out their beef, which would clear the way for Brian to join us."

I had so many questions, I didn't even know where to start, except to say, "Damn, you've given this a lot of thought."

Rowdy gave me the most Rowdy smile ever. "I'm not just a pretty face."

For years, Rowdy had embraced the role of small-town hockey god. No fucks given for anything except hockey, parties, and getting laid. And then he'd met Tressy and Krista, and it was like he'd morphed into this stable, business-minded guy who thought about things like the mechanics of the business and the ramifications of bringing his best friend and his brother's nemesis into the family team.

"I had no idea you were considering Brian for a coaching position."

He shrugged. "Maybe you just had other things on your mind."

And there was the snark I expected from my older brother. I flipped him off again, though my heart wasn't really in it, and my brain was doing some gymnastics of its own. If he took the job, he'd stay in St. David. And we would work together every day. And we'd live happily ever after, like in that book I was telling Brian I'd read.

Which was a fantasy, of course. Nothing ever worked out so easily. There were always snags.

"Rebel would have to sign off on this."

"Yep." Rowdy nodded. "And if he won't, it could push him away. It could push Brian away too."

"It's a no-win situation."

"Unless they get their shit figured out." Rowdy's gaze slid to the window again, but I don't think he saw the pretty landscape. "I'm not sure Brian's Dance of Contrition is going to heal that rift completely."

No, I didn't either. Shit. *Shit.*

Hell, I wasn't even sure Brian would want to stay after the season was over. I mean, that's what I wanted. What I was hoping for. And if he took the job Rowdy was offering, he'd be here all the time.

But...did he want to be here all the time? Hell, we'd just started...well, I couldn't even call it dating. Did having sex every chance we could constitute a relationship?

And with his sister getting out of rehab, she was going to need help and support.

"What are we going to do?"

Rowdy looked straight at me, dead serious. An unusual state for Rowdy. "We're gonna talk to Rebel and Rocky. We'll tell them today that we want to talk and that they should come prepared."

"When?"

"How about Monday?" Rowdy's grin returned. "Over lunch."

This time I didn't even bother to give him the finger. He had to know it was implied.

"Monday it is."

"HEY, I didn't expect to see you today."

Brian walked through my front door Friday afternoon, carrying a bag from Luigi's that smelled amazing. Fresh bread and marinara. I took it from him with a smile

"I wasn't sure I was going to be here today, but then I said, fuck it. You give me more incentive to play than any fucking extra practice."

I laughed, carrying the bag into the kitchen with Brian following. "Aw, that might be the most romantic thing a man's ever said to me. That he picked me over practice."

I felt him still behind me as I set the bag on the table. When I looked over my shoulder at him, he had a strange look on his face.

"What's wrong?"

"If you think that's the most romantic thing I've said, we need to go on a real date."

My breath caught in my throat. All the reasons I wanted to say yes were on the tip of my tongue, while all the reasons we shouldn't played through my brain like a herd of pissed-off cats.

I really wanted to go on a date with Brian. An actual date that involved getting dressed up and going to a restaurant and then coming back to my house and screwing our brains out. But almost every one of those pissed-off cats had Rebel's name on them. And no, my brother shouldn't be the reason we didn't go on that date.

But there were other considerations too. My dad hadn't been thrilled when I'd dated Mo Zelinksy. My brothers even less so. Even my mom hadn't been happy. That should've been a huge red flag. And had I listened? No, I had not.

Would they be just as unhappy for me to be dating Brian? Maybe I didn't want to know, which was why I didn't want to tell anyone. But they all loved Brian. They thought he was a great guy. Why wouldn't they give me their blessing to date Brian?

Why do you need their blessing?

I looked into Brian's eyes, seeing the questions forming because of my silence.

"I would love to go on a date with you." I was completely sincere. "I really would. Even though my schedule's crazy right now. The Winter Carnival is coming up. We've got this decision to make about the team, and there's no way my brothers and I are going to be able to come to a unanimous agreement. Like, ever. And you've got Maddy and school and your sister and hockey, and I know it sounds like I'm making excuses but—"

"Rain, I get it." His grin softened any edges his words might have had, as did the hand he lifted to run his thumb along my jaw for a brief second before pulling away. "I do. I know there's a lot going on. I know we're going to have to wait. I just want you to know that I'm planning on it."

The relief that flooded me made me feel worse. Because all those roadblocks still felt like excuses and if we really wanted to, we could make this work now.

But then he stepped closer, and closer, until he was only centimeters away from me but still not touching. I wanted him to touch me. I craved it, like I sometimes craved chocolate ice cream. I don't allow myself to eat ice cream whenever

I want because it isn't good for me. But I can't stop myself from gorging on Brian.

"What else are you planning?"

His eyes narrowed, and he leaned down until the tip of his nose brushed against my cheek. I shivered as he put his lips close to my ear.

"Right now, I'm planning to strip you naked." My breath hitched as his teeth nipped at my earlobe. "I might start right now."

I sucked in air because he'd stolen every bit left in my lungs.

"Hell, I might decide to take off all your clothes and lay you out on the dining table. I'll make you lift your arms over your head and grab the edge. Your tits will look amazing, and I'm going to suck and bite them until you want to scream. I want you to be so fucking hot for me you're burning from the inside out."

My heart pounded so hard, I heard its beat in my ears. And I was wet, so wet, my panties were soaked through already. I swallowed hard.

He pulled back and our gazes met and held. "Are you with me so far?"

I nodded because I wasn't sure I could form a coherent sentence. I was absolutely with him. All the way.

"Good. Because I'm definitely not done."

Grabbing me around the waist, he turned me and walked me backward. Toward the table. Excitement boiled in my belly as I let him guide me backward. When my thighs hit the table, I sucked in a breath. My sex clenched, and my hands settled on his shoulders, fingers digging into the muscles. Those muscles bunched and flexed, the long length of his neck drawing my gaze. I wanted to run my tongue along his skin, dole out a little torture of my own.

But before I could lean in, he lifted me onto the table, and I lost all capacity to think rationally.

"After I've made you scream my name, then I'm going to kiss my way down your body and put my mouth between your legs and make you come with my tongue. You taste better than anything I've ever had in my mouth.

"Then I'm going to play with your clit and fuck you with my tongue until you think you can't take anymore. But I know you, Rain. You can take it. You can take everything I give you. And I'm going to give it to you. I'm going to hold you down," his hands spread around my waist, sliding under the hem of my shirt until I felt his heat seep into my skin, "so you can't move. And you're going to love it."

I already loved it. I loved everything he did to me.

"Then, when you think I'm done, I'm going to lean back on one of those chairs," he nodded toward the table, "I'm going to pull down my zipper and take out my cock and let you ride me."

And then he did everything he promised.

"SO, what's Uncle Brian gotta do?"

"They call it the Dance of Contrition."

"And he has to wear some costume?"

"The Tutu of Shame."

Maddy gave me a look like she thought I was insane. Hey, they weren't my rules. They were the team's rules.

"All because he lost some race. Seriously? What? Are they, like, eight?"

I laughed because Maddy wasn't wrong. It did seem childish. But it was tradition. And it had solved some of the worst intra-team fights.

"Our league does have some, um, unusual traditions, but it works for us. And the fans love it."

Maddy shook her head, her expression doubtful, as she slumped back in her chair in the family box. She'd been a little more withdrawn tonight. I knew she and Brian had seen Lin on New Year's Day. Maddy was probably missing her mom even more now that she'd seen her and had to leave. As we'd eaten lunch today, he'd told me that their visit had gone well and that Lin had looked good. Better than he'd been expecting. But Maddy had been quiet when they'd left and hadn't wanted to talk. So he hadn't pushed.

He must have channeled his stress into giving me the most intense orgasms I'd ever experienced today. On my kitchen table. I wouldn't be able to sit there ever again without thinking about what he'd done to me with his mouth.

Afterward, we'd reheated the food and eaten every bite while he'd talked. Then Brian had kissed me hard and left to take a nap before the game. I'd thought about telling him to stay at my place, but he wanted to be home when Maddy got off the bus from school.

And now I couldn't stop thinking about Brian, and I'm sure anyone in my immediate vicinity would be able to tell I'd gotten laid this afternoon. Hell, my mom was only a few seats away, talking to Tressy while Krista played with her dolls. My brothers swore she could read minds. I thought she was omniscient. Like all the knowledge of the universe just filtered through her brain.

Neither was true. My mom just knew her kids. If I was trying to hide something, she'd know. Nothing I could do about it. So I concentrated on what was happening on the ice.

Brian's Dance of Contrition would take place during warm-ups. Word must have gotten out because there were more than the usual number of fans already in the arena. Small towns disseminate gossip like the flu. Fast and furious.

The teams hadn't made their way onto the ice yet, but our in-arena announcer, Kath Sweigart, had just started her safety announcement, which meant the guys would be out in a few seconds.

I should be making my rounds on the concourse and through the boxes, but like everyone else, I didn't want to miss Brian's performance. Mostly, I didn't want to miss what would come after.

Rebel's acknowledgment.

The warm-up light show began, and I sucked in a breath as the guys skated out through the benches and onto the ice. Both teams took one lap around their end of the ice. Then everyone skated to the benches and lined up along the boards. Except for Brian, who remained at center ice.

All the lights in the arena went down and the catcalls started. Whistles, mostly. Foot stomping and hand clapping, disjointed until they all got into a rhythm.

Beside me, Maddy leaned forward in her chair, her gaze focused on Brian. But my focus had switched to Rebel. I thought he'd be an ass and let Brian stand out there alone while he took his time grabbing the tutu. But my brother surprised me.

He took the tutu from the trainer on the bench and skated to center ice. He and Brian stood face-to-face for several seconds, while the crowd got louder. From where I was sitting, I could just make out Rebel's expression. He didn't look as snarky as I thought he would.

In fact, he looked uncomfortable. Rebel didn't like to be the center of attention. He loved to play hockey hard and fast, but give him an award or recognition, and he glowered until he could retreat to his lair, otherwise known as his cabin.

Right now, he looked like the dentist was pulling his teeth without anesthesia. Then again, Rebel looked like that a lot of the time, so...

Finally, Rebel reached out to wrap the pink, sparkly tutu around Brian's waist then skated backward to the boards. Now the arena went dark for several seconds and so quiet I could hear Maddy suck in a breath, before a single spotlight shone on Brian at center ice. He simply stood there, like he was waiting for a bus.

Finally, the music started, and the crowd began to cheer.

And I started to smile.

NINETEEN

Brian

THE MUSIC BEGAN, and I smiled. The winner got to pick the music, while the loser just had to skate around the ice and fuck around until the song was over. But I'd taken an educated guess at the song Rebel would choose. And I'd gotten it right.

Because I knew Rebel. He'd been a damn good friend until that night all those years ago. I knew I should've tried to heal this rift between us sooner. I'd tried a few times, but life had gotten in the way. And I'd been a shitty friend. Sure, Rebel had played his part, but I'd just let it go.

Maybe after tonight, we could start over.

Once you tell him about you and Rain.

Probably shouldn't think about that right now. It'd just fuck with my head.

So I did my dance.

"I'm Too Sexy" by Right Said Fred blasted out of the

speakers. It'd been a staple at hockey practices and warm-ups because hockey players were dorks. So I knew the beats, and I knew every fucking word.

And I'd put in some thought as to what I was going to do. Hell, I'd even admit to doing a little practice when no one else was on the ice. Because this was going to be the best fucking Dance of Contrition ever.

But there was only one person I was dancing for.

I looked up into the arena and found the Lawrence suite, where I knew Rain would be. And there she was, a huge grin on her face and clapping her hands above her head. Beside her, Maddy was shaking her head, but her smile was wide.

Now, I'm a pretty damn good skater. And while I don't normally show off my skills, I've got moves. I wasn't going to embarrass myself out here. I let the music play out for a few seconds before I pushed off.

If I had to classify my dance, I'd call it late-night bump-and-grind, college style. My technique was a little rusty, but my feet were sure as I moved around the ice. I didn't do any pirouettes or anything where my feet left the ice. But I put on a fucking show. Because if I had to do it, I wasn't going to half-ass it.

Rowdy probably recognized some of it. I'd been hot for a girl in college who'd been an ice dancer. She'd taught me a few moves.

The crowd loved it. But I was skating for an audience of one. Because, honestly, if I thought about the fans in the arena watching me, I'd probably trip over my feet and face-plant. Couldn't think about Maddy either. Didn't know how I was gonna live this down with her. At least, it'd be good for a laugh between us. Hadn't been many of those this week.

Our meeting with Lin had gone well, I'd thought. Lin had looked good. Sober. And she and Maddy had been so happy to see one another. But Maddy had been quiet these past two days, and I didn't know what to do to make things better. Honestly, I was hoping Rain had been able to get Maddy out of her head for a little while.

I lost my rhythm for a second and pushed those thoughts out of my head before I tripped and fell.

The hooting and hollering and stomping in the crowd complemented the music as the song wound down. Stopping at center ice, I bowed toward the bench then turned and did the same to both ends and the penalty box side.

Now, I let myself take in the ear-splitting noise coming from the arena, but my gaze sought the owners' box. Anyone watching would think I was smiling at Maddy. And I did. At first. But for the last split second, my smile was all for Rain. She jumped up and down, cheering and circling one hand over her head like she was roping cattle. Her expression made me long for the moment we could be alone together.

Movement from the bench drew my attention as Rebel stepped onto the ice and skated toward me. The audience quieted as he stopped a couple of feet away.

Shaking his head, he sighed. "Nice moves. And take off the goddamn tutu."

"I don't know." I shrugged. "I wear it pretty well."

"No, you really don't."

"We good?"

A pause, then something that looked almost like a smile. Probably just gas.

"Yeah."

I guess that was as good as I was going to get for now.

"Then let's play fucking hockey."

———

"BRIAN."

I turned at the sound of Rebel calling to me just before I was about to leave the locker room. I'd been the last man off the ice because I'd been named First Star of the game and had to give an interview to the radio announcer. Not only had we won the game, but I'd gotten assists on both goals. I felt good and the only thing that could make it better was to spend the night with Rain. But, of course, that wasn't going to happen.

"What's up?"

Fuck, that had sounded like I was angry with him, which I wasn't, and I could see him stiffen.

"Shit, sorry. I didn't mean that to sound pissy. It's not you." I shook my head. "What do you need, Reb?"

He didn't answer right away, just stared at me, like he was trying to read me. "I just wanted to say you had a good game. And you're a good sport. And I haven't been. So, yeah, sorry."

Hell, he didn't even look like he'd said any of that grudgingly, but like he actually meant it. So I didn't want to light fire to any of the bridges we may have just started to repair.

"Thanks, man. There's blame on both sides. You're right. I let my bias cloud my judgment. That's on me. Sorry I wasn't a better friend."

"You were a good friend." Reb shook his head. "And I took all the shit I was dealing with out on you. I never forgave you for something that wasn't your fault. And I never said sorry for thinking it was."

Alone in the room right now, I could say exactly what I'd been thinking since we'd had that fight two weeks ago.

"It wasn't all your fault. And you're right. I was dealing with a lot of shit then, and I'm dealing with a lot of shit now. But I don't want to fucking fight with you anymore. I don't know that you'll ever let me close enough to be friends again, but I never hated you. And when you cut me off like you did, it felt like I'd lost a limb. It was fucking hard, Reb. My dad's an alcoholic. Linny is too. I couldn't do a damn thing about my dad, but I can fucking be there for Linny and Maddy."

"Is Maddy doing okay?"

"Hell if I know. I'm a poor fucking excuse for a fill-in father, but I'm all she's got, because her own dad's a deadbeat and hasn't seen her in years. And if the bastard came around today, I'd probably knock that fucker into next week."

"Like you did to Zelinsky for my sister?"

When I didn't say anything, Reb just shook his head.

"I know you've got a lot on your plate right now," he said. "I don't want to add any more shit to it. I just want you to know I'm done being angry with you. I should've been done a long time ago, but I'm an asshole who can hold a grudge for a fucking long time."

Nodding, I gave him a hint of a smile. "No shit."

"How'd you learn how to skate like that, anyway?"

"Why? You want me to teach you?"

Now Rebel actually cracked a smile. "Fuck you, man. I got my own moves."

We walked out together like maybe our friendship could still be saved.

Even if I was having a secret affair with his sister.

"HI THERE." Rain smiled at Maddy and me as we walked through the door of Crack One Open Sunday morning. "I didn't expect to see you this morning."

Smiling, I walked up to the counter, opening my coat to let in the warm air of the bakery. Maddy had asked to come here for breakfast, and since it'd been the only thing she'd asked for since seeing her mom, I couldn't say no. Maddy had been quiet all day yesterday, though she did ask me where I learned to skate like I had Friday night. She'd seemed less than impressed when I'd said I did it to get a date with a girl.

"I think Maddy just wanted to get out of the apartment. And I need about a gallon of coffee."

The last two games against the Saltersburg Seagulls had been grinders. The Seagulls had a couple of enforcers who took one look at me and decided it was Christmas all over again. And I was the gift. We'd had some run-ins over the years that made this game a little more...physical than some of the others this year.

Consequently, I had a few more shades of color on my skin than normal. Especially one on my jaw, which I saw Rain's gaze glance over.

"Erin just made some chocolate chip muffins and blueberry scones. I could get you an ice pack for that too."

"Sounds good."

The bakery was quiet this morning, only a few people at the tables, all of them reading the local newspaper, probably because Erin printed it next door and set it out for free on all the tables.

As Rain filled a large cup with coffee, I turned to check on Maddy. And jolted when I realized she wasn't in the room.

"Shit. I'll be right back."

Rushing for the door, I shoved through and exhaled when I realized she sat on the bench in front of the empty store-front next door, the one Erin and Rain were going to turn into a bookstore. Shoulders hunched, head down, she stared at her feet.

"Maddy."

She didn't move, didn't acknowledge me in any way.

"Hey, kid. You okay?"

"Yeah. I guess." She took a deep breath and blew it out, mist forming in the air in front of her. "I don't know. I'm just..."

Fuck. Just...fuck. I didn't know how to deal with this. Didn't know what to say. What to do to make this better for her. I didn't want to say the wrong thing, but I had to say something. I couldn't just watch her twist herself into knots.

Jesus, how had I let it get to this? What had I missed? She'd seemed okay after seeing Lin. I'd figured she needed some time to decompress. I should've known. I should've asked. I should've paid more attention. I should've done *something*.

So, what the hell did I do now? She was twelve. Did I lie and tell her everything was going to be okay? But that wasn't right. That was a page out of my dad's playbook. And no fucking way was that the right thing to do.

I took a breath and sat. "Okay, then let's figure out how you're feeling."

She looked up at me with wild eyes, like a cat trapped in a cage. And shivered. Shit, it was cold out here.

"But not out here," I said. "Let's go back inside where it's warm and talk."

She looked over her shoulder through the window. "There's people in there."

"Yeah, but I'm pretty sure Rain will have somewhere we can talk in private."

Putting my arm around her, I stood, bringing her with me, grateful she didn't put up any resistance. When we walked through the door, I caught Rain's eye. She and Erin were talking, but they stopped to look at us. Rain walked around the counter, her expression calm.

"What do you need?"

"Is there somewhere Maddy and I can talk?"

She nodded immediately. "Sure. Follow me."

Rain led us through the kitchen then opened another door that led into the building next to it. The bookstore they were planning to open in a month or so. They'd done a lot more work than I'd realized. Bookshelves lined the walls, though there were no books in them yet. There were two huge, comfortable-looking leather chairs. And it wasn't cold.

"If you need anything, just let me know." Rain's smile eased some of the tightness in my chest. Then she disappeared back into the kitchen, closing the door behind her.

We sat in silence for a few seconds, our breathing only sound in the room.

"All right, Mads. Tell me everything you're thinking. Just

spit it all out. No judgment. If you just want me to sit here and listen to you spew words, I'm here for that."

She didn't speak right away, and it took all my self-control not to push her. Because I wanted to help. I wanted to be the person she needed right now.

Finally, after at least a minute, she said, "I'm angry. And I don't want to be angry."

I saw the anger in her face, but I also saw the guilt and the sadness and the fear. I understood all those emotions because I felt the same.

"I'm angry too, hon. And I'm scared."

Her eyes narrowed a little. "Why are you scared?"

"Because I don't know what's going to happen. No one does, and that sucks. I hate being scared, but it doesn't mean I'm not going to keep moving forward. And keep believing that things will be better."

Her lower lip trembled. "Mom looked good. But—"

She cut herself off and looked away, her cheeks flushing, like she was ashamed.

"But you're worried she'll fall back into old habits when she gets out. I feel the same way."

Now her eyes widened. "You do?"

"Yeah, but you weren't there when she asked me to care for you before she went into the program. She looked determined. She looked ready to fight. Now you and I have to show her that we believe she can do it. This is just part of the process."

She sat and breathed for a few seconds. "You really think this time she can do it?"

I realized we hadn't had this discussion the whole time she'd been with me. I'd been avoiding it and that was on me.

"I believe she can, yes. But I also think she has to know *we* believe in her."

Maddy's gaze slipped away, and her voice went quiet. "What if I don't?"

"Then you look your mom in the eyes, and you tell her you do. Because she needs to hear that she can. And honey, I know part of you does believe it. Just like I do."

"Isn't that lying?"

I thought about it for a few seconds then shook my head. "No, it's positive reinforcement. Sometimes all you need is someone to believe in you to help you realize you can do it. Make sense?"

She really thought about that one, her gaze dropping to the floor as she chewed on her bottom lip.

"I guess. Yeah."

"Good. The next time we visit, we're gonna tell her exactly that. That we believe she can do it."

She took a second then nodded, glancing up at me for a few seconds. "Sure. I can do that."

"Good. Now, you ready to get some breakfast?"

"Yeah. I'm ready." She grinned at me. "Love you, Uncle Bri."

"Love you too, Mads."

As we walked back into the bakery, I realized the decision I was going to have to make was almost here. And that avoiding it was no longer an option.

Because I was going to have to choose. And I didn't fucking want to.

TWENTY

Rain

"SO," Rocky sat at Rowdy's dining room table, twirling the ECHL proposal on the tabletop with one finger, "I read through the material, and it looks like a slam dunk. More visibility. More money. Higher quality of play. Why wouldn't we want to do this? What am I not seeing?"

Rowdy, Rebel, and I exchanged a grin around the table before we all looked back at Rocky.

"When did you get so smart, Rambo?" Rowdy asked. "Must be all that Ivy League learning."

The fifty-year-younger carbon copy of our father held his middle finger at Rowdy for the nickname he hated.

"You all can go fuck yourselves." Rocky leaned back in his chair, sprawled like the lanky teenager he'd been a few years ago. He'd added a few pounds in the past couple of years, and now he rivaled Rebel for height and muscle. "I'm being serious. I read through everything, and it looks like a good deal on paper."

"What about you, Reb?" Rowdy looked to his left. "How are you leaning?"

Reb had played his cards pretty close to the vest on this. Then again, he and I hadn't spoken about it. I'd pretty much made up my mind, but we'd decided among the four of us that this had to be a unanimous decision, or we didn't do it.

"I think it's now or never." Reb laid his arms on the table. "If we don't, we're letting fear control us."

"Damn, Reb," Rocky laughed, "that's more words than I've heard you say at one time in years."

"Shove it, kid."

"What about you, Rainy Day?" Rowdy nodded in my direction. "What's your vote?"

Damn it. I really didn't want to do this. I didn't want to go against my brothers. But I also knew what I felt.

"I don't think it's right for us. Not at this time."

Reb blew out a breath and rolled his eyes to look at the ceiling, while Rocky leaned forward, his gaze narrowing.

"Why?" Rocky asked. "Is there something specific you don't like about the terms?"

I glanced at Rowdy then back to Rebel. "It's not the terms of the contract. I think it's everything that's not in the contract. Financial concerns we need to consider. And I think it'll change the entire culture we've built here, not to mention what it will do to our league. And...some of our guys won't make an ECHL team."

"Sounds like you're selling our guys short." Rebel's voice held an edge that put my back up.

"That's not true. I'm just saying our league is built differently than the ECHL. Not better. Just different. Dad and the other owners have created something here to be proud of. And bigger isn't always better."

Rebel stared at me for a few long seconds. "True, but I still think most of our guys would make the cut."

"And what about the ones who don't?" Frustration started to bubble up and I had to work to shove it down. It wouldn't help. "Wellar and Denny? We give guys like them a home in the game. They feel safe here. We give guys like Bonesaw and Brian a second chance."

"Is that a good enough reason to turn down what could be a one-time offer?" Rebel stared at me, his eyes narrowed and his expression tense. "To stifle everyone because of a couple of players?"

Did he know about Brian and me? At that moment, I swore he did. But now definitely wasn't the time to address that.

"There's also the financial concerns."

"The team makes money, right?" Looking between Rebel and me, Rocky ran a hand through his shoulder-length hair. The damn kid had prettier hair than I did. "I mean, the ECHL wouldn't have wanted us if we didn't make money, right?"

"True," I nodded, "but we'd also be putting out more money than we are now. We might get more butts in seats, but it also means more concession workers, more food, more maintenance, and that's just the start of the list. I know this seems like a great opportunity, but I don't think it's the right one at this time. We've got to look at staffing concerns. Can we hire enough staff to handle bigger crowds? We have trouble hiring enough people to maintain the place now."

Rebel and Rocky exchanged a look, as if asking each other if they'd known that. I didn't want to be snarky and tell them they didn't know because they didn't give a shit. But they didn't. Rebel had made it clear he just wanted to play. He left the running of the team and the arena to Rowdy and me. Rocky got a pass because he was still in school.

"Why didn't I know about this?" Rocky said.

Rebel actually answered before I could.

"Because we didn't ask."

"Hey, we're not playing a blame game." Rowdy put his hands up like he was negotiating a treaty. "We've all had our roles to play. What we need to figure out now is how to move forward."

I looked at Rowdy, knowing that if he voted with our brothers, I would go along with their decision. Not because they would steamroll me, but because I wouldn't be the one to tank this deal if they wanted it. And then I'd do my damnedest to make sure it worked.

Rebel and Rocky turned their attention to our oldest brother, as well. Rowdy looked at each of us in turn, his expression serious. He looked like a grown-ass adult. Impressive.

"Guess it's a good thing I made pulled pork for lunch because we've got more talking to do." He shot me a glance. "I'm with Rainy on this. I think there's more to consider than just the prestige of moving up a league."

Holy shit. I honestly hadn't expected him to say that. My mouth hung open for a couple of seconds before I snapped it shut.

"Then I guess you should know." Rebel sighed and

dropped an atom bomb. "I got a player tryout offer from the Redtails a couple days ago."

I DROVE HOME from Rowdy's after the meeting with my brothers, still reeling from Rebel's announcement. Happiness warred with the sense that change was coming and maybe I wasn't equipped to deal with it.

For so long, my brothers and I had been a team. I always knew Rowdy would be here for me. And when I said "here," I meant right here, in St. David, working for the Devils. With me. And for all the sniping Rebel and I did at each other, I thought he'd be here too.

I'd been prepared to lose Rocky, though it would hurt my heart when he moved away to work at some impressive research facility. The kid's brain was way too smart to use in any capacity other than curing cancer or ending world hunger. Yes, he loved hockey just like the rest of us, but personally, I thought the world needed him more than we did.

But Rebel leaving hit me harder than I'd thought it would. I guess because it was a surprise I hadn't been expecting. And when I say surprise, I mean it was a fucking heart-stopping shock.

Not because I didn't believe he could do it but because I just didn't think he'd ever *want* to leave. Maybe I didn't know my brother as well as I thought I did.

After Rowdy and Rocky congratulated Rebel and peppered him with questions for the next ten minutes, I'd given him a hug and told him I was so happy for him, that he absolutely deserved it. Then I'd left to go home, but not before I stopped at the arena to grab a few files I'd forgotten. I walked to the window that looked out over the empty ice. In a few hours, the youth hockey club would have practice, and later tonight, the ice skating classes given by the Y would start.

The knock on my office door made me jump and gasp. I turned to see Rebel standing there.

"Hey."

I slapped on a smile, but I'm pretty sure he could see it wasn't completely true. "Hey. Congrats again. It's such a great oppor—"

"You looked like I kicked your puppy."

Arms crossed over his chest, Rebel stared at me. Trust him to cut straight to the chase.

I shook my head, my smile wry. "It was a shock."

"What? You don't think I can hack it?"

I made a face. "Don't be an ass. Of course I think you're good enough. I think it's a great opportunity for you."

"Then what's going on? I would've thought you'd be the one who'd most want us to do this. To push us forward."

"Maybe I think we're doing just fine where we are."

"Or maybe you're afraid if things change, Brian won't stick around."

I refused to give him the satisfaction of a response. "Maybe I'm worried that half our team won't stick around. And that they won't have any other place to go. That offer is a great opportunity for you, but maybe you're the one who wants everything to change for you. Why would you want to stay here and play for an ECHL team when you've got AHL interest?"

The muscle in his jaw ticked, and his gaze narrowed. "Maybe because this is my home."

"I know that. It's mine too." Anger had started to burn in my gut. "And I'm not sure I want to completely fuck it up by conforming to another league's rules. I can't believe you, Mr. Leave-Me-The-Fuck-Alone, suddenly wants to be a joiner."

"Maybe because this is my home. And I want to stay with my family."

"And maybe you're just afraid to leave." Fuck. *Fuck.* I'd fucked up. "I'm sorry. Shit, I didn't mean that. Not the way it sounded. Reb—"

"No, I think you meant it." Amazingly he didn't look angry. "And maybe I should think about that. But maybe you should think about the fact that you're holding the team back for your selfish reasons."

He turned and walked away, and I let my head fall back as I stared at the ceiling that really needed to be painted.

Fuck.

BRIAN

You home?

RAIN

No not yet. Be there in a few

BRIAN

Lunch?

RAIN

Absolutely

I'D JUST LEFT the arena to work at home this afternoon because it was Friday, and we had a home game tonight. I hadn't seen much of Brian for the past two weeks, except at the arena during practice. Something kept coming up. He'd had a meeting with Maddy's teachers Tuesday. Wednesday, Rowdy and I went ring shopping because that was the only day Rowdy could schedule it so that Tressy wouldn't realize we were going to Harrisburg to meet a jeweler.

And OMG, the ring. I literally sighed when he picked it out. It was so pretty. Not gonna lie, I shed a few tears, which made Rowdy laugh. Then I smacked him on the chest, and he grabbed me in a bear hug, kissed my cheek, and told me I was the best sister ever. And we left to have lunch before making the trip back.

I don't think Tressy suspected a thing.

The team had left Thursday for a three-game weekend in New York and hadn't gotten home until late Sunday night.

Something had come up every day this week. Monday and Tuesday, I'd had a meetings for the Winter Carnival, which would be here in two weeks. Since the event had been running for almost a decade, all I had to do was make sure everything ran smoothly during the lead-up. Mom and a team of volunteers did most of the heavy lifting, but I coordinated all things Devils.

Which meant wrangling the schedule of a team of guys for various activities, including a charity game at the town park pond on that Saturday night, featuring the youth hockey groups and our guys.

I'd only seen Brian at the arena this week. A few stolen

kisses in a couple of dark corners of the arena had not been enough for me. When my doorbell rang, my thighs clenched because I ached for him.

WI really should tell Brian he could just walk in.

I opened the door and barely had time to smile and say, "Hi—" before he caught me around the waist, lifted me off my feet, and slammed the door behind him with his foot.

His lips landed on mine, hard and demanding, and I practically melted against him. I let him shove all the shit out of my head with his lips and his tongue and the heat of his body wrapping around me.

I gave back as good as I could, but he seemed to be on a mission to consume me as fast as possible. Since I didn't have any objection to that, I let him. I held on as he walked me up the stairs to my bedroom, his mouth on mine. I ended up sprawled on my bed naked while he kissed his way down my body, tossing clothing aside as he came to it.

I could barely catch my breath, but I didn't care. I wanted to lose myself in him just as much as he seemed to want to do the same with me.

My pants slid down my legs, giving him the ability to put my knees over his shoulders, his hands on my ass, and lift me to meet his mouth. I sucked in air as he made me come with his mouth, my body shaking with a desire I couldn't seem to quench around him.

"If I have to face off against that asshole on the ice, I'm going to do it after I've made you come so many times you can't walk right."

Oh my god, I hadn't even thought of that. The Devils played the Anderstown Animals. Mo Zelinsky was the Animals captain.

And no way in hell was I going to let anything about that man invade this moment.

"More sex. Less talk."

Brian chuckled as he bit the inside of my thigh before letting my ass hit the mattress as he fell over me, caging me with his arms on either side of my head.

"Absolutely, sweetheart."

I already had my hands on his pants, pushing beneath the waistband and shoving them and his boxer briefs down just far enough for me to release his cock. I gave him a few pumps before flinging my hand toward the bedside table and trying to grab a condom out of the drawer. Brian got there before me, grabbing a condom and putting it in my hand before using his hand to cup my breast and squeeze.

Arching into his hand, I reveled in the sensation of his flesh on mine. But I didn't forget that there was a bigger prize to be had. Fumbling with the condom packet, I tore it open with my teeth, then handed it over for Brian to take care of.

Sitting back on his haunches, he rolled it on, not bothering to take off his clothes, and sank deep on the first thrust.

Brian seemed to be on a mission, and I was happy to go along for the ride. Because the ride was amazing. My body gave in to his dominance and let me drown in pleasure. Any woman who claims not to enjoy having a big strong guy make her whimper with his hands and his mouth and his cock was lying.

His first thrust made my body tighten around him like a fist. The next sent shudders through my body as my nails scratched down his back.

The next sent me over.

"DID you talk to your brothers about what you're going to do?
"

"Yeah, but we didn't decide anything. We're meeting again before the carnival. Reb's going to be home for the weekend."

"Guess there's a lot to talk about."

"There is, considering we don't agree on the direction we should take the team."

"And your dad's letting it up to you and your brothers? He's not giving you any advice at all?"

"No. I kinda think it's a test to see if we do the right thing. I just don't know what the right thing is."

"What's your gut telling you?"

"That it's the wrong thing to do at this time."

"You don't sound sure."

I sighed, loving the feel of his naked skin against mine as we lay in my bed. "I am. But I also know this could be a huge deal for my brothers. And..." Shit, I couldn't tell him about Rebel. He'd sworn us to secrecy. "...we're talking about a decision that could affect hundreds of lives, not just ours."

"You sure there's nothing else going on with you about this?"

"What do you mean?"

"Rain, you're always the first person to jump into something new with both feet. Why is this any different?"

"Because it's not just my life we could screw up if this goes wrong. We're not starting from scratch here. And we wouldn't just be screwing up our team, we could be screwing up the league. Dad and the other owners built this from the ground up."

"I feel like I've fallen into one of those inspirational sports movies."

I smacked him on his chest then kissed it better. "I don't know why we can't expand this league on our own. We don't need to follow anyone else's rules. We can make our own. Why are you smiling at me like that?"

"Because you're cute when you're channeling the plucky heroine of some cheesy movie."

"Plucky? Seriously? What the hell kind of word is 'plucky'?"

"The kind that perfectly describes the look on your face right now."

Scrambling to my knees, I straddled his lap and mock-glared down at him. Even though his naked body made my mouth water, and my sex clenched at the position I was in and what I could be doing to him right now. His hands landed on my hips and his lips curved in a grin. And when I wrapped my hand around his hardening cock, I had the satisfaction of seeing his expression harden with lust.

"Do you want me to tell you what your face looks like right now?"

"If it's not telling you how fucking sexy you are, you're not reading me right."

Then he showed me just how sexy he thought I was with his hands and his mouth.

TWENTY-ONE

Brian

LIN

I know you know I get out Thursday but I wanted to double check the time. 3 pm Please bring Maddy. I miss her. Miss you too Bri. But I can't wait to see my Mads again

BRIAN

We'll be there. Thought you weren't allowed to use your phone?

LIN

I can with the therapist. Be happy to sleep in my own bed

BRIAN

I'm sure. See you soon

LIN

> Love you Bri. Can't thank you enough for everything you've done for us.

I SAT in the car down the street from Rain's house Tuesday morning, probably long enough for a neighbor to call the cops on me. Lin's text had come through right as I'd been parking. But I'd been dreading this conversation for the past week.

Neither of us had spoken about what happened when Lin got out of rehab. I'd purposely avoided the subject. But now it was happening. And I couldn't put it off any longer.

I'd planned to stay and finish out the season. It's what I'd told Rowdy. It's what I'd let Rain think. But now that the time was here, I knew I couldn't just take Lin and Maddy back to their apartment in Allentown, drop them off, and leave again. I couldn't do that to them. Not until I knew they'd be okay.

And that meant going to back to Allentown And, since I'd given up my apartment, it meant sleeping on Lin's couch for a while. I could handle that. What was tearing me up inside was the conversation I had to have now. With Rain.

Fuck.

I shoved open the car door and slammed it shut behind me. Anger and regret and disappointment and a whole raft of other shit rolled around in my stomach, making me want to scream.

Because I'd been such a fucking idiot.

And now I was going to pay for it.

I walked to her door, knocked and waited with a lump in my throat. When the door opened, the smile on her face nearly cut me off at the knees.

"Hey, come in." She turned, heading back toward the kitchen. "I've got to turn off the stove before I boil all the water away. I swear..."

"Rain, we need to talk."

TWENTY-TWO

Rain

I'D KNOWN this day was coming. Honestly, I had. But somehow, I thought maybe it would all work out for Brian and me.

You know, like the ending of a Hallmark movie where whatever conflict the couple had disappeared like smoke a minute before the credits roll. Brian's sister would miraculously be cured and all better, and she and Maddy would move back to Allentown or wherever, and Brian would stay here and...

I was an idiot.

Brian and I sat on the couch in my living room, He stared at me like he wanted me to get angry. Waiting for me to blow up.

He should know me better than that. When things don't work out, I don't melt down. I see it for what it is. A miscalculation on my part. Of course he was leaving. He'd never mentioned staying after his sister's program was over. And I had never asked.This was totally on me.

"So you're going back to Allentown."

It wasn't a question, because I knew that's where he was going.

His jaw tightened and I saw frustration in the flat line of his mouth and the clench of his hands on his thighs. Did he want me to get angry? Cry? Beg him not to go?

Wasn't going to happen because I totally understood why he had to leave.

Even if I'd hoped...maybe...there might be some way—

"I made a promise to Maddy." Each word sounded like a vow. And an apology that he didn't want to give. "I promised Maddy I'd be there for her. And she needs me now. My sister needs me."

And what about me? The words sat on the tip of my tongue, but I wouldn't say them. I couldn't. I couldn't be that selfish brat who melted down when I didn't get what I wanted. I was a goddamn adult and sometimes you were disappointed.

Yeah, that was a good word. Disappointed. Definitely not heartbroken.

I nodded, my expression carefully constructed to be supportive. Definitely not clingy. I wasn't clingy.

"Then you need to keep that promise. They need you."

His frustration grew, probably at the steady sound of my voice. "The rehab helped line up a new job for her in Allentown. A better job. She starts next week."

"That's great. And what about you? Do you have a job lined up?"

Damn, I wished I could do that one over. It sounded a

little edgy. Maybe a little pissed off. Nope, not gonna do that either.

Now he looked guilty, though that didn't make any sense.

"I called the lumberyard yesterday. They always have openings."

Ah, and that's why the guilt. He'd known yesterday and hadn't told me.

I forced a smile and hoped it looked somewhat natural. "Well, I hope everything works out for you and Lindsey and Maddy. You all deserve to—"

"Rain—"

"—start fresh. I'm glad you came to say goodbye this time." I made sure my expression was pleasant. Such shitty word. "Thank you for that. I appreciate you not—"

"No. Not goodbye." His expression set in lines of determination as he leaned closer. "I'm not walking away this time. Not after the last few weeks. You and I can make this work. I just need time to get my sister set up. Just a couple weeks."

That didn't sound so bad. A couple weeks. But I could tell he didn't believe what he was saying. I saw the truth in his eyes. He knew it would take a lot longer than a couple of weeks to get this sorted. His family needed him. I knew all about family needing you.

But right now, I wasn't feeling generous and understanding. Because anger continued to build. Anger at him for leaving and anger at myself for not realizing what'd been coming.

"I'm sure you already talked to Rowdy about releasing you from your contract."

He grimaced. "With Rebel leaving too, I can't ask him to hold a spot open. The team needs players. And I don't know exactly how long this'll take. I need to make sure Linny and Maddy are okay before I leave them."

But he knew I'd be okay when he left me. Because of course, I would. And even though my heart was shriveling into a tiny little ball of anguish, I forced a smile and nodded. "Of course you do. I hope everything works out for them."

"Rain." The growl in his voice made my thighs clench, which pissed me off. He shouldn't get to talk to me like that anymore. He was leaving me. "Don't count me out this time. I know I fucked up last time by not sticking around, but I'm not giving up that easily now."

Sure. I nodded. Smiled. As if I believed him and he hadn't walked away last time.

"Tell Maddy I said bye. Tell her she's welcome to come to a game whenever she wants. Same for you. Just let me know if you want tickets."

The frustration on his face made him even more handsome. That shouldn't be allowed.

"God damn it, Rain." He leaned closer, the longing on his face nearly making me crumble. But I couldn't. I was so pissed off at myself that I'd allowed myself to believe him. That I'd let myself fall for another hockey player who wasn't as committed to me as I was to him. "I'll be back. I know you don't believe me, and I don't blame you. And I don't expect you to wait for me. But I will come back, and I will show you that you can depend on me. I'll earn your trust. And I won't leave again unless you fucking tell me to go."

Then he turned and walked out the door.

"HI, sweetheart? I was wondering if you'd like to go to lunch."

I looked up from my desk at the arena, surprised to see my mom in my office doorway.

"What are you doing here?"

Her wry smile and raised eyebrows made me want to take back my words. Even I'd been able to hear the shortness in them.

"Last I checked, I still was a majority owner in the team."

I shook my head, trying to shake the frown away. "Sorry, I didn't mean—That didn't come out right." I rose and walked around the desk to give my mom a hug. I hadn't seen her for a few days. Actually, I hadn't seen her since Brian had left. The team had been away all weekend, and I'd turned down her invitation to dinner Saturday night, pleading a headache, which had seemed lame even to me. Mom had taken my rejection to easily.

Which explained her unusual visit to the office.

She hugged me tight and patted my back, like I was a child in need in comfort. She wasn't wrong. I just didn't want to cry in front of my mom.

I had managed to stave off tears so far. This situation was my own fault.

"Hi, Mom."

"Hello, sweetheart. How are you?"

I took a step back and managed a smile. "I'm fine. What's up? What can I do for you? Did I miss a meeting for the carnival?"

Shit, had I missed a meeting? I'd been so focused on the team and our decision—and yes, trying not to think about Brian—that maybe my famous laser focus had finally failed me. And that was unacceptable.

"I don't think I have anything written—"

"Rain, honey. It's okay you haven't missed anything."

I took a deep breath, realizing now how frantic I'd sounded, which is probably why my mom was looking at me with that sympathetic stare. I didn't need sympathy.

"Good. That's...good. I know we've got a lot to do in the next couple of weeks. I don't want to fall behind–"

"Honey, you're not falling behind. Take a breath. I'm here because I'm worried about you."

Yeah, I knew that. "I'm fine, Mom. Really."

"So you're not upset that Brian left?"

Why did I feel like a knife just slipped through my ribs? "No. Of course not. He has other responsibilities. His sister and Maddy need him."

"Very true." Mom nodded and made that face, the one that let me know she could see right through me. And maybe she could. But that didn't mean I had to acknowledge it.

"And I've got more important things to worry about right now. We still haven't made a decision about the team. And Erin and I need to do more work on the building to get it ready. The carnival is in less than two weeks and there's still a lot of work to do there. Plus all the regular work for the team."

"You do know there's more to life than work?"

"I do have a life. I've got friends. I've got you and Dad. I've even got my brothers."

"So you're not missing Brian at all? Have you been in touch? I'd love to know how his sister's doing."

"I've been so busy, I haven't had time to check in. And he's got enough on his plate."

Not to mention that every time I decided to text him

back, I had no idea what to say. It hurt to think about it, and I didn't want to hurt. So I just shoved it all aside.

Mom just nodded, like that was exactly what she'd expected me to say.

"Let me take you to lunch, hon."

Another bright smile I didn't really feel. "Thanks, but I've just got so much to do."

After a few seconds, Mom smiled and nodded. "Okay, babe. Try not to work too hard."

"Sure."

Damn, I hated lying to my mom. But I hated this ache in my chest even more.

TWENTY-THREE

Brian

> Sorry I haven't texted back. Busy here. Carnival prep in full swing. Games this weekend. So much work

THE TEXT HAD COME AROUND eight this morning, almost a week after Maddy and I had moved back to Allentown with Linny.

I'd felt my phone vibrate but had been in the middle of loading a truck for a customer at the lumberyard. The manager had taken me back, no questions asked. He'd actually seemed happy to see me. He was a good guy, and the job paid decent...but I didn't want to be here.

I thought I'd been able to hide that from Linny and Maddy. The three of us were living in Linny's old apartment until I could find my own, hopefully close by. And hopefully soon because sleeping on the fucking couch had already messed up my back. For right now, though, it was all I had because I'd given up the lease on my old apartment.

Add my frustration at not hearing from Rain and it was getting harder every day to hide my frustration. Linny looked at me sometimes like I wasn't hiding it well enough. I needed to work on that. She didn't need to worry about me along with everything else on her plate.

I'd wanted to reply to Rain immediately, but the day had been busy. And when lunch had rolled around, I didn't know what to say. I wanted to tell her how much I missed her and that I fucking ached to hold her. But that felt unfair. I still didn't know what I should send back when I walked into the apartment to find my sister sitting at the dining table. The expression on her face... My stomach dropped.

"Hey." I stopped to take off my boots. "What's wrong?"

I breathed a little easier when Linny's lips curved in a tiny smile.

"Nothing, actually. You have a visitor."

"What? Who?" Who the hell could be visiting—

From the corner of my eye, I caught movement in the doorway to the kitchen.

"Hey." Rebel stood there, hands shoved in his pockets.

I just stared at him as my sister got up from the table. "I'll give you guys some privacy. Nice to meet you, Rebel." Then she disappeared into her bedroom.

I stared at him for several seconds before I spoke. "What are you doing here?"

"Probably being an unwanted pain in the ass." He sighed as he took a few steps closer. "I talked to Rain yesterday. And

I don't know what you did to her, but you better fucking fix it."

"What the hell are you talking about"

Had Rain told Rebel about us? What had she said? And why wasn't Rebel trying to beat the shit out of me?

"Bullshit. Don't be a dick. I know my sister well enough to know she cares about you and you hurt her when you left."

That cut through my gut like a knife. I hated to think that I'd hurt Rain.

"Mom said Rainy's been quiet. When have you ever known my sister to be quiet?"

Hell, she wasn't even quiet in bed, but I definitely wasn't going to tell her brother that.

Rebel took a step closer. "Look, man. I love my sister. She may be the second-biggest pain in my ass in my life, but I will fuck up anyone who messes with her. And apparently, you're messing with her."

Fuck. "This is none of your business."

"My sister is my business." Reb lifted a hand and stuck an index finger right in my chest. "And you are my business, asshole. You're one of the only friends I've ever considered as close as a brother. I can handle the distance between us, but she fucking misses you. So you need to be the bigger person and tell her how you feel."

"The bigger person, huh?"

Rebel rolled his eyes. "For some unknown reason, she cares about you, asshole. And not like she cares about everyone else. You're special." His jaw flexed. "And I'm not going to be the asshole who stands in the way of what she wants. So if you're avoiding her because of me, knock it the fuck off."

"I'm not." I grimaced and ran a hand through my hair, which definitely needed a trim. "I texted her the night we left. I texted her the next day. You know when she got back to me? Today. I'm not fucking avoiding her, but when she doesn't text for a week and then only to tell me how busy she is, I'm not an idiot. I get the hint. Why the hell do you care anyway? I figured you'd be glad she was getting rid of me."

"Is that what you think? That I'd be happy you hurt my sister? You think she wants space? Did she *actually* say that?"

I tried to shake some reason back into my head. "Reb, what the actual *fuck* are you doing here?"

For a second, I thought he'd turn and walk out the door, because that was how he usually handled conflict. Or punch me. I might've preferred that because at least I'd have a response.

Instead, he took a deep breath. "I'm checking on you," he spoke way too slowly, as if I was an idiot and couldn't understand him, "because my mom is worried about my sister and my sister's worried about you. I was close. So here I am. Checking on you." He shook his head. "I don't know what was going on between you two. And I don't want to know. What I want is for my sister to be happy again so my mom doesn't worry and ask me to check on you. Text. Her. The. Fuck. Back."

I nearly choked on a laugh, because the situation was just too absurd.

"You drove here just to say that?"

Now Rebel looked like he was going to punch me. "Yeah, actually, I fucking did." He stopped to suck in air and glance at the ceiling for a quick second. "Look, I know how important family is, okay? I get it. But," his jaw worked, like he was having trouble forming words, "we're your family too. I might want to punch you occasionally because you're an asshole, but then I do the same with Rowdy. And ..." He sighed. "I don't like when my sister's upset."

Fuck. I didn't want to cause her any pain. "I thought it'd be easier on her if I didn't text all the time. You don't know how many times I've picked up the phone to call..."

"So why haven't you?"

I shook my head. "Because I'm an idiot. Is that what you want to hear? Because maybe she doesn't want to talk to me. Because the one and only time she texted was to tell me how busy she is. Maybe she's just too fucking busy for me."

Rowdy rolled his eyes. "Jesus, maybe if you both weren't so fucking blind, you'd be able to see you're making excuses not to be the first one to put their heart on the line and risk getting it smashed."

I just stood there and looked at him for several long seconds. "Dude, who the fuck are you?"

Rebel didn't take the bait, even though I was being fairly serious.

"I—"

The door opened, and I turned to see Maddy walk through.

She gave me a smile that quickly turned into a wide grin when she noticed our company.

"Rebel! What are you doing here?"

With an ease I hadn't seen in a while, she walked up to Reb and gave him a hug, which he returned.

"Good to see you, Mads. How's school?"

She shrugged, her gaze sliding away. "It's okay." Maddy had agreed to go back to her old school, so she wouldn't be home alone while Lin and I were at work. But I could tell she hated it. Another item to add to the worry list. "Uncle Bri said you're playing for another team now. He said we could go see you when you play here."

"That's another reason I'm here." He reached into his pocket and pulled out tickets. "The Redtails play here tomorrow night. I hope you'll come."

She looked at me. "Can we?"

"Of course, if you want to go. Why don't you go tell your mom. She's in her room."

Maddy knew when she was being dismissed. "Good. I miss hockey. See you at the game, Reb."

Once she disappeared into the bedroom and closed the door, Reb crossed his arms over his chest. "You need to text Rain. And then you need to figure out what the fuck you're doing. Because whatever it is, neither of you are happy."

"Will Rain be at the game?"

"No. The Devils play. Mom and Pop will be though. And you're sitting with them."

I huffed out a laugh. "Thanks for the warning."

"I gotta go. I hope you use the tickets. And don't disappoint my sister again. She cares about you."

TWENTY-FOUR

Rain

"WHY DON'T you just call him?"

"So he can swipe me into voicemail? Nope. Not happening. If he missed me, he'd text me back."

Erin and Caity exchanged a glance as we worked in the kitchen of Crack One Open, finishing up the s'mores kits for the carnival. We'd already finished the hot chocolate mix and were moving onto snowman kits. Giant marshmallows that I would shove in their faces if they continued to talk about Brian.

"When was the last time you texted him?"

I shrugged, not meeting their eyes. "A few days ago."

Which was more like a week, because his first text had been:

BRIAN

Hi. Busy here. Getting Maddy squared away at school and Lin in her new job. Getting my workout in at lumberyard

Nothing about missing me. Of course, I hadn't given him a great send-off. I'd basically told him to have a nice life. I was surprised he even texted at all.

And yet he had.

And I'd let him hang for a week.

Now who was the asshole? That would be me.

"She's doing that thing." Caity nudged Erin, as they both stared at me like I was an exhibit on display.

"What?" I frowned at them. "What thing?"

"You're thinking too hard." Caity cocked a hip. "Second-guessing everything. And you're using work as an excuse."

"I am not. I'm busy. The carnival is this weekend, and I've got way too much to do and not enough time to do it."

"Do you ever think you do all this stuff for everyone else so you don't have to confront the loneliness of your own existence?"

Caity and I looked at Erin, our expressions mirror images of WTF.

"Girl, what the *hell* have you been reading?" Caity shook her head. "Seriously, you need to lay off the dystopian and read more romcoms."

Erin wrinkled her nose and grabbed the bin with our next project, the snowman kits.

"I just mean, I think you're in avoidance mode. Doing all this stuff gives you an excuse to not do anything else."

"It's not an excuse." Except it probably was. "If he wanted to contact me, he would."

"Maybe if you'd sent something other than 'gee, I'm so busy,' he would have some idea of how much you miss him." Caity held up the scissors she was using to cut ribbon. "And don't even say you don't miss him. You've been moping ever since he left."

My nose wrinkled. "I have not. There's just a lot going on right now."

It sucked that I couldn't tell my friends what else weighed on my mind. My brothers and I were planning to talk again Thursday, the night before the carnival started. Rebel didn't have a game until Sunday, so he was able to come home. We'd agreed to make a decision then, no matter what.

"I don't know, Rain," Caity said. "If you want the guy, maybe you need to tell him. *Have* you told him?"

"Of course I did."

Hadn't I?

Or had I been a selfish brat who expected him to make all the effort?

"Rain, just call the guy, for fuck's sake." Erin clasped her hands in front of her, her expression overly dramatic and hilarious. "Put us all out of our collective misery. Besides, you know you want to."

I did. I really, really did. "What if he doesn't want to talk to me?"

Caity leaned on the counter, staring at me. "And what if he's just been waiting for you? Maybe he thought you didn't want to hear from him. Like, because you didn't text him back for a *freaking* week."

"I don't want to be that girl. The clingy girl. The one who doesn't get the hint."

Caity threw her hands in the air and huffed. "You're just scared! Get over it."

"Okay, so maybe I am. I haven't exactly had a good track record with hockey players."

"You just haven't found the right one." Erin spoke low and steady. And absolutely right. "Until now."

———

"SO, we've all made up our minds?"

Rowdy looked around the table at each of us, stopping with me. Because he had to know I had something to add.

Rebel and Rocky had walked through the door to the arena conference room just a couple of minutes ago. Rowdy had shut the door behind them, and they'd barely had time to sit before Rebel took a chair and started.

"Before we do this," I said, "I want to say this. If you three decide you want this...I'm in. I love you all, and I want what's best for you. Not just for the business. But for you guys. Personally."

Rowdy stared at me, for long moments, his gaze not giving anything away. Then he looked at Rebel, who nodded, and Rocky, who grinned. Then they all looked at me and smiled.

What the hell? "Okay, now you're just freaking me out. What's going on?"

"Don't freak out, but we met behind your back." Rowdy held up a hand to stop whatever was about to come out of my mouth. "Yes, I know we agreed not to discuss this unless we were all together, but there were some things the three of us had to say. Most of it was the fact that you were right, and they didn't want to have to say it to your face."

Rebel rolled his eyes and stared at the ceiling, but Rocky took the bait, just like Rowdy knew he would.

"Hey, that's not exactly true." Rocky gave me a smile that would totally melt any woman's heart in a five-mile radius. "Okay, maybe it's a little true. We love you, Rainy. You just scare us a little sometimes. You're usually right about everything."

No, I wasn't. Look how badly I'd screwed up my relationship with Brian. I still hadn't texted him to tell him how I felt. That wasn't exactly me being right about everything. That was me being stupid. And indecisive. Two things I typically wasn't.

"Just to be clear," I said. "We're going to turn down the offer?"

"Yes. Because you're right." Rebel finally stopped staring at the wall to look at me. "This team and what Pop built here is more important to our players and our fans than jumping to another league."

I looked at Rocky. "You're sure?"

"Yeah. I'm sure. And I trust that when I decide I want to play here, you and Rowdy will be running the best damn team in the Northeast Professional Hockey League."

"Rowdy? Are you really sure this is what you want?"

"It is." He nodded, his expression as serious as he ever got. "I know you and I are gonna butt heads sometimes, but there's no one I would rather run this team with. We're gonna kick ass, Rainy."

My smile widened.

"We will."

Now, I just needed to figure out how to fix the mess I'd made of the situation with Brian.

TWENTY-FIVE

Brian

THURSDAY after a long shift at the lumberyard, I walked through the apartment door to find Linny at the table, laptop open, shaking her head.

She didn't even look up when I said, "Hey," just kind of hummed a sound and went back to frowning at her screen. I walked around her to get to the sink to wash my hands and get a glass of water, then leaned against the counter to peek at her screen.

Banking app. And it didn't have a negative balance. Which was great. Still...

"This isn't working," I said.

Linny went still, her fingers freezing over the keyboard before she turned to face me. She didn't say anything for several seconds before she took a breath, her expression resigned.

"I know," she said. "I just...I don't know how to fix this. Maddy hates that school. I don't exactly hate my job, but I know you do. I hate that you aren't playing hockey. And I hate that this is all my fault."

Shit. My heart stopped beating for a second as I thought of all the implications of that statement. Had she relapsed?

"Brian, breathe." She actually smiled a little. "I haven't started drinking again. And I hate that you immediately went there. I hate that I made you go there. I'm just stuck, and I hate it. I need to do what's best for Maddy and me and you—"

"I'm fine. You don't need to worry about me."

"But this isn't working for Maddy, and I can't live with that. I don't know what to do, Bri."

I paused for a second, knowing I had to get this out there. "Maybe I do."

She looked at me with so much hope in her eyes that I sincerely hoped I wasn't going to steer her—steer us—wrong. Because this wasn't just about Linny and Maddy. It was about the three of us. I wasn't willing to leave them behind again. We needed each other. But I had another family out there who I knew would be happy to take us in.

I missed hockey. I missed the Devils. I missed St. David and the fans.

I fucking ached for Rain every night we'd been apart.

Pulling out the seat across from her, I sat, watching her closely for any hint that she'd been drinking. I couldn't help it. The therapist said that mechanism could last forever but might eventually fade. Unfortunately, that could take years, but it wasn't odd or even uncommon. It just was.

"Are you going back to St. David to play? At the game, I overheard the Colonel say you'd be welcome back any time. I think you should go."

"Yeah, I've been thinking about it. I'm going to contact Rowdy about finishing out the season in St. David."

Linny took a deep breath and nodded. "I know that's the best thing for you—"

"And I want you and Maddy to come with me."

She blinked. "What?"

"Maddy actually liked the school there, not that she'd ever admit to it. She'd made a couple of friends and didn't hate going every day. But she will never say that to you because she loves you, and she doesn't want to do anything to upset you."

"I know. And I hate it."

"But it doesn't have to be that way. You hate your job. I'm pretty sure you can find something better in St. David. We'll make it work."

"You make it sound easy."

I shook my head. "I know it's not gonna be easy. I know it's going to be hard to leave behind everything you know here."

"Leave all this splendor?" Sarcasm dripped from every word. "How could I? Bri, I know I'm supposed to be older and wiser, but that's always been you. You've always been the one looking out for me. And I know you have our best interests at heart. If you think moving is our best option, I'm with you."

Then she paused. "And if it will put a smile back on your face to be nearer to the girl you left behind, I'm all for it."

I'D CALLED Rowdy after Linny and I had talked last night. He'd laughed and said I was right on time.

"I was waiting for you to call. We haven't filled your spot yet, and I even rolled the dice and paid another month on your apartment. And I might have a lead on a job for your sister."

Things seemed to be going in our favor.

Except the text I got from Rain this morning made me wonder if she'd even care that I was back.

RAIN

> Sorry I didn't get back to you sooner. Busy but also didn't want to make your life more complicated than it already is. I hope everything is going well with you and Maddy and Lin. Just want you to know I'm thinking about you

If I didn't know her better, I'd think she was blowing me off. And for a few seconds, maybe I did. But we were here now in St. David. We'd talked to Mrs. Travers, who'd taken one look at Maddy and smiled. Actually smiled, like she'd missed the kid.

Then she'd wanted to talk to Lin, which had kind of freaked me out, but Lin had smiled afterward and told me everything was fine. I was dying to ask what they'd talked about, but Linny had told me we needed to have boundaries. Not badgering her about a private conversation was probably one of those.

After that, we put away the clothes and stuff we'd

brought with us, and now I was counting the minutes until we could leave for the carnival. I knew Rain would be there. I'd been stressing over what to say to her when I could look her in the eyes and explain myself.

I still hadn't figured out exactly what I was going to say.

"Are you finally going to teach me how to skate, Uncle Bri?"

"Sure. We can rent you a pair of skates at the pond."

Good thing I'd remembered to put my skates in the car.

We parked at the school, where half the parking lot was already filled. The Winter Carnival was a big deal in St. David, despite the fact that it was freezing cold. Luckily, there wasn't a lot of wind. Luminary bags lit the path from the parking lot to the street and then to the borough hall, where the carnival was held every year in the park.

Lights from the rides glowed above the hall, and music got louder as we joined the steady stream of people heading for the park.

"Damn, they go all out, don't they?"

Linny's comment held a hint of amusement, but Maddy had already caught sight of the food stands and started dragging her mom toward those. That's not where I wanted to go, but I didn't want to abandon Linny and Maddy the second we got here.

"Bri, it's okay." Linny shooed me with her hands. "Go find Rain. We'll be fine. We're just going to get some food. Play a few games. We'll meet up with you later."

"Mom, come on. I'm hungry."

I didn't think I could eat anything anyway. Tension had settled into my stomach, making it knot. But when I finally caught sight of Rain after making a circuit around the grounds, that tension became something else. A certainty I hadn't felt until just now.

Carrying a large plastic bin, she hurried from the back entrance of the hall to the bakery stand, set up near one of the larger firepits. Fires gleamed from pits all around the park, tended by the local volunteer firefighters, of course.

I stopped to watch her hand over the bin to Erin, laugh at something her friend said then walk to the next stand. And the next. Checking to make sure everything was running smoothly. I didn't want to interrupt her while she was busy, but I didn't want to stalk her like a creep either.

So I took a deep breath and made my way through the growing crowd. I lost sight of her for a second, but the pink puffy coat she wore made her easy to spot when she moved back into view.

Before I could reach her, she disappeared into the town hall again.

I thought about following her, but someone tugged on my coat, I turned and frowned because there didn't seem to be anyone there. Then I looked down.

"Hi there. What can I do for you?"

"Are you Mr. Whiskers? My mommy said your name is Mr. Whiskers."

The little girl, who was probably around four or five, stared up at me like I was a problem she needed to solve. "My cat is named Mr. Whiskers."

The seriousness of her expression made me bite back a smile.

"Did you name it after me?"

A pout. "She's not a it. She's a girl. I wanna know why you have the same name as my cat."

A girl cat named Mr. Whiskers. Okay then.

I went down on my heels, thighs surprisingly not giving me a hassle. "Well, a friend gave me the nickname Mr. Whiskers and it stuck a long time ago."

"Stuck where?"

My grin got bigger. "It stuck on me. He called me Mr. Whiskers because at the time, I was growing a beard. And I wasn't doing such a good job of it."

She patted my face. "You don't have whiskers now."

"No, because I still can't really grow a beard. And Whiskers rhymes with my last name. Fiskers."

"Your name is Whiskers Fiskers?"

That adorable little face looked at me with so much disbelief, I just shook my head. "No, my name is Brian. Sweetheart, do your parents know where you are? What's your name?"

She shrugged, white pom-pom bobbing on her purple hat, which totally clashed with the sky-blue coat. "I'm Desi. My moms' are over there."

She pointed over her shoulder, but none of the adults I saw appeared to be missing a little girl. Since I couldn't leave her alone to pursue Rain, I said, "How about we go find your parents."

Without hesitation, she held out her arms and let me lift her onto my hip. Seconds later, we weaved through the crowd in search of a police officer to find Desi's parents. I didn't need to say anything as we walked because she kept up a running commentary about the Devils. Not about hockey, but about the uniforms. Apparently, she had some suggestions on how to make them better. Mostly the use of colors like pink and purple. And unicorns.

No more than two minutes later, we found a cop and a pair of distressed moms, who rushed me like a couple of professional linebackers. One of them grabbed Desi, the other grabbed me. I thought for a second she was going to deck me. Instead, she gave me a hug that nearly cracked my ribs.

Another few minutes and many thank-yous later, Desi and her parents walked off to get hot chocolate, and I could continue my pursuit of Rain.

"Hey, Mr. Whiskers."

I was grinning as I turned, the voice coming from behind me.

I had a split second to see Rain covering the distance between us at speed before she launched herself at me. I wrapped my arms around her and held her tight, her arms around my shoulders.

"I heard someone was looking for me." She spoke directly into my ear, her breath brushing against the lobe and raising gooseflesh all over my body. "I really hope it was you."

Pulling back so I could stare into those beautiful eyes, I smiled, watching her lips curve in an answering grin. "I've been looking for you all my life, Rainy. I'm here to stay this time."

"I'm sorry—"

"I'm sorry—"

We laughed as we spoke over each other, and I set her on her feet. Then I bent and kissed her.

And the town cheered.

THE CROWD HAD DWINDLED DOWN to mostly adults by around nine o'clock, and the park looked magical.

White twinkle lights sparkled everywhere, from poles and trees and draped overhead between all the little stands. Couples gathered around the firepits, drinking spiked hot chocolate and beer and something Mitzi, the Tea Room owner, called Fire in the Hole. I didn't have a clue what was in it, but holy hell, it definitely warmed up your insides.

I'd gotten Maddy out on skates on the pond earlier in the night, but she and Linny had left a few minutes ago. Not to wait up for me. And I'd find my own way home. Eventually.

"Come skate with me, Rainy."

I glided to the edge of the frozen pond and held my hand out.

"I don't know." Rain put her hands on her hips and smiled at me. She'd already put on her skates. "You have some pretty fancy moves, if I remember correctly. And I'm not sure we have the right music."

Something slow and full of guitar played over the speakers. A few other couples skated around the perimeter of the ice, but I only had eyes for her.

"I promise not to show off my moves if you hold my hand."

Her smile widened as she stepped on the ice. But she skated past me, hands behind her back until she was as few feet away, then turned and skated backward, holding out her hands.

"Come on then, make it worth my while."

Grinning, I skated up to her, scooped her off the ice as

she gasped, and spun her around like we were pairs skaters. I owed that ice dancer in college a beer if I ever saw her again.

Rain continued to laugh as I lowered her back to the ice, then turned and took her hand, pushing off and tugging her along on a leisurely path around the outside of the ice.

"I want you to know," I said, "I had already decided to come back before Rebel came to talk to me."

She blinked up at me. "Wait. What?"

"He didn't tell you?" I snorted. "That figures."

She looked mystified. "I had no idea. Why?"

"Because he loves you, and he said I made you unhappy. Then he threatened to punch me if I didn't make it right. I want to make it right."

"Brian—"

"I thought you were happy to see me leave. The way you looked at me when I walked out your door... It felt like you were already wiping your memories of me."

Grimacing, she released my hand to thread her arm through mine, bringing her closer. "I hate to be wrong. I mean, I'm not always right, but I thought *we* were right. That we were meant to be together. And when you left, I just thought...I'd screwed up again."

"You didn't screw up. I did. I should've made it clear nothing would keep me from coming back to you. I missed you. Every single day. I missed you." I didn't bother with subtlety now. I just needed to know. "It felt like my heart was being crushed."

She looked up at me, eyes sparkling. "Me too. Every day."

"I love you, Rainbow."

"I love you too."

From across the ice, someone yelled, "We love you, too. Now get a room!"

We looked at each other.

Rainy said, "Damn good idea. Race you," and took off back to the edge of the pond.

I let her win, but only because I already had my prize.

Her.

EPILOGUE

Rebel

OH FUCK, my head hurt.

I stayed horizontal on the unfamiliar mattress, a hangover currently making my skull feel like someone was in there with a pickaxe.

For a second, I couldn't remember why the hell I had a hangover.

And then it came back to me.

Rowdy. Tressy. Wedding. Reception. Shots. So many shots.

Something niggled at my brain, something...important. I'd done something last night, something I shouldn't have.

I thought back over what I did remember. The wedding had gone off without a hitch. I hadn't lost the ring. I hadn't fucked up my best-man speech. Apparently I'd had way too much to drink, but that was to be expected at the wedding of your brother, where nearly half of the audience were hockey players.

I remembered dancing late into the night. Hitting the bar with a few of the other members of the wedding party—

Movement from the other side of the bed.

Holy fucking shitballs.

My eyes flew open, and I stared at the ceiling of the resort hotel.

"Oh fuck me, my head hurts."

My eyes snapped shut again as I recognized that voice.

Paralyzed with shock, I couldn't get out of bed and out the door before the woman next to me opened her eyes. Because I was naked, and there was no way in hell I was going to run through the halls with my dick hanging out. Although that might be better than the alternative.

"Where the hell—oh fuck!"

I turned my head and met the horrified eyes of the one woman in the world I didn't want to wake up next to.

Erin Wright.

ALSO BY STEPHANIE JULIAN

DEVILS HOCKEY

Rowdy Hearts

Rainbow Kisses

Rebel Secrets

FAST ICE

Bylines & Blue Lines

Hard Lines & Goal Lines

Deadlines & Red Lines

REDTAILS HOCKEY

The Brick Wall

The Grinder

The Enforcer

The Instigator

The Playboy

The D-Man

The Machine

The Ghost

OFF ICE PLAYS

(First Person Editions of REDTAILS HOCKEY)

Netting the Goalie

Pucking the Grinder

Falling for the Enforcer

SCANDALOUS DESIRE

Invite Me In

Reserve My Nights

Expose My Desire

Keep My Secrets

Rock My Heart

WICKED & CHARMING

Seducing Whitney

Claiming Ellie

Sharing Brianna

INDECENT

An Indecent Proposition

An Indecent Affair

An Indecent Arrangement

An Indecent Longing

An Indecent Desire

LOVERS UNDERCOVER

Lovers & Lies

Sinners & Secrets

Beauty & Brains

ABOUT THE AUTHOR

Stephanie Julian is a USA Today and New York Times best-selling author of contemporary and paranormal romance.

Visit her website at www.stephaniejulian.com for more information.

Rainbow Kisses

Copyright © 2025 by Stephanie Julian

All characters in this book are fiction and figments of the author's imagination.

www.ingramcontent.com/pod-product-compliance
Lightning Source LLC
Chambersburg PA
CBHW050549190726
48283CB00007B/2071